Catalyst

A Collide Novel
Book Three

SHELLY CRANE

1

Editing services provided by Jennifer Nunez
Naming contest for 'Rylee' winner is Jennifer Snyder
Printed in paperback December 2011 and available in Kindle and E-book format as of December 2011 through Amazon, Create Space and Barnes and Noble.

Printed in the United States

10 9 8 7 6 5 4 3 2 1

More information can be found at the author's website

http://shellycrane.blogspot.com

ISBN-13:978-1468120257

ISBN-10:1468120255

"When you're a catalyst for change, you make enemies. and I'm proud of the ones I've got."

Rupert Murdoch

For my family
who we've missed while on the road. We were thinking
about you. Out of sight doesn't mean out of mind.

Fit For Battle
Chapter 1 - Cain

"Listen, you don't worry about me. I'm trained for things just like this. I've *done* things just like this. I'm ready. I'll be fine," I told Lillian for about the fifth time.

She hadn't said anything but her hands were shaking in mine. I knew she was upset about the whole thing. The Lighters had taken Sherry to 'interrogate' her, which was just a pretty word for torture. I had volunteered to go into the enforcer's containment unit with Billings to retrieve her, undercover as a recruit for the enforcers program. I was the only one who could and was equipped to do so. I was immune to the Lighter Speak and couldn't be detected as a Special for some reason. I was unemployed. I was with Billings. It would work. It was a good plan.

Still, Lillian was freaking.

"I know. I'm trying really hard here, Cain," she said, her voice scratchy from fighting tears.

"I know you are," I replied and pulled her to me, wrapping my arms around her in an effort to calm her somehow.

It was morning. We'd been up almost all night planning and plotting, learning. Merrick was sick, absolutely sick with grief. Like a zombie, he just watched from the stairs in an anger cloud. I pulled him aside sometime during the night and tried to talk him out of it; tell him that I'd get her back, no matter what.

"You know I'll do everything I can, man. I'll bring her back."

"I know that. I've just never felt so helpless in all my existence. If you weren't here, there'd be no way to get her back. I- none of us could go and make it out alive. Not to say I wouldn't try but..." He bent over from the stair where we were sitting and put his head in his hands. "Oh, God, please let nothing happen to her. Please," he begged to no one in particular.

"She'll be ok."

He looked up at me sadly.

"I know what they are doing to her in there, Cain. I know what the purpose of those facilities are. They're torturing her. God knows all the horrible things they're doing to her," he grit out through his teeth, looking like he might throw up.

Then, too fast for my eyes to see, his fist went through the plaster of the wall beside us.

"Don't, man," I told him. "We need you. You'll be right there when I bring her out of the building. We need you to finish out the plan. Everybody's got a purpose."

"Bring her back, Cain. Bring her back."

"Absolutely."

Lily ran in and jumped into his lap. No one had told her what had happened with Sherry and she kept asking for her.

"Whewre's Shawwyy? Whewre's mommy?"

"Soon, baby. You'll see her soon," he promised and buried his face in her hair.

Danny had blown a gasket at being told he couldn't go into the facility at all. Lighters can still sense Specials, all but me for some reason. He was unhappy to say the least. He wanted to leave then - right then, no waiting until morning. He shouted, he cursed and pushed Jeff and Merrick off as they tried to calm him.

Only Celeste, who was still wrapped up in her own grief for her mother, had been able to reach him and get him to settle down. They eventually huddled together in the corner in a pile of arms, legs and heaving and comforting whispers. Man, it hurt to watch.

I had never been close to my own family. I didn't have any brothers or sisters. I didn't understand the pull, the need to protect and comfort. But I felt it now and it was a fierce thing.

And Margo. We had to put her in a room. No one could or would deal with her right then. There were too many other things going on. She was silent and waiting. Whether she knew her fate, understood what was happening to her or not, the rest of us did. And it was one I wasn't ready to deal out.

Lillian looked up at me with eyes glistening.

"That's it." She wiped her eyes and took a deep meaningful breath. Her eyes were full of decision as she said, "I'm coming with you."

"No," I said and grabbed her upper arms gently. "You most certainly are not."

"Yes. I am," she said firmly and pulled away from my grasp, even as I tried to stop her.

She walked further into the commons room right up to Billings.

"I'm coming with you."

"Uh..." He looked at me, walking behind her. I'm sure he was trying to decide if the glare was directed at her or him. "I'm not sure about that."

"I am. I'm coming. One more person to help in the search, right? We can cover more ground and be in and out faster."

"L, no," I said turning her to me. "Why? Because you're scared for me? Remember what I told you about not risking yourself? I meant it."

"You need me. You may not want to admit it but you do. Women can be enforcers, can't they Billings?"

I turned my glare on him full force and silently dared him to speak.

"Uh...well," he stammered and I could tell he wanted to bring her, to use her.

"Don't even think about it, Billings," I growled.

"What? If you want the truth, we could use her. A pretty thing like her would-"

"Don't say another word!" I bellowed.

"Fine. You asked."

"Actually, I don't think I did."

"Hey! I'm right here, you know," L said clearly annoyed. "Don't talk about me like I'm not here. Cain." She turned to me, pulling me from facing Billings. She grabbed my face in her warm long fingers and looked into my eyes. "I lo-" She closed her eyes and licked her lips. I wondered what she was going to say. "You mean a lot to me. A lot. But you are kind of making me crazy right now. This isn't just about you and me, nothing is anymore. This is Sherry we're talking about." She quirked a brow and I wanted to drag her to her room and demand that she explain what she meant by that. Did she really think I still had feelings for Sherry? "She would do what she could for us. We all have to do what we can for her. You can't make me sit on the sidelines when I know I can help."

I leaned closer to her so no one would hear but her.

"I know what you're insinuating, but I'm not doing this for some hang-up on Sherry."

"I know that." She looked stricken. "I didn't mean it like that at all. I meant that I know you care about her, we all do." She rubbed her temple. "I'm not trying to start a fight with you right now. I know we have things to do. All that I'm saying is that it's not fair and it's not right to make me stay here when I can be helping and doing some good out there. That's what Mitchell tried to do."

Dang. Girl fought dirty.

"L, you're putting me in a bad place here. You see that right? Once again, you're going to be out there and I'm going to be freaking out over you getting hurt. This isn't some club we're going to. This is right in the middle of the Lighters. I don't want you there. Not because I don't trust you, but because if anything happened to you, I'd..." I sighed and balled my hands into fists.

"That's exactly how I feel about you," she said with clear inflection. "I want to be with you. I feel safer and better about you when I'm with you. Ok?"

"No, it's not ok," I sighed again, "but I'm not gonna make you stay."

She nodded but still didn't look pleased. She understood where I was coming from. I understood where she was coming from. Neither of us liked it, but there was no budging as we both thought our side was important. I was pleased that she took no joy in winning.

"Billings, when are we leaving?" I asked, glancing back at him.

"Fifteen minutes."

"Go get dressed," I told Lillian. "You heard him, fifteen minutes, which means you've got twelve to be ready to go."

She turned and walked down the hall without looking back at me. I wondered what it meant that I'd never felt this bad about a fight before with any other girl. I really wanted to go to her room and apologize, tell her it was all alright, but that would have to wait for later.

"Billings? Do we have everything we need?"

"Yep. You, Lillian and I will go in. Merrick, Jeff and Miguel are riding for the muscle if we need it. Ryan, Danny and Marissa are gonna come and sit tight, just in case, for back-up."

"Ok, good."

The Keepers went over the regular rules with us: no thinking of home, we need to pretend to be thinking about the job, be anxious about our new placement, wonder who our boss will be. Normal human worry so that when they read our thoughts, it wouldn't be suspicious.

Then it was time to get the show on the road.

I saw them at the stairs, all ready to go. I went to Lillian's room to get her. She was already coming out of her room by the time I got to the hall. Something in me hurt - physically hurt - looking at her. I didn't want this life for Lillian, not like this.

I walked right up to her and begged her with my eyes to understand what my mouth couldn't say. I pulled her to me with a hand on the back of her neck. She didn't stop me. I thought she might since she was mad, but she kissed me back just as eagerly, her small arms gripping me tightly to her. I pulled back first, taking her face in between my hands.

"None of this is about any feelings for Sherry," I said firmly.

"I know that."

"You promise?"

"I promise," she assured me firmly.

"You're going to give me lots of gray hair, you know that?"

"I know," she whispered and smiled sadly.

"Let's go."

She followed close beside me. I held her hand to the stairs and as we made our way up to the van. Her warm long fingers squeezed mine every few seconds.

She was nervous but she needed to come. I let it go and didn't call her on her shaking.

We'd talked about it and if we were going to rescue Sherry, we might as well rescue any other prisoners if we could. Billings described the holding cells to us and the layout of the hallways. He said he'd only been present for a couple of interrogations and such, he just sort of avoided that wing, so he didn't know exactly what went on in them or what we'd find, but he knew it wouldn't be good.

We loaded up the van. Billings, Lillian and I had our concealed stakes in our boots under our pant legs. We would be given a uniform shirt to wear so we couldn't take any other weapons with us.

The van ride was long and quiet. Except for the occasional word or tid-bit from Billings if he had forgotten or thought of something we might need to know.

Merrick and Danny were two of the most sullen and anxious people I'd ever seen, faces of stone and bobbing knees and legs restlessly. Even me, I was worried sick about her. I didn't want anything to happen to her. When I heard what Margo had said, that they wanted a fragile person to take, one that we'd go after, I wanted to hurl. I didn't want to think about what she was going through or what they'd done to her.

One thing the Lighters didn't count on was us having Billings. We had a way directly inside. We weren't trying to break-in in the middle of the night, tripping alarms and bumping into guards like they expected us to do.

No, we were walking right through the front door.

We pulled up behind the facility where Billings said was an employee's only section and recruitment office. Lillian and I followed him and we left the rest of them in the van. They were close enough to the door that they could see a commotion or hear the alarm, but stay in the back. The back seats were still removed and there was open space back there.

"Listen." I pulled Lillian to a stop. We couldn't touch after we went through the door and I needed to touch her and make her understand one thing. "You be careful. I mean it. Follow my lead. No hero stuff, got it?"

"I understand. I'll stay behind you."

"You are..." I started, but couldn't think of how to word it. "You are really important to me. I need you to stay safe, ok?"

She looked slightly taken back. She bit her lip.

"Cain," she breathed my name and it made my heartbeat skip. "I promise I'm not here to prove anything. I just need to be with you, even if it's in the backdrop. Ok?"

"Ok."

"You don't do anything crazy either."

"Me? Never."

She smiled, which was what I was going for. I touched her cheek with my hand and she closed her eyes. I kissed her again quickly and then we dropped our hands to follow Billings like the good little recruits that we were.

Billings took us through the side door and into a little room with a round middle aged older woman with a smile a mile wide. She was more than delighted with Billings with his two new recruits.

We filled out miniscule paperwork and she gave us our uniform shirts. We followed her to a small back room and changed into them. It was customary that whoever you brought in to the enforcers was your responsibility. Hence, why Billings said he would be my mentor.

It was the perfect setup. Lillian and I were to work with him directly for the next two weeks - yeah right - and then we'd be turned loose on our own. So for today, he was to show us the ropes and daily routines. We even had a little green patch on our pocket that indicated we were in training.

We went through an hour or so of a presentation with a couple other enforcers. They went on and on about rules and such, the mission statement, blah, blah, blah. Then they took us through the stale doughnut and crappy coffee room.

The building wasn't impressive. They had taken over the old Sheriff's office. It had windowless rooms all along the hall after a couple of administrative rooms. Nothing was distinguished. No signs to point where to go or what each wing or room was for. No plaques on the doors. No colors either. Everything was white floors and walls.

We passed a few Lighters in the main hall and my body twitched with a need to pull Lillian to me, to keep her far away from them, but instead I stayed directly behind her, guarding her back as she walked next to Billings and we made our way around.

It was strange to say the least. The Lighters didn't look at us and we tried not to look at them. To them, we weren't important. We were humans, less than nothing. What had Piper called us? Vapors.

It was like they were regular old superiors on any other job. Nobody questioned how they got in the position, you just knew to respect it. It was plain as day compulsion. The Lighters weren't even wearing uniforms. So how did everyone know to tell the difference between them and the rest of us? The human enforcers were in so deep they didn't question anything. They were just mindless.

I followed Billings down to the end of the hall. He informed us that it was a little after 11:00 in the morning. Interrogations were handled right before lunch so we should see them exit once they were done and then we could check the rooms for Sherry and anyone else.

"After the interrogations?" I asked, once what he said clicked.

That did not sit well with me.

"Yes. I'm sorry. They'll be too many of them, several people to each room, but only one guy guards this hall at a time when they aren't conducting business down here. Once they're done, most of them will leave. We'll have a better chance at it then."

"You mean Sherry is in one of these rooms being interrogated right now, right this second, and we just have to sit out here and wait?" Lillian asked quietly.

"I don't like it anymore than you do, but it's our only chance. We can't fight a whole mess of them. We have to get Sherry and whoever else out and to the van undetected. It's going to be hard enough as it is without alerting the Lighters, let alone charging on in there with guns blazing," Billings answered.

I hated that he was right.

We all grabbed some literature from the table and pretended to read and study while we waited for the torture to be over.

After about thirty five minutes, they started exiting the rooms. There were five from a room on the right. Then another room on the right had a few come out and they had a woman with them. She was panting but didn't seem to be too bad off from the back, but I hadn't seen her face. She wasn't bleeding or anything but her clothes and hair were wet.

She was blabbing about telling them anything they wanted. I looked at Billings and he shook his head sadly.

"The ones who crack," he explained. "The ones that give information are taken directly to Malachi."

"And the ones that don't crack?" I asked, fearing that I didn't want to know the answer.

He crossed his arms, watching the hall.

"They stay," he sighed, "and repeat everything tomorrow."

"Just what are they doing to them in there?" Lillian asked angrily.

Her hands were shaking. We'd talked about it before we came in. She and I didn't need to touch each other or show a weakness for each other in case everything went bad, they couldn't use us against one another. We were all supposed to be acquainted but nothing more. And I wanted to hold her so bad right then, because she was scared and furious and it pissed me off that we had to be here in the first place.

"I don't think you-" Billings started.

"Don't you dare tell me you don't think I want to know!" She inched forward, crossing her arms and spoke low. "I want to know, that's why I asked. We need to know what to expect so we'll be prepared. We can help her faster, especially when we get her in the van if we know what's wrong with her and what to tell Miguel to do for her."

Billings looked thoughtful for a minute with his brow furrowed.

"Alright. I haven't been back here much except in the beginning for training. I didn't like it so I chose to work elsewhere but the few times I was back here they used heat and freezing air. They refused them food and water and sleep."

"What do you mean heat and freezing air?"

"First, they get the room so hot, you can't think straight. Then they throw ice water on you and turn the air down to freezing cold. Your body more times than not goes into shock." Lillian looked sick but nodded for him to go on. I wasn't much better. I could feel my body shaking. "They don't feed you or let you sleep either. Other than that, except for a bit of slapping around and such, I personally didn't witness anything else. We always heard crazy stories about the stuff going on down here but..."

It was hard to get a good breath. I couldn't think of Sherry in the next room being slapped or anything else. It wasn't right to just stand out here in the hall and let it happen but, we had to. And it frigging sucked.

We waited. We were almost about to go check the rooms when another group of them came out of a room on the left. Five Lighters, two enforcers. Instantly, I recognized one of them and put my arm on Lillian's back to remind her stay calm. I heard Billings utter a low curse under his breath. I heard Lillian take a swift intake of breath but kept quiet.

It was Daniel. Daniel, the Lighter, who saved us and fought for us. And it was too late to turn around, he was already looking right at us the second he exited the room. His gaze jolted in a double take to us quickly then away. Other than that he didn't act any different than the others as they filed out of the hall.

I noticed that no one came out of the room with them, which meant that they must have not have given in. Good for them, whoever they were.

I held my breath, knowing Daniel was going to rat us out any second, but he just followed the others out of the hall and out into the main part of the building.

One of the enforcers, a big German looking dude, stopped and took up residence in a big chair on the end and immediately picked up a racing magazine from the table. He crossed his ankles and looked bored.

About half a minute later, Daniel came back and spoke to the guard. We couldn't hear them all the way at the other end of the hall, but whatever he said, the guard left quickly with a nod.

Daniel turned to us and I could've sworn he almost smiled. He walked to us slowly and easily. I looked and saw no cameras or anything around, but Lighters couldn't be filmed anyway. That would kind of give them away to the enforcers when they didn't show up on surveillance, now wouldn't it?

He reached us, stopping a couple feet away and kept his voice low but looked right at Lillian with a look of awe and affection. I tried to remember he was a Lighter and it wasn't like I should be jealous. It wasn't like he had a chance with her even though he clearly had some feelings for her, though he may not have understood them.

"What are you three doing here? I never thought I'd see you again."

"They have our friend," Lillian answered quickly. "What are *you* doing here?"

She sounded disappointed and I understood why. If Daniel had some kind of revelation, like he told us, why would he be back here hurting people again?

He winced like her words physically hurt.

"I'm here because it's the only place I can be. The only place I can do any good. Your friend?"

"Sherry."

He closed his eyes and shook his head.

"Your Sherry is a tough one."

"What does that mean?" Lillian asked anxiously.

Billings stepped up.

"Alright, let's do this. Daniel, you gonna try to stop us?"

"You are here to take back your friend," Daniel said with understanding.

"And the others if we can."

Daniel nodded like he already knew that.

"You beat me to it. I have been feeding them and releasing a few of them. I can't save them all or the others will notice. A couple a week, I say they died at night or something. The enforcers believe me, anyway. It's only a matter of time until I get caught. Sherry was going to be my next try, for tonight."

"Really?" Lillian asked. "You've been really doing that?"

"Yes," he sighed and took a deep breath. "I told you I wanted to be different and I am."

"Ok, well," Billings started and stepped forward, "I don't want to get you in trouble so... What do I need to do? Punch you or something so they think you fought us? We can grab Sherry and go?" Billings asked Daniel hurriedly.

"No. A punch wouldn't take me down anyway. I'll help you. I think they are starting to catch on to me in any case, like I said. It was only a matter of time before I'm found out."

"How many captives are here?" Billings asked, back to business and I was grateful for it.

"This is the only captive wing and there are only two left; Sherry and another woman. They haven't gotten to the other one yet. She was only brought in this morning. Sherry is in that room, on the left." Lillian started towards the door quickly but he grabbed her arm to stop her. It irked me a little but I let it go. "I warn you, it's not pretty. I did all I could, but I couldn't be with her every second."

She nodded and I moved to get in front of her as I grabbed the door knob and unbolted the lock.

"Nuhuh, I go in first remember? And, Lillian, let me handle this, ok? Nothing crazy."

She rolled her eyes and smirked a little.

"I'll take Billings and we'll get the other woman," Daniel said and took position in front of the door opposite us in the hall.

Then we opened the doors together and we got our first peek of Sherry, soaking wet and shivering, sprawled out awkwardly on the concrete floor lying on her back. Blood was mixing with the water swirling around her. Her bloody legs were bent underneath her. Her skin sickly white and blue all over. She had a massive bruise on the side of her face and her nose was bleeding. Daniel wasn't lying.

It definitely wasn't pretty.

Now or Never
Chapter 2 - Sherry

They were still pumping in the heat. I'd not been fed anything else since that water and granola bar, and I was beginning to wonder if I was even supposed to have that. I'd not been allowed to sleep. Every time I closed my eyes they banged on the door or blared a horn into my room from a speaker in the ceiling.

I continued to sing in my head. Anything to keep my mind from running. I didn't know what else to do. I was sweating so much and my face felt flushed and burned. The water and granola I'd eaten were long gone, burned up in my body from the heat. I felt lightheaded and foggy, my knees ached, my head hurt, my eye was swollen. All I wanted to do was go to sleep but they wouldn't allow it.

I didn't know how much longer I could hold on without passing out, and then I wondered what they'd do.

I didn't have to wait long for the answer. I just couldn't stay awake. I tried. I heard the banging. I heard the horn, it roused me but not fully and I couldn't open my eyes. I heard the door, I felt the cool air from the hall blow over my damp skin and it was almost painful with relief. It caused me to shake and have gooseflesh.

Then I felt someone grab me by my shirt back. I was dragged across the concrete floor, my knees scraping on the way. I was taken to a room a little ways down across the hall. I tried to wake, to see what was going on, but before I could succeed, my face was immersed in freezing ice water.

I felt a hand on the back of my neck, gripping tightly and bruising. I tried to fight but he was too strong. I struggled and wiggled and kicked and scratched. I saw a burst of light from the corner of my eye where I broke the skin on his hand but he still didn't let go.

Just when I thought that this was it, he was just going to kill me this way, he pulled me up and held me by my hair, which was no longer in a bun but a sodden mess. He was right in my face.

"Awake?" he barked.

I couldn't say anything as I spit and sputtered and gasped. I blinked and tried to focus but, no good. I could barely see him right in front of me. The curtain of hair in my view didn't help either.

He pushed my face back into the sink of water again, this time he held me under for less time but it was enough. I again sputtered and choked.

17

He pulled back from me some and slapped me across the face. It felt so different from the last time I'd been slapped, this one was openhanded, wet and close and quick. It stung and pounded through my head. I forced my eyes open all the way so he wouldn't do it again.

"Awake?" he asked again gruffly.

"Yes," I croaked.

"Hey!" The Lighter holding me turned and we saw another one had yelled from behind us. "Don't damage the goods. Malachi may want her."

"She hasn't been *processed* yet. She needs to be handled before he can have her."

I worried about that word 'processed'.

"Where did this one come from?"

They talked like I wasn't in the room. Like I was nothing, nobody.

"No idea. Who cares? She's not a loyal, right? Out there way back from town? Only rebels that way, and if not, well then Malachi gets a nice new plaything."

"I guess. Well, take it easy on the face anyway. He likes them pretty."

I saw the water beneath me was red in the sink. I looked up to the mirror on the wall above it and there was blood running down my nose and chin. From the slap I guessed. I also noticed that I looked absolutely horrible.

My eye and cheek were swollen, red and bluish. I remembered the elbow to the face in the car and the car window. The rest of me was paler than usual. I had bruises on my arms and neck. I had no idea how they got there, must've been from when I was passed out and they dragged me. My pant legs were ripped and bloody, as were my knees. They were crusted with dried blood and new blood and dirt. I hurt so much all over I could barely stand up.

The Lighter who had me by the hair dragged me with it to the same room I was in before. I felt the heat on my skin from the hall, then he pushed me in and let me fall to the floor from the release of his hand.

"Stay awake or you'll get another dunk. They'll be in soon enough to ask you some questions."

He slammed the door.

I lay there, waiting for- what? I knew I wasn't going to die. I could see that now. They wouldn't kill me, yet. Not until they'd tortured me for information. I blanked my mind and hoped beyond hope that I could withstand the pain. That I wouldn't cave, wouldn't give them what they want.

What I thought was a few show tunes and a couple hours later, they came in. Five of them; three Lighters and two enforcers. They all looked so normal, so human. Even with the dark hair and eyes. The two enforcers were blond and tall and regal looking. They refused to meet my gaze. I did recognize one of the Lighters as the one who'd said he would help me, who brought me food and water.

Daniel.

Right now, he didn't look like he'd be much help. He stared blankly at the back wall.

They closed the door and gathered around me in a loose circle as I still sat half sprawled, my legs under me, on the floor in the middle. I tried to keep my breaths steady and not show them how scared I was. They had two five gallon red buckets and I wondered what was in them.

My hair was still wet from my dunk and scraggly all over my head and face and shoulders. My pants and shirt had blood that had dripped down from my nose. And though I was so hot I felt like I'd pass out, I wanted to shiver from fright.

This was it. Whatever their end game plan was, they were putting it to action.

The two enforcers grabbed the buckets and came one after the other and dumped them on top of me. The water was freezing cold. There were even some ice cubes that fell beside me but melted quickly on the hot concrete. Then I felt the air change. They were no longer heating me, they were freezing me.

The air vent directly above me blew in frigid air in a fast current. I tried to inch over so the air wasn't right on me but one of them kicked me in the leg to halt me.

"You'll stay right where you are."

I shivered and my teeth chattered. I wanted to tell them they didn't have to try so hard to freeze me. That I got cold really quickly anyway but I knew it didn't matter. My head seemed to float and my ears were waving in and out of hearing. The lightheadedness made my vision swim. I blinked to stop it but I felt myself slip, I couldn't stop it.

I blacked out.

I was awakened with another slap across the face. I gasped and focused with everything I had in me. This time it was the enforcer. I looked him right in the eyes. It wasn't the Lighter that hit me. This was the human.

He held my shirt in his fist and waited for me to steady myself. He didn't even flinch when I felt the hot tears stinging the flesh of my frozen cheeks, which made me wonder how long I'd been unconscious to be so cold. He just watched. This was his job. He'd been made to believe he was doing good. I guessed I shouldn't blame him for it. It wasn't the enforcers' faults. They didn't know any better.

19

He let go once he saw I wasn't going to pass out again and I laid there, freezing, shaking and hurting. I wiped my face to remove all traces of crying, my fingers were white and stiff.

"Now that we have your attention, we want to know all the names of the people you live with," one of the Lighters asked me, bending down on his haunches to be at my level.

I blanked my mind, though Daniel told me he'd block me, I was scared to believe. I said the first thing that came to mind.

"My brother Richard and I l-live with my grandparents. I w-work at the store you found me at," I chattered.

"Wow. You are an absolutely horrible liar. It's like you're not even trying." He laughed humorlessly but the others stayed silent. "Why don't we try this again? Who do you live with?"

"I t-told you," I said quietly and looked up at Daniel.

He was watching me now and nodded, a small movement that no one else saw. He was telling me to keep it up. I looked away before someone saw me staring and pulled my knees up to my chest for warmth.

"I don't believe you. Do you know what we are going do to you?"

"N-no."

"Lot's of bad things if you don't tell us what we want to know. We can keep you in here as long as it takes. Or until the lack of food and water kill you. Either one ends badly for you."

"There's nothing else to t-tell."

"Tell me the truth." He looked at me directly and spoke slow and steady. I knew he was trying to use the Lighter speak. "Who do you live with?"

"I told you already," I answered softly.

I tried to think of inconspicuous things while they all just sat there and watched me. A cheese sandwich. My high school prom. President T. Roosevelt. When no one's expression around me changed, I decided to test the theory. I pictured myself sticking my tongue out at the jerk Lighter in front of me.

Nothing, but I did see Daniel crack the tiniest smile and he shook his head just a bit. I sent him a thought.

I guess you weren't lying about blocking me.

He gave me a look that said 'I told you so'.

What's gonna happen to me?

He looked sad and shook his head slightly and we all sat there as they continued to study me. Finally I couldn't take it anymore. I had to say something.

"If I knew anything about rebels, I'd t-tell you. That's what you're looking for, isn't it? I'm not one of them," I said and saw my breath like a fog in front of my mouth.

"What do you know about it, little girl?"

"I saw it on the n-news. You're offering a reward for them. If I knew I'd t-tell you. I c-could use the money. Believe me."

"Why?" he asked and stood up looking around at the rest of them. "How are they all so blank and unresponsive? It's like they know what to expect from us." No one answered. It wasn't really a question, he was just venting. "I've had it with this." He bent down, grabbing my shirt and slapped me across the cheek again, much harder than the other two had done. When the stars cleared I wondered if my cheeks would ever feel the same again. "You will tell me exactly what I want to hear or you will die, understand?"

I didn't. I didn't understand anything. I was in a haze of pain and miscomprehension. I lay limp in his grasp, waiting for him to slap me again and wake me from my stupor.

"I-" I heard myself stammer.

"They're all dead you know. We found them and they are all dead."

I knew he was lying. Not only could I tell but I also knew that if that were true, he wouldn't be asking me for information that he already had. I tried to keep my face blank, which wasn't too hard since I was on my way to passing out anyway.

"Alright. Times up," Daniel said and strolled forward. "Let's go get lunch. You'll get nothing from this one today."

"It's not time," the jerk said looking at his watch. "We still have five minutes."

"Mine says time. Let's go."

The jerk picked me up from the floor in his grasp. Both hands fisted my shirt front, my head lulled back as I was unable to hold it up. My feet were at least two feet off the floor. I was so cold, so utterly numb but painfully aware at the same time. It seemed to be worse than the heat.

"Tomorrow. The time will not save you, little girl, and I will get my answers."

He dropped me all the way to the floor and I crumpled under my own weight like a doll. My head and back hit hard on the solidness of the floor and I gasped and tried to roll over but couldn't. I couldn't make my body move.

I don't know if it was the concussion, or the heat and then cold or all the hits but I was molded to the floor, uncomfortably laying there, watching through barely there slit eyes as they all made their way out of the room, leaving the freezing blowing air and violent shivering to be my only constant reminder that I was even alive anymore.

Daniel was last to leave, holding the door. He looked at me but I fell into a sleep or blacked out again. Something. The last thing I remember was his boot and then the door closing behind him with an audible final click of the lock.

I woke up with a warm hand on my cheek and I immediately grabbed at it like a lifeline.

"Merrick?" I said but my voice was scratchy and rough.

"No, Sherry, it's Cain. Open your eyes."

My eyelids fluttered opened slowly and unsteadily at the request and I saw Cain leaning over me, looking distraught and angry.

"C-Cain," I squeaked and stuttered and when I tried to reach my arm up to him, but it wouldn't go.

"Shh. I've got you. Gah, you're ice, Sherry." He gathered me up in his arms and I moaned out loud at the warmth of him. My fingers wouldn't bend as I tried to grasp his collar and pull myself closer. "Hang on, sweetheart."

I heard someone else murmuring in the room. Lillian.

"Lillian?"

"I'm here, Sherry. We're going to take you home, ok. Just hang on."

Then other voices, one I knew but couldn't put a face to it and the other was Daniel. I wanted to look but couldn't, not just yet. My head was muddled and tired, uncooperative.

"Come. We've got to get out this way-" Daniel said but was cut off by a yell.

"Hey! What are you doing?"

"Prisoner transfer."

"I don't have a transfer on my schedule f-"

I heard scuffles and grunts and it felt like Cain was running, as I was being jostled. He set me down in a big scratchy cloth chair. I opened my eyes to see what was going on and the hall was blurring and swirling. I blinked to focus.

Daniel was fighting someone, and Billings and Cain were fighting another. I couldn't tell what they were: human or Lighter. Lillian was on the other end of the hall. She appeared to be looking for something or someone.

I was finally able to move my limbs some, my bones and veins still cold and stiff but they went when I told them to now, painful as it was. I sat up in the chair and watched with horrid fascination. It all came to a screeching full on understanding.

Cain, Lillian and Billings had come to save me. Daniel was helping them and now, the Lighters had been alerted and were coming to stop them. I felt so useless and scared for them.

I looked again and saw a woman, no, a girl, with Lillian at the other end of the hall now. The girl was leaning on the wall, sitting on the floor, looking as scared as I felt.

I saw blurs of banging fists and legs. Daniel threw one of them into the wall and broken pieces of dry wall fell off in chunks to the concrete floor. Billings was kicked in the stomach and doubled over but quickly recovered, upper cutting the one he was fighting in the chin sending him falling backward into a table with papers and brochures on it. The papers flew up into the air in a cloud and rained down all around him on the floor. I saw that he was a human.

I heard a loud crashing and looked to my left to see the door to the rest of the building had been banged open. A couple of people came through it and jumped into the fight, down on Lillian's end of the hall was the same. Three enforcers ran out of the door at the end and started swinging.

Cain was a force all his own. He took them down easily, one after another and I knew he had his gift to use if need be but I was sure he was trying to not use it to draw attention to us.

I was surprised there wasn't an alarm or something. I stood up on shaky legs and leaned on the wall. I might need to run and if that's the case, I need to get my baring before that happens.

I was grabbed from the side and I screamed out of surprise. He gripped me around the throat and I surprised the heck out of myself by using the hold break maneuver Miguel had taught me, out of instinct. I slammed the heel of my hand into his inside elbow and he let go. I ducked under his arm but before I could run or do anything else he gripped me again and slammed me into the wall before grabbing me from behind to hold my arms down.

I looked up and saw that Lillian was being attacked too from her end. An enforcer had her by the throat but she wasn't fighting back, she didn't know how. I screamed to Cain, who had just put down an enforcer.

"Cain! Lillian!" I screamed to tell him to go to her and was surprised to hear that my voice worked again.

He looked to me first, eyes wide, then Lillian. She was watching just like I was. His gaze switched from me to her several times, his face twisted. I realized he was struggling with who to save. He was making up his mind on who to run to, making a choice.

Then he made it.

He took off running for Lillian fast, his boots pounding on the concrete; I could hear them all the way from where I was standing. He grabbed the enforcer from behind and wretched his head back, throwing him to the ground. Then grabbed Lillian in his arms and turned back, taking a step toward me. The woman still sat on the floor with her eyes shut and her ears covered.

The enforcer who had me was trying to pull me out of the hall. I say trying but, he was succeeding. I could barely stand and he was practically dragging me. Then I saw Daniel take a stake, one of ours from home that Cain or Billings must have brought, and drive it through the stomach of the only other Lighter in the hallway.

I saw the bursting light. Daniel ducked down as the bolt of lightning shot forth and out of the Lighter's chest straight through the roof of the building. The boom was massive and my ears were ringing. Lights flickered and a couple big fluorescent ones hung down from the ceiling on their hinges. Plaster and wood pieces fell all around us in a shower of debris.

The enforcer who had me had stopped moving to watch with horror on his face but now in the aftermath had started dragging me again. Daniel blurred my direction and punched the man in the nose, who fell back bleeding and confused. Daniel grabbed me under my legs and back as I started to collapse. The man took one more look at Daniel and ran the other way.

I heard Daniel yelling to the others.

"If they didn't know you were here before, they definitely know now. Out this way. Let's go."

I buried my face in Daniel's chest. Yes, he was a Lighter and yes I felt awkward at his whole turn-around attitude, but I'd heard the story of what Cain and Lillian had said about what he did. I'd seen him help me and he was helping us now. And right that second, he was holding me carefully like I was fragile and important enough to worry about.

The most important of all the reasons I was clinging to him was because I was still freezing cold and even though Lighters are cold skinned themselves, he was still warmer than I was.

He was still wearing that big jacket from earlier and I tried to sleepily snuggle into it as he crept down the hall. I heard footsteps behind us and stiffened.

"Don't be frightened. It's just your companions," he whispered to me as he set me in a chair in the hall, took off his jacket and wrapped it around me, even did the buttons for me.

Cain came into view.

"How you holding up, kiddo?"

"I-" I tried to speak but couldn't, my mouth was cotton and my vision started to blur again, so I tried for a smile, but it must have looked more like a grimace. Then I was being swiftly picked up once more in cold arms and carried down the hall.

"Faster. We've got medical supplies in the van," Cain ordered.

We reached the door and Billings told Cain the code to get it to open. He too had his hands full, trying to coax the girl to follow us and be quiet. She looked

24

frightened beyond belief. Her dark eyes were wide and shallow and dark rimmed. She whimpered behind us as he pulled her along.

Billings yelled something to Cain about a room next to us. They opened it and started rummaging through.

Daniel made it out the door first with me still in his arms and rounded the corner. I didn't see Cain or Lillian, not even Billings. It was so bright I couldn't keep my eyes open. My ears were still ringing from the lightning blast.

I heard yelling in front of us. I felt the vibrations in Daniel's chest as he yelled back. I made myself peek and saw Merrick. My heart immediately went off the charts, skipping violently, but I was still too weak to move much. I tried to tell Daniel it was ok but he couldn't hear me over Merrick and Danny's yelling.

Danny. Danny was there, too.

I realized what that must've looked like to them. I had just come out of the enforcement facility after being kidnapped, unconscious and bloody, carried by a Lighter with no Billings or Cain in sight. Crap.

I raised my hand slowly and heard them all stop.

"It's ok."

Daniel walked slowly and carefully to Merrick a few feet away and held me out for him to take.

"I believe this belongs to you," Daniel said and passed me to Merrick's warm arms.

Before Daniel could get staked by someone, I made sure to let them know he was not gonna hurt us, that he was one of us now.

"Merrick-"

"It's ok, baby. I've got you," he said and his arms settled and tightened around me.

"No. This is Daniel. He helped me," I creaked.

Merrick looked up to him. I looked between the two as they stared each other down. No matter how much Daniel may have changed, I was sure it wasn't easy to be face to face with a Keeper, your known enemy for thousands of years, and not still feel a pang of needing to do something about it.

Danny stood off to the side glaring at Daniel, too.

Luckily, Cain and Billings came around the corner just in time to diffuse and Cain started telling everyone to get back in the van. Now. As if something was about to happen and we needed to get out of there.

Lillian grabbed Daniel's arm beside me and started pulling him to the van.

"Come on. Come with us."

"No, Lillian. I can not go with you."

"Yes, you can. They don't care. They'll understand."

"I believe you are mistaken about that."

25

She looked at Merrick.

"You would stop him from coming with us after he helped Sherry? You need to hear what he's done. You have no idea, but there's no time. Don't stop him from coming with us, Merrick. He saved Sherry's life."

Merrick looked at Daniel sharply for a moment and nodded.

"Let's go."

I was so incredibly proud of him. As I was sure it wasn't easy for Daniel, it wasn't easy for Merrick either, to put away all that old rivalry, but Merrick would do anything for me. And he just kept proving it over and over again.

I heard Daniel and Lillian talking back and forth as Merrick walked away. Billings was putting the girl in and handing her to Ryan, who he explained to her was a good guy. She clung to him and buried her face in his neck to cry. He was startled, but he leaned back against the front seat and settled in with her.

Once settled in the van, Merrick placed me on the floor in front of Miguel.

"You just can't keep out of trouble can ya, love?" Miguel asked me and smiled. I tried to smile back but my face hurt something awful. He touched my arm. "You're freezing, Sherry. And your face!" He looked up to Merrick to explain.

Merrick shrugged.

"I have no idea. Ask him," he said and nodded toward Daniel, who was climbing in and everyone got really quiet.

"What's he doing in here?" Jeff said angrily and Miguel grunted in agreement.

"Hey," I croaked and it was so quiet in the van that everyone could hear me. "He saved me. Ask him all the questions you want, but he risked his life to save mine."

Merrick nodded to me.

"I know that, I'm sorry. Thousands of years of habit are gonna be hard to break." He looked back up to Daniel. "I'd shake your hand but..." Lighters and Keepers couldn't touch each other's skin, so Merrick just tilted his head to him, "but thank you."

It was like everyone held their breath.

"You are more than welcome."

I couldn't help but think this was the first time in history that a Lighter and a Keeper had called truce. I wondered if it would be a recurring event.

Daniel looked down at me as Miguel threw a blanket over me and started looking at my face.

"I'd like to come but I'm needed out here. There are other enforcement facilities nearby. I'll go to them and continue to help if I can." He touched my shoulder and I saw Jeff tense beside me. "I told you to be strong and everything would be ok, didn't I?"

26

"Thank you." I reached over to grab his hand. "You could just come with us."

"I could. Maybe one day," he said and patted my hand, creeping out backwards. "But for now, I have a lot to make up for."

Lillian pulled him in for a hug. He looked awkward and unsettled by it but patted her back before stepping back to let Cain and Billings in the van. Billing turned before shutting the door.

"I would head for the hills if I were you. We rigged the place."

Daniel nodded, looking first at Lillian for a long second, then back at me.

"We'll meet again someday. Be safe."

Billings slammed the door and whoever was driving jerked us into first gear and away from the building. I heard a faint siren or alarm going off and felt a rush of panic. I heard Billings counting down softly looking at his watch.

"I set it for five minutes. That should be plenty of time for the innocents to get out."

"Get out for what?" I asked and Miguel told me not to talk and got me to sip some water.

Billings made a show of an explosion with his hands. I understood. That's where they were when Daniel had me by the van. Setting a trap. A bomb.

The alarm got louder and then I heard yelling.

"Dang. I thought we'd make it," Billings barked. "Well, we brought you for muscle. Let's go guys. They already closed the gate but I only count six of them, all enforcers."

"Let's do it fast," Cain ordered as the van screeched to a stop and the door slammed opened.

He jumped, then Billings, then Miguel.

Merrick looked down to me.

"Be right back."

He was gone before I could say a word to him in protest. I was still foggy and groggy and essentially exhausted. My blood felt thick and sluggish in my veins but I struggled to stay awake. I tried to sit up, but Lillian stopped me.

"No, no, no. They'll be fine. They are handling them."

"What's going on?" I rasped.

"They're fighting the enforcers at the gate blocking our way. It's ok." She kept looking out the window and not at me. "They are doing fine. Almost all the enforcers are down now."

"And now?"

"Here they come."

I felt the movement of people jumping in the van.

I tried not to think about the enforcers out there. They were innocent, but under a spell. It wasn't fair to them. Maybe we could help them somehow, learn how to break the compulsion from the Lighters, change the persuasion. We could show them how it really was.

I felt a hand on my forehead as the van jerked into movement again and felt strange for worrying another second about anything that didn't have black hair and green eyes and was looking at me with such concern it made me ache, right at that moment.

We slammed through the gate and I saw pieces of it flying around the windows from my spot on the floor. And then we were home free, I assumed.

"Hey," Merrick said with concern. "I know this is a dumb question, but do you feel alright? Where do you hurt the most?" he asked running his hand over my hair.

"Everywhere," I answered truthfully. "Come here."

He lay down beside me without hesitation, though there was barely room, and wrapped his arms around me under the blanket Miguel had given me. I barely had the strength to snuggle in but I did my best.

You have got to stop doing this to me.

I nodded. "I know," I countered and pointed to my lips limply. Asking. It felt like déjà vu all over again. He smiled and pressed a careful easy kiss to my upturned lips and then rested his forehead against mine.

No more. I mean it this time. You can not leave my sight. I hope you enjoy watching me shave and talk Keeper talk, because you are attached to my hip from now on.

I laughed silently, but could feel the movement of it. He chuckled too and I loved it so much that I didn't let on how much it hurt my body to laugh.

"I don't care anymore. If that's what it takes, then so be it. I just know I never want to be away from you again." I saw Danny watching me with concern and worry from out of the corner of my eye. "That goes for you, too, brat."

He chuckled and shook his head. "At least you still have your sense of humor."

"Humor? You *are* a brat."

"I missed you, too, little sister."

I smiled and felt Miguel pouring something onto my knee, antiseptic of some kind. I sucked in a breath through my teeth, wincing. Merrick bolted upright and glared at Miguel.

28

"Hey," Miguel held up his hands in surrender. "Just a little peroxide."

"It stung a little, that's all. It's fine," I said.

Then we heard the explosion.

Everyone turned to look but Merrick kept a firm hand on my shoulder to hold me down. I didn't want to see it anyway. I had enough of violence and death. I just wanted to forget it all.

I pulled Merrick back down to me and let him fuss over me as I was so exhausted and couldn't do much else. He tucked the covers around us and kissed me somewhere where there wasn't a bruise every thirty seconds. He tucked my wet hair behind me ears, rubbed his hands up and down my body to warm me, murmured sweet things in my mind.

Ryan detangled himself from the girl, who still refused to talk, and leaned over us.

"Hey, there. How are you doing?"

"I've been better."

He looked aghast. "Oh, Sherry. I'm sorry. That was stupid-"

"I'm just joking, Ryan," I calmed him. "I'm ok. I'll *be* ok," I corrected.

For whatever reason my mind waited until that moment to let it all crash over me; everything that had happened, thinking I'd never see my family again, how much I hurt all over. All the things that the Lighters had done to me. All those human enforcers. All my family members surrounding me, who came to save me. All the people who had come through those rooms and didn't make it out. My lip started to quiver.

Ryan leaned down to half hug me and it was the last straw. I started to cry.

I didn't try to hold back this time. I couldn't anyway. The tears spilled out and I felt Ryan stiffen. He rubbed my arm. "I'm sorry," he whispered.

"I'm ok, Ryan. It's not you. I just can't..."

"I know."

He pulled back and Merrick enveloped me in his arms once again. And I cried. I cried long and painfully. My body shook with the force of it and it just added to the already very present pain, but I did it anyway.

I needed to.

I felt someone rubbing my leg, another person rubbing my hair. Merrick was in my head and surrounding me with his arms and his love, which was warm like the sun.

I decided it was time to stop and felt Merrick wipe the last of the tears away. I looked around the van, embarrassed by my meltdown, and saw Jeff at my head and Marissa behind him, her arms around his neck. They both smiled sadly at me when they saw me looking. Danny was still watching me and I tried to smile at him again. He didn't look at all convinced that I was ok.

Miguel kept working on me and Billings was talking to whoever was driving. The woman was back to gripping Ryan's shirt as if he were her only lifeline, his arms were awkward and loose around her.

Cain and Lillian were both in their own world in the far back. She was in his lap and they both looked asleep, but I doubted they were. He held her close and tight, their faces resting against each other.

I remembered him agonizing over which one of us to save. I hoped that he didn't feel bad about that. I understood. Between the two of us, she had been the worse off. Plus, she was the one he loved. And he did love her, I knew that, but I wondered if he knew.

It all worked out in the end. We were all safe, for now.

It's Just A Sandwich
Chapter 3 - Lillian

We'd been home for about an hour.

Sherry fell asleep or passed out, maybe. She was carried into the bunker by a relieved Merrick. Danny trailed sadly behind and everyone fawned all over them.

Celeste met Danny at the stairs and wrapped her arms around him, kissing him frantically as he lifted her in a hug. Margo was nowhere in sight.

Jeff and Marissa slunk down the hall to get away from everyone as Ryan toted that poor frozen stiff girl to a high back chair in the corner.

She refused to let him go, clinging to his shirt collar and begging him not to leave her there as she looked around frantically at all the even newer faces. She was in hysterics. We didn't even know her name. He settled in on the floor beside her chair and she seemed to find that acceptable, though she kept his hand in between hers. Her eyes darted from one face to the other.

Merrick carried Sherry to the couch and Miguel told everyone to stand back just as Lily bolted from her room yelling for Merrick.

Danny grabbed her before she could reach him, picking her up in his arms.

"Whoa," he crooned, "slow down, bug."

"Shawwy? Where's Mommy?" she called loudly, searching all around with her eyes and a few people jerked up their heads.

Even I had never heard Lily call Sherry 'mommy' before.

"She's here."

He took her over to where Merrick stood so she could see Sherry on the couch. Merrick leaned close to Lily, touching her cheek.

"Mommy's ok. She's just not feeling very good right now. We have to let her sleep for a little while and then I promise you, you can have her, ok? She missed you so much."

Lily didn't look happy or eager about Merrick's explanation, but nodded and rested her head on Danny's shoulder as he and Celeste carted her away.

We only brought minimal supplies with us in the van so Miguel ran to get more. He wrapped Sherry's knees in gauze and pushed a needle in her arm with some yellow clear liquid in it. He spread a cream across her face. She slept through all of his ministrations.

31

I overheard him say to Merrick that he was pretty sure she had a concussion and a fractured cheek bone, but he couldn't be sure. We needed to wait until Sherry woke up and told us what happened to her.

Cain just stood by me and watched everything happen around us. I wanted to get away, let Merrick and Sherry spend some recoup time together. But I wasn't sure if Cain was ready to leave, if he was worried about her and needed to make sure she was alright first.

I knew he felt bad. I hated it that he had to choose between me and her in the facility; to save her or me. I hated it that he had to deal with it like that, it wasn't fair to him. As jealous as I got about the situation, it still wasn't fair for him to have to go through that. Though I was surprised that he chose me.

I reached over and took his hand. He looked at me and cracked a small smile.

"Do you want to stay or..." I asked quietly.

"No. Let's go make some sandwiches for everyone. None of us have had any lunch anyway," he suggested.

"Sure," I said, glad for the distraction.

So we went and made about twenty turkey sandwiches and three gallons of sweet tea. Then Cain called everyone to eat.

I took Merrick a plate since he was in no way interested in leaving Sherry's side. He took it and grabbed my hand.

"Thank you," he said looking right into my eyes and I thought I'd never seen eyes that green before.

"You're welcome, Merrick. It's just a sandwich."

"I'm not talking about the sandwich," he said meaningfully. "Thank you."

"No problem. She would have done it for me."

He nodded and let me go and then called out to me before I walked off.

"Oh, and thanks for the sandwich, too," he said and smiled.

"You're welcome," I said and smiled back.

I went to Cain in the kitchen. He was sitting on the counter finishing off his sandwich and drinking tea out of a big Mason jar. Billings was just walking out and I heard him mumbling about going to his room, that there were too many people in this place. I walked up to Cain and stood between his knees.

"Well," he said and put his arms on my shoulders. "Had enough excitement?"

"Definitely."

"Good. Me, too."

"Sherry got lucky."

"Yeah, I know she did," he said softly.

"If Daniel hadn't been there-"

32

"I know," he said. I sighed and let my cheek rest on his chest. He spoke into my hair. "I'm glad you're ok, L."

"I'm only ok because of you," I told him and he took a deep breath. I decided to go ahead and get it out there. "I know what you did. I saw you and I'm really sorry you had to choose between us like that."

"I'm not," he replied surprising me. "I mean, I'm not glad that we were in the situation, but it made me see once and for all what's the most important thing to me." He cupped my cheeks and looked straight into my eyes to relay his conviction. "You."

I licked my lips that had suddenly become parched and tried to breathe normally.

Oh my. I was in love with him. How long had I known him? A month? Could you fall completely in love with someone in a month? I guess you could, because I was so in love with him. And he must feel something for me because he told me he was in love with Sherry before and he chose me over her.

"You aren't still angry with me, are you?" he asked quietly.

"No. I thought you'd be angry for having to choose. For choosing me," I said bluntly.

"I'm not and I never will be." He hopped down from the counter and grabbed my hand. "Come on. Come sit with me for a while. There are some things I don't know about you that I'd like to."

"Like what?" I asked wondering if he was thinking of something specific.

"Everything. We have some time to kill. Everyone's gonna be so wrapped up in Sherry for the rest of the day we won't even get a word in with them. I want to know everything about *you*."

"And I can have some questions, too?"

"Of course. Though I have to warn you, prepare to doze, my life was mundane and boring."

"As was mine."

"I'll be the judge of that. Sit here."

He'd walked us to the second room and sat me on the loveseat. He went and turned on the radio and then came back to settle in on the end opposite me, putting my feet in his lap.

"Ok. So, you're an only child, right?"

"Yes."

"And your parents were missionaries." I nodded and he looked pensive. "Did you go to prom?"

"Yes. Did you?"

"No. With who?"

"Michael. Why didn't you go?"

"I was working, but didn't have the money to rent a tux anyway. Both my parents were laid off from work at the time. They were laid off a lot. Ok, how about extracurricular?"

"I was on the dance squad."

"Really..." he drawled and smiled deviously. "That I'd like to have seen."

I laughed and shook my head at him, tucking the hair behind my ear. Not only did I roll my eyes at his typical male response, but I was blushing furiously at the look he was giving me.

"You? Wait- football?"

"Yes," he sighed. "Cliché quarterback dated the head cheerleader."

"Aha. So, how long did that last?"

"We got engaged right after high school."

"Really! You were engaged? Wow. So...what happened? You're not secretly married are you?"

"Nope. I called off the wedding. She was more interested in her boss' tongue than she was in marrying me."

Oh, no. She cheated on him.

"Oh, I'm sorry."

"It's ok. I didn't love her." He held up his hands. "I know that sounds bad, but we'd been together so long, it was just routine or habit for us, you know? Neither of us cried when it was over." He squeezed my foot. "So, did you and Michael have a big wedding?"

"Nope. My parents were gone already on a mission trip and I didn't have any other family. And Michael's dad had passed away a few years before. His mom came to the church with us, but she was less than thrilled about him marrying me. We had a small ceremony with only about fifteen people. Mostly our school friends."

He nodded, thinking. Rubbing his bottom lip with his thumb.

"Favorite color?" he asked, raising an eyebrow.

"Red. Yours?"

"Don't really have one. I'm eclectic, easy to please."

"Uhuh. What's your least favorite food?"

"Ok. Don't laugh, but it's birthday cake."

"What?" I laughed. "How can you not like birthday cake?"

"Easy. I hate it. It's too sweet and spongy then gooey and always has those annoying sprinkles. I can't stand it." He made a face like he was imagining taking a bite and was disgusted making me giggle. "What's yours?"

"Bananas."

"Texture or taste?"

34

"Both, but mostly texture. Matter of fact, I love banana flavored candy, just not bananas themselves."

"You are strange," he goaded in his familiar sarcastic way.

"Hey!" I kicked my foot gently into his stomach and he tickled my foot making me giggle harder. "So, I already know you play guitar and you were a Sergeant in the Marines. I know you love kids and like to work. You have a green thumb and really love your sweet tea. What else?"

"There's not a lot left to tell you."

"Oh, come on," I pleaded. "What is something nobody knows about you? I won't tell anyone," I said sweetly and smiled at him.

"Hmmm." He touched his tongue to his lip ring, thinking. "I once prank called a girl I liked in the ninth grade. I was trying to get her to meet me at the movies without knowing who I was because I thought she'd say no. She hung up on me. The next day at school she got this other guy in trouble for stalking because she thought it was him. I never told anyone it was me. No one."

"Wow. I'm so happy to be privy to your big bad secret," I said with mock seriousness.

"Yo," he said and pointed at me, "back in the day, I was bad boned. I was tough, ok? Rugged. People feared me."

"I'm sure they did," I said blandly to goad him.

"Are you doubting my mad badness?"

"Oh, no. Now way. Certainly not."

"Oh, L." He shook his head. "You are skating dangerously close to skepticism."

"Oh, I'm not skating. I'm there." I laughed at his playful scowl.

"You are gonna pay for that, lovely." He jumped up and grabbed me as I made a try to run, but he overpowered me, bracing himself over me on the couch length wise. "You may be cute, but you are not immune to the rules."

I giggled. "And what rules are you referring to?"

"The rules of opposite sex etiquette. Don't challenge the manliness of the guy that is within tickle range."

"Ooh. Good rule. I'll remember that."

"You better. I'll let you off with a warning this time."

"What's my penalty?" I asked and bit my lip to tease him.

"What do you think?" He leaned in so close his lips were almost grazing mine.

"I think...that you are awfully cheesy, mister," I crooned sweetly.

"That's it! Last straw!" he yelled and began to tickle me on my sides.

I screamed and giggled and squirmed, but there was no getting loose.

"Ok! Ok! I give. You are so, so manly! You are rugged and handsome and…" I stopped to gasp and scream as he intensified his assault. "So manly! Please! You are so manly!"

He smiled at me in triumph and stopped tickling. He let his weight press me further into the couch.

"That's right, and don't you forget it."

"How could I with a display like that?"

He chuckled and continued to look at me. He brushed the hair off my face that had fallen over my eye then he ran his thumb over my bottom lip making my heartbeats gallop. I decided to take the initiative this time. I pulled him down to me by his shirt collar.

He seemed pleasantly surprised, given by his smirk.

I kissed the hollow of his neck and had the pleasure of hearing his breath catch. I kissed my way up and bit his lip ring playfully. He chuckled before taking over and pressing our lips together. He stayed braced over me on his elbows as his mouth ravished mine. After a few minutes he pulled back quickly. I was confused by the sudden change of pace, but he just scooped me up and took me to the bed on the far wall.

He probably wasn't too comfortable sprawled out with me on the loveseat I imagined. He placed me gently to the bed and picked up right where he left off.

His mouth was eager as his hand took a tour of my body in caresses and chaste advances. His fingers went just under the hem of my shirt, but no further, and he pulled me closer to him by my belt loops.

It seemed we stayed like that for hours. My lips were swollen and my jaw was chafed deliciously from his stubble. My fingers were sore and stiff from fisting his shirt for so long. It was the first time we'd just been able to completely be alone and together like that.

Eventually, we stopped to breathe, but he kept his hands on me. Our noses were touching while we lay on our sides. I drifted off into a sleep, restful and needed.

When I woke up some time later, I smelled dinner cooking. Cain's face was pressed into my hair and he was still asleep. Our arms and legs were tangled. I knew there was no way to get free without waking him up, so I stayed there. It was where I wanted to be anyway.

An Undulated Fate
Chapter 4 - Merrick

Sherry slept for hours. I didn't move her again because Miguel wasn't sure of the extent of her injuries. So, there she stayed on the couch in all her broken splendor.

Lily was anxious and persistent to wake her. She didn't understand what was going on and Danny wasn't much better. He drifted our way every few minutes or so, peeking over the couch and pursing his lips. I assured him I'd call him in his mind the second she woke up.

I didn't leave her side. This surprised no one, including me. This was standard conduct for me; Sherry watch. I just couldn't leave her. So I stayed watch and held Lily for a while before she tottered off to more fun ventures, and fended off questions for and about Sherry.

Well after supper was done, Cain and Lillian came into the room looking disheveled and incandescent. They walked hand in hand over to me and acted extremely happy. I tried not to take it personally on Sherry's behalf.

"Hey, how she doing?" Cain asked, sobering and sitting on the couch arm.

"Same. Miguel gave her some morphine so she'd sleep."

"That's good. She'll be ok, man."

"I know." I looked up at him. "Thank you for going in after her."

"Don't thank me. I didn't do anything you wouldn't have."

"This isn't the first time you've saved her life."

Cain's face changed. He looked down and made a noise in his throat like he was uncomfortable. Lillian squeezed his hand. "It's fine, dude, really. So...*Daddy*."

"Yeah," I laughed and smiled, embarrassed, but I couldn't quite put my finger on why. "She finally said it. And then she wanted to call Sherry mommy. It's unreal."

"It's sweet," Lillian said. "She wouldn't want to call you that unless you were good to her, you know. Kids are smart."

I laughed again, feeling a little semi-giddy. "Thanks. She is smart. She's incredible. Sherry thought she'd never have kids and Lily is so perfect for her."

Danny and Celeste came up and joined us, taking the chair near Sherry's feet.

"Why did she think that?" Lillian asked quizzically. "I know Sherry didn't think she was gonna be a spinster."

"Not with that bone structure she wouldn't have been," Celeste blurted. "Sherry is so petite and sweet looking. It's not fair really if you think about it. I have the legs for a model, but not the hips. If I can't be a model, why can't I at least be dainty and wholesome like someone I know?" She leaned forward a bit on Danny's lap and spoke to Sherry conspiratorially. "That's right, Sherry. I'm talking about you like you're not here. And I called you dainty. Wake up and yell at me," she sang.

We all laughed then I turned to answer Lillian's question.

"Sherry can't have children. She found out when she was fourteen. She was pretty upset, even at that young age."

"Yeah, I remember that," Danny chimed sadly. "She cried for a whole day straight. I thought she was crazy. I kept asking what she wanted to have kids for anyway. And Mom and Dad weren't big on sympathy. Mom told Sherry every reason why that had happened to her; the universe, karma, poor diet from sneaking animal products when we were away from home. They made it sound like it was her fault."

"But that's how Sherry handles things," I said firmly. "She freaks out, she cries, she moves on. She tries to find the positive in everything. In fact, I don't remember her ever telling anyone about it. She just acted like it didn't matter, it didn't exist. She didn't beg for sympathy, didn't tell all her friends so they could feel sorry for her. She just dealt with it."

"What's that like?" Lillian asked suddenly and looked at me intensely. "Knowing everything about her? Remembering all the same memories, every birthday, every milestone, all the crazy stunts she pulled as a teenager."

Danny laughed and I tried to hide a chuckle.

"'Crazy' and 'stunts' aren't in Sherry's dictionary. The craziest stunt she ever pulled was the one time she snuck out of the house when she was thirteen, but she got caught. In fact, she came back and pretty much told on herself."

"Really? Nothing crazy?"

I squinted, trying to remember, but came up with nothing.

"Moving out. Her parents didn't want her to but she was determined that if she got out she would be happier. So she did. But other than that, she's pretty clean."

"Squeaky," Danny said smiling.

"So, she really is a saint. But you didn't answer my question, Merrick."

I sighed, hoping she would let that one pass. It wasn't something I was exactly proud of; watching Sherry when I wasn't supposed to.

"It's normal for me to know everything. It's all I've ever done was watch people. But, I have to say, Danny and Sherry were by far my favorite. And I'm not just saying that because one of them is listening," Danny laughed, "and because I was crazy for Sherry. They were just so...I don't know, the opposite product of their environment. It was fascinating. They are so grounded and easygoing where as their parents were very over reactive, uptight, and against the flow."

"That's putting it mildly," Danny muttered darkly.

"I mean there's nothing wrong with being different, nothing wrong with being proactive, but they didn't have any balance of the causes and their own children. And they didn't have any other family so, Danny and Sherry just were kind of on their own."

"What did Sherry think when she found out you were a Keeper? That you'd watched their lives? I remember Michael was kinda furious at first, but he was guy, so that's different I guess."

"I thought she'd be angry, but she surprised me. She was upset with herself, for not showing a better example."

I laughed remembering her turning the situation in on herself.

"That's Sherry. Our little martyr," Danny said loudly. "I'm talking about you. I'm gonna tell everyone about the time your bikini top fell off at the beach. No one knows what you had to do but Merrick and me," he said in a sing-song voice, trying to rouse her.

I chuckled and felt myself turning a little red. Ha! I was blushing! I wondered if anyone else could tell. I thought Lillian could. She was smiling at me, knowingly.

"Danny Patterson. Sherry will kill you," I said trying to stifle a laugh.

"Yeah right. I can take her."

"I can hear you, brat," Sherry said suddenly, her voice raspy her eyes still closed. Then she smiled, but winced and grabbed her cheek.

Danny and I both jumped and knelt beside her and everyone else crowded around the back of the couch.

"Hey, baby. How long have you been eavesdropping, huh?" I joked, pushing her hair back from her face.

"That depends. How long have you been talking about me like I'm not here?" She tried to smile again. "What are you all doing?" She cleared her throat.

I grabbed her water glass with a straw and offered it to her. She drank eagerly.

"Waiting for you," Celeste said happily. "Duh."

"How long have I been out?"

"Not long enough," I said with a tone so she'd know I disapproved.

"Help me sit up?" she asked and I shook my head about to protest, but she stopped me. "Please. I can't sit here like this anymore right now. I've been lying down for..."

I think we all knew what she meant; lying down on the concrete alone for hours and hours.

"Ok. Don't overdo it. If you feel like you need to sleep or whatever, you tell us to shut up and leave. Got it?"

"Got it."

She smiled again, letting me lift her and set her up at the end. She tucked her legs under her and pulled me down next to her. I went easily, trying not to jostle her and she snuggled right up against my chest. I pulled my arm around her and kissed her forehead. She felt just right in my arms. I tried not to think about how she was almost taken away from me, again.

"Cain." She looked up to him and smiled again. "Thank you, guys. Lillian, I can't believe you did that." She held out her hand and Cain took it as she pulled him down to squat in front of her, then she hugged him. Any lingering weird feelings of jealousy I had about those two, forced by Piper and her compulsion plot to make us doubt each other, were completely gone. I'd seen the way Cain looked at Lillian. And I no longer had doubts of Sherry's feelings either. "You shouldn't have come and got me. You had no idea what you were getting yourselves into."

"Are you kidding? We stick together, shorty," Cain said and winked.

"I promise to try really hard to stop being the trouble maker of the group." Everyone laughed, more for her benefit than her being funny I thought. "I'm sorry. Maybe I should've tried to...do something, but I thought if I didn't go with them, they would find you guys and I couldn't have that. Thank you for saving me."

Cain looked down at the floor again, looking...guilty?

"Hey," Sherry said softly and when he looked up, she leaned forward and whispered something in his ear.

It took about a full minute before she pulled back and he nodded and smiled sadly. I wondered what it was about as I was sure Danny did, too, given by the look of intense curiosity, but we stayed quiet.

She released his hand and waved Lillian to her for a hug. Then Danny came over and hugged her so hard she winced and he apologized, but looked really peeved. Celeste hugged her too before resuming her spot on Danny's lap in the chair. There was an uncomfortable silence and Sherry sighed loudly.

"Will everyone please just sit down and relax? I'm fine, really."

"Yeah, that's why you can barely see out of your left eye and I can't even hug you without hurting you," Danny said angrily.

"Danny," I said to stop him and he sighed and nodded.

"I'm sorry. You're fine, Sherry, I just can't believe what they did to you."

"Well, I'm not talking about it, ever. The last thing you need is one more reason to be angry. So, what were we talking about?"

I watched her. She looked pretty normal. Except for the bruises and trauma to the skin on her face, neck and arms. But she looked normal. She didn't look traumatized, didn't look upset. This was how Sherry did it; freak out, cry, move on. Just like I said before. She was a rare breed.

"You," Celeste said matter-of-factly. "Danny was just about to tell us a story about a bikini top."

Sherry gasped and looked at Danny in disbelief. "No, you are not!"

Everyone laughed and hung on every word she said with watchful, fearful, careful eyes. Everyone was worried, but let her talk and laugh and add her own anecdotes for Danny's stories for a while until she fell back sleep after an hour or so on my shoulder during a story Danny was telling about a camping trip of theirs.

"Ok," I whispered, "that's it for her." I guess she wasn't too bad off because she moved by herself before. So I decided to take her to our room. "I'm taking her to bed so you can still talk."

I picked her up and she lay there in my arms, loose and exhausted but trying so hard to not induce sympathy, trying to be strong. At least look strong.

Our room was a little chilly so I lay down with her under the blanket for a while, just watching, making sure she was comfortable. She was dreaming. It must've been a good dream. She kept smiling and then wincing because of her cheek. She whispered my name a couple times as she snuggled closer, making my human heart jump in exhilaration.

I smoothed her hair, rubbed her arms, fiddled with her necklace charm that made it through her debacle intact somehow. Anything to let her know I was still there.

After a while, she still slept soundly so I crept out. It was late. I wanted to check on Lily and make sure she got to bed. I knew someone had taken care of her, that's how it always was. Everyone loved to do things for her, but I wanted to make sure she wasn't up somewhere fretting for Sherry.

I found her asleep in her room. Joy, her doll, was tucked under her arm and her pajama shirt was on backwards. Danny. I knew it right then that Danny had put her to bed.

I chuckled and backed out.

I decided we'd all waited long enough for a certain situation. Celeste had been studiously avoiding the topic and even walking around smiling and acting normal, but we all knew what had to be done. Margo had to be dealt with and there was only one way. And I so didn't want to be the one to start the execution.

I called the Keepers in my mind. It was kinda late but not too late. Most people would still be awake and it might even be better for people to sleep through it. Except Celeste. She had to know.

41

Brothers, sisters? I'm sorry, I know it's late, but you know there's one more matter to deal with.

I felt them agree. They were coming to meet me in the commons room. I called Danny in his mind and told him to bring Celeste. I also told him to prepare for a bad time.

I saw them coming down the hall. Celeste was smiling and oblivious. I wondered how in the worlds she could be so unconcerned with the situation with her mother.

"Danny, did you tell her?" I asked curiously.

He leaned in close as Celeste walked over to Kay.

"No, not yet. I did something you may not agree with, but we were leaving and she was freaking out. I didn't want to leave her here so messed up over her mom and Sherry and me leaving so...I used compulsion to make her not worry."

"Danny," I breathed angrily, "I can't believe you did that. Just because we gave Marissa permission that once wasn't a license for everyone to start compelling everyone they crossed paths with."

"I didn't. Merrick, you didn't see her. She was out of her mind, completely in hysterics. I couldn't get her to go to sleep at all that night. She cried and begged me not to go with you, begged me not to let you kill Margo. I had to do it so she would be ok while I was gone and could get a grip before she hurt herself."

"I understand, ok? I see why you did it, but Celeste isn't going to like that you did that to her. And the others aren't going to like that you used your gift on her without her knowledge or consent."

"I know. I'll take the consequences."

"The consequences are to leave the bunker, Danny. That was the punishment we set to detour people from doing this to each other." I sighed in frustration and pinched the bridge of my nose. "Ok, we'll deal with that later. For now, take off the compulsion. We've got to deal with Margo. She'll only get worse and it's cruel to let her suffer like that."

With the mark, the patch, the Lighters control you with a compulsion as well. The patch just makes you their eyes, but the compulsion does the deed they want done. Once the deed is done, the compulsion is still there because of the patch and can't be reversed or removed without death to the subject. Because the compulsion is still there to finish a task, but there's no task to be done anymore, it drives the subject crazy. Margo had been slowly degrading in that back room and it was only right to end her suffering, though it meant her death. Technically, she was dead already, but it would be hard for Celeste to understand that.

He nodded and walked to Celeste. He framed her face with his hands. She smiled up at him.

"I'm sorry. I did what I thought was best for you," he said softly and then closed his eyes, his mind reaching out to hers.

Her smile changed and so did her eyes. If I hadn't been so wrapped up in Sherry, I might have seen the compulsion in her eyes making them glassy and blank. She understood everything immediately. With Danny's kind of compulsion, that was how it worked. Since he had to tell her to stop, it made her aware that something had happened. Therefore, he didn't have to explain anything to her. Her mind was already aware.

"Danny," she squeaked. "You shouldn't have done that."

"I'm sorry. I'm so sorry, baby."

"I could've spent the day with her while you were gone. I could've gotten a few more hours with her! And now, they're going to kill her!"

"She's not herself, Celeste. She's not your mom right now."

"Yes she is! It's not fair. I should get to say if she lives or dies!" She looked around at us all, all the Keepers standing around, to her looking very much like executioners.

Right then, I felt like one.

"Baby, listen," Danny tried again, "you know she wouldn't want this. She wouldn't want to be stuck in some Lighter compulsion making her do things that she doesn't want to do."

He tried to hold her, grabbing her upper arms, but she wrenched away.

"You don't know! You don't know anything about it. She wants to live." Her tears streamed down her face. "That's what she wants; to live and not to be murdered by the people who claimed they were here to help us! Murderers!"

She collapsed despairingly on the floor, heaving and sobbing loudly. Danny sat next to her and pulled her close. She only fought for a few seconds and then clung to him and sobbed even louder into his neck. He looked nauseas and regretful, but it wasn't his fault.

She was out of her mind over Margo, he was right about that.

I would never say anything to him about it, but looking at the situation like that, I thought he did the right thing. She was too grief stricken to be left alone like that. With all of us leaving, she needed to be stable while we were gone. Now, she could deal with her grief and Danny was there to ferry her through it.

Kay came to kneel beside her and rubbed her back.

"Ok. Come on, Celeste. Let's go see Margo," she suggested and tried to coax her to stand.

Celeste looked up at her and nodded reluctantly. She let Danny pull her up off the floor and then pull her under his arm as we all walked together in a sad procession.

43

Margo was squatted down leaning on the wall in a corner. Her hair was all scraggly like she'd been pulling at it. She was scratching long lines down her arms and some of them were bleeding. Her hands twitched.

"Oh, mom," Celeste said in a sob and then turned towards us with fresh tears rimming her eyes. "Oh, God, help her, please. I can't- I was wrong. I'm sorry about all the stuff I said. Please, just help her."

Merrick. Who?

I knew what Jeff was asking. Who? Which human was going to do it because the Keepers couldn't touch the patch.

I'll call Miguel.

I did and explained why we needed him. We waited for a minute while Celeste tried not to look at her mom. He came and looked at Celeste sadly for a second before coming to stand by me.

"Don't look at her eyes," I told Miguel, remembering he'd been scratched before by a Marker as well as Sherry.

It hurts the ones who had been marked.

"Wait," Marissa materialized in the doorway, "maybe I can help."

"Sweetie," Jeff said slowly. "You can't help this, don't get Celeste's hopes up."

"No. No, I'm sorry, not that. I mean...I can help with something else. Remember at the Mayor's manor you told me that one compulsion overrides the other?"

I knew where she was going with it and so did Jeff, he shook his head.

"Normally, yes, but not this. The patch is...it's like it's hard wired into their brain. We've tried before. There's no way to reverse it or stop the compulsion. You might be able to stave off the pull for a few seconds if you concentrated all your focus on it, but-"

"Yes! That's what I'm talking about. I want to do that; let Celeste and Margo have even a few seconds where Margo is coherent. To say goodbye."

It's worth a try.

Jeff apparently didn't agree with me. He looked at me sharply.

I still think it's getting Celeste's hopes up. And it'll drain Marissa of a lot of energy to pull that off.

She wants to. She wants to help.

Would you let Sherry?

Could I stop her?

His mouth pursed and he quirked an eyebrow.

Touché.

He looked at Marissa for a long minute. "You know what this will do to you, don't you?" he asked her softly.

"Yes. It's worth it."

"What are you talking about?" Celeste asked fretfully. "What can you do?"

Marissa looked to Jeff and he nodded, then she explained it all to Celeste; about how compulsion works, about one compulsion canceling out the other. About what she thought she might could do so she could have a minute with her mom before we had to let her go.

Celeste nodded, understanding and stepped towards her mom a little bit.

"Ok, why don't we give them some space?" I said and we all started to move out.

"Merrick, Kay, stay," Danny said, not looking our way.

"I'm staying, too," Jeff said and took up a stance near Marissa that dared someone to tell him otherwise. Marissa knelt beside Margo on the floor.

So, Miguel, Danny, Celeste, Kay, Jeff, Marissa and I watched and waited to see if Marissa could pull off what she proposed.

She touched Margo's hand carefully so as not to scare her. Margo looked at her like she didn't know her at all. Then she looked at Celeste with the same expression.

"Mom?"

"Who are you? I need to... I'm supposed to tell someone. I'm supposed to... I'm important. To save her. To catch her. To take her," Margo mumbled and Celeste whimpered.

"Do it," Celeste ordered in a whisper.

Marissa closed her eyes and her whole body convulsed as she tried to undo the compulsion on Margo. You could almost see the energy surrounding them, the power of it. Marissa began to breathe heavy. Jeff moved forward to stop her.

Wait. Just a few more seconds. I think she's onto something. Can't you feel that?

I could literally feel a little current on my skin and a hum of static in the air. Jeff looked pained, but listened to me and held off. He moved to sit behind Marissa and steadied her as she began to sway. Then, what we'd all been waiting for happened.

Margo sat up straight and looked right at her daughter.

"Celeste," she breathed.

"Momma?"

"Oh, Celeste. I'm so sorry."

"It's not your fault, Momma," Celeste said crying and sniffling. "None of this is."

"But I hate it just the same." She grabbed Celeste's hands. "It's coming back. I can already feel it. Listen-"

"No, Momma, just hold on, ok?"

"I can't, honey. It's coming. I need to tell you some things. I'm sorry for what I did to Sherry...so very sorry." She let the tears fall from her eyes and didn't wipe them. "But, the Lighters didn't see. They put too many patches on too many of us, all spread out. They didn't know which location we were at, they didn't know what they were seeing. You'll be safe here."

"Mom, no," Celeste croaked.

"Did you find Sherry?" she asked me.

"Yes. She's here. She's ok."

"Oh, thank God. Ok." She nodded and swallowed, then pressed on. "Also," she looked at Celeste and held her gaze, "I don't want this. Let them let me die."

"No!"

"Yes. Baby, you don't know what it's like with this thing in my mind. I'm being pulled in two, trapped inside myself. Please. I know I screwed up. I'm so sorry. I thought I was protecting you."

"Momma, just wait. We can figure something-"

"No, Celeste. I want you to be happy. I don't want you to be angry and resentful. You know where I'm headed and I'm ready." She turned and took Danny's hand. "I'm so glad she met you. I couldn't have asked for a better son-in-law. Be good to each other." He nodded and she reached up and hugged Celeste tightly. "I love you so much. I am sorry. I want you to know you were the most precious thing in my life. You were so..." She trailed off and the glassiness and blankness returned to her eyes instantly, she looked up at Celeste. "Must be afternoon. I feel a nap coming on, but I'm so busy. So very busy. The store. Must save her. Must take her."

Celeste turned her back on Margo as the gibberish returned and she let Danny fold her in his arms.

Marissa collapsed into Jeff's arms just as she let go of Margo's arm. I knelt down beside them.

"It was a lot, but you did it didn't you," Jeff told her with clear fascination and awe and then looked up to me. "Did you see that? That was incredible."

"I saw and I agree. Marissa, that was genius. I've never seen anything break that kind of compulsion before."

"Thanks," Marissa whispered, she grimaced. "Jeff, I think I'm gonna be sick," she groaned.

He scooped her up and carried her out of the room with her head lolling to the side. It looked like she passed out. She would be ok, but using that kind of power always took all the energy out of you. Like when Marissa put the Muse's wrath on Sherry, Sherry wasn't normal again for a few days.

"Celeste? Do you want to be here for this?" I asked her, telling Danny in his mind that I really didn't think she should be, maybe he should persuade her to go, but it wasn't needed.

"No." She knelt down beside her mother who continued to mumble and whisper. "Bye, Momma. I love you, too."

Impatient Patient
Chapter 5 - Sherry

It was daytime and hot, which was surprising. The sun was bright and casting long dark shadows on the ground and landscape before me. The buildings looked too shiny, too new and unused. The trees were too green and the sky was bluer than ever. Not a cloud in the sky and no birds. There were no noises, no horns, no traffic.

It was eerie and unsettling. I don't like the quiet. The power lines above me were swinging in the wind, lulling me into a false sense of normalcy. But things were far from normal.

Where were my parents, for one? I hadn't seen them in weeks. Usually, I moseyed on over every couple weeks and suffered through a tofu dinner with them, but they hadn't answered the door in a while, or the phone.

And Danny, he was still a loafer, but I hadn't seen him either. And Matt, no. I'm not dating him anymore. He's mean.

I pull from the ridge. I wondered about it because I never go there in the daytime. I don't understand why I went there this time. I decide to see if Danny is working. Maybe I can get him to help me find our parents.

I get in the drive-through and wait, and wait. The guy in front of me is just sitting there. After an insane amount of time, I tap my horn, which I hate to do. He still sits there.

I get out to see if he's ok, but the car is empty. What? What is going on here? I get back in my Rabbit and reverse it to the parking lot, where I pull in to a spot near the exit. I go up to the window for walk-ups, but there's no one inside. I ring the little bell, but no one comes so I pull out my cell phone to text Danny. No signal. What?

I get back in my car. My lunch break is over by now. I drive down North Lake Shore Drive, hanging a left at Wacker Drive, headed for the office. Ugh. I hate this part of town. The Trump Tower looms over me ominously as the Rabbit sputters and spits in lunch hour traffic.

I'd kill for air conditioning. Kill for it. I grab my emergency hair band out of the glove box and shake my hair back, attempting to tame the beast of curls. At a standstill in traffic I decide to check my phone again. Still no signal, but I've got a message. I click on the little envelope and read the words so clearly meant for me.

'Meet me at the ridge'

What? I was just there. Who sent that to me? No one knows I go up there but Danny. I close my phone and look up. All the traffic is gone. My car sits alone in the middle of the street. Absolutely every person is gone. No cars on any streets or parking spaces. No people walking the sidewalks, nothing. What is going on?

I decide the only logical thing to do is go to the ridge and find out. I make my way quickly with the clear streets. I park and get out, leaning on my hood overlooking the city.

I hear someone's steps crunching in the gravel behind me. I turn to see Merrick, my one and only. Surely he'll know what's going on.

"Hey, baby," I say sweetly, happy to see him.

"Honey," he crooned softly. "Have a good day at work?"

"No, not really. Something very strange is going on today."

"Yes. Very strange."

"But I'm glad you're here." I wrap my arms around him and smell his shirt. He smells clean and mountainy. "I missed you," I crooned and he laughed.

"You just saw me three hours ago."

"I know. It's been too long. You didn't miss me?"

"You know I did."

I tried to pull him down to kiss me, but he wouldn't budge. "Are you ok?" I asked.

"Yes, but we can't do that here."

"Why not?"

"Because this isn't real."

I thought about what he was saying. "Wait. How did you text me? You don't have a cell?"

"I didn't. She did." He pointed behind me, but before I could turn he grabbed my arms and looked into me. "I'm sorry things aren't as they should be."

"What do you mean?"

"Listen to them. They miss you."

"Who?" I turned and saw a group of people standing behind the Rabbit. My parents. Mrs. Trudy. Aaron. Phillip. Mitchell. Margo. Matt.

Matt? Whoa, weird. I look between the two of them. Both have the same dark mess of hair, the same build. The same face, but so very different. One, so obviously adoring and honest, the other so inherently self-absorbed and controlling.

How had I ever mixed up the two even once? The one with brown eyes watches me, too. I look at him and see a large spot of blood on his undershirt, under his button up over his heart. So that's how he died, an injury to the heart...almost fitting. He takes a step towards me but stops.

"Sherry, you didn't let me in." I try to think what he means. Oh, the night he was drunk and he was banging on my door, the day before he died. Does he blame me for his death? "Things would be different if you had. I don't know where I am."

"Oh, shush. She didn't come all this way to hear you cry like a baby," Mrs. Trudy said and pushed him aside to come hug me tightly. "Hey, sugar, you pretty thing. You still keeping Merrick in line?

"Yes, ma'am."

"Good. How's that Lily?"

I grinned. "She called me mommy."

"Awww. What a sweet girl. She has just what you need, you know."

"What do you mean?"

"Just what I said. Lily is the key. She's everything you need, Sherry."

"Yes, she's very precious."

"More than you know. Give my love to the family."

"Ok, I will."

For some reason, none of this seemed strange to me. I remembered everything from my previous life. I remembered everything from the present, too. They both melded together and for some reason, in my mind, this seemed normal, seemed to fit.

Mom and Dad came forward, not touching each other, and looking very much rebuffed and noncommittal, like they were made to be here.

"Dad, Mom, what are you doing here?"

"Seeing you it would seem," Mom said. "How's your brother?"

Typical.

"He's fine. He met a girl."

"I expected nothing less. He's a handsome boy."

"I got married. And I adopted a little girl."

"Did you get her from China?"

"Uh, no. We found her here."

"Well, there are way more females waiting to be adopted in China than here. You should have gone there and set a good example."

"I said I'm married, Mom, did you hear me?"

"I heard you. How old is he?"

"Twenty four."

"Hmm. A little old for you. What does he do?"

"That's all you have to say? Dad?"

"Your mother's right. It's a huge age difference. Hey," he said and smiled, "you're still wearing my necklace."

"Of course I am, Daddy. Why wouldn't I?"

"Waste of metal if you ask me," Mom mumbled.

"Where did you go?" I asked.

"It doesn't matter now. You're safe, for now. That's all that matters," Dad said and put a hand on my shoulder. "Tell Danny we love him."

"Sure," I said exasperatingly, having no idea what the meaning of all this is.

They walked away and Merrick put his arm around my waist from behind just as Phillip stepped forward smirking.

"I got nothing to say, sweetness. No cute anecdotes. Sorry."

"It's time to go," Merrick said and waved his hand in front of us.

Everything started to shake and bleed away, just like all the dreams I'd had before. All the colors bled in to the ones below it and faded away until only we were left. So, this is a dream. Makes sense now.

"But I haven't learned anything. Why am I here?" I asked him.

"To remember," he said steadily. "To remember all the things that have happened and all the people you knew. To remember past mistakes, yours and theirs. We must learn from history or it is doomed to repeat itself."

"Oh, don't you talk riddles to me, too," I pouted.

He laughed. "My Sherry, so eager to learn. You'll know all you need to know when you need to know it."

"That doesn't make any sense at all, Merrick. You know that right?"

"One day, it will. In the mean time..." He pressed his lips to my ear, giving me shivers of pleasure. "Wake up."

I woke with a start. I was lying on my back, alone in our room. My body felt heavy, but I wasn't quite as achy as before. I remembered every detail of the dream like it was a memory. It was a strange dream for sure.

I stretched my body slowly, testing myself. Feeling my muscles groan and complain and my joints pop. Yesterday had been good. Today, my third day home since my rescue, looked to be even better.

Yesterday I was bed ridden and slept most of the day away. I only got out of bed once- correction - I was only *allowed* out of bed once to go to the bathroom and I was carried there and back.

Danny had poked his head in once, but didn't stay. I was a little surprised by that but chalked it up to him believing I was fine.

Merrick fed me, sponge bathed me, rested with me and talked for hours. He even cooked lunch for everyone since it was supposed to be my day to.

He brought Lily to me that afternoon after her nap. Oh, that was a sweet, sweet reunion. I've never felt so loved and needed. She chattered on endlessly about everything she could think of. About how uncle Danny had read her a bedtime story about an old woman who lived in a shoe and had lots of cats with a mole on the end of her nose and hated pie. She also had a pet wolf name Marco.

Merrick and I laughed so hard we cried at her explaining it to us. I made a mental note to teach Danny a real bedtime story.

She told us that Aunt Rissa and Uncle Jeff - the kid had a lot of aunts and uncles - had done a puzzle with her. And Uncle Cain and Aunt L had played hide and go seek with her in the dark second room with flashlights.

I wondered where in the world she got the idea to call Lillian L from.

Lots of people came to visit me, like I was in the hospital or something, faces so sullen and uncomfortable. I laughed at them and told everyone to stop acting like I had an incurable disease.

But today, I was getting out of this bed. People walked around with concussions and besides, I felt like I was about to get muscle atrophy.

I got up and eased on some clean clothes, jeans and a loose low hanging green top. Merrick had scrubbed me with a sponge bath yesterday morning and night. He was so thorough I doubt I'd ever been so clean. To be honest, I think he enjoyed it more than I did. He kept smiling and trying to hide it. He watched me with a look of fascination, to see if I'd like what he was doing or not. I did like it, but he wasn't about to do anything about me liking it so it was a moot point.

I brushed my hair out with my fingers and twisted it to the side to hang over my shoulder. I creaked open my door. I had no idea what my face looked like. Merrick had assured me the bruises weren't that bad, but he was prone to stretch the truth for my benefit which made it hard to tell if he was lying or not.

So I just lifted my chin. Why did I care? I wasn't vain, I just didn't want people to see me really good in the light and put on the sympathy face. I was tired of the sympathy face.

Marissa saw me coming and pulled away from Jeff to meet me at the mouth of the hall. She grabbed my hands and pulled them out to my sides to look at me.

"Oh, my goodness! You look so great."

"I can tell when you're lying, Marissa," I teased.

"Then you'll know that I'm not," she said and winked at me. And I could tell. She did think I looked great which helped my fears about my facial issues. "Come on. Jeff has been worried sick about you."

Marissa however did not look great. Mean, I know, but this was like she was sick or something. Her eyes were very dark with big rings underneath and she was so pale, almost yellow. Maybe she hadn't been sleeping well.

Jeff jumped off the couch and pulled me into a bear hug. I hugged him back with enthusiasm. He held me for a long minute, patting my back.

"Thank you guys for coming to get me, and taking care of Lily. She loves you guys."

"She loves you. She's been worrying like a pro. She must have picked that up from someone else I know." He smiled. "And don't thank me. We weren't about to just let you get away from us."

I made sure to find Ryan and Miguel as well and thank them for my rescue. They were both equally embarrassed by my hugging and praising and willing to throw the heroism on someone else. The girl who we brought home had still not stopped following and clinging to Ryan. I basically had to pry him away so I could get my own hug. But Ryan didn't seem bothered by it. In fact, I think he liked it. He liked to feel human and have someone want comfort from him.

But then I saw Polly coming my way. I made a scampery move to get away, but wasn't fast enough.

"Sherry, wait." She looked at my face for a second before saying, "Is there something I'm supposed to be doing?"

"Uh…no?" I said in confusion.

"Nothing you need help with?"

"Nope. I think I'm good."

She nodded and walked away. I shook it off as bizarre and tried to help in the kitchen a little, but not too much. I still felt not quite tip-top, but needed to at least act normal.

I made some hot tea and waited for it to steep in the kitchen at the counter. I felt Merrick put his arms around me from behind.

"Sneaking I see."

"You can't keep me locked up forever, warden."

He chuckled slowly and squeezed me.

"Do you feel ok?"

"Yeah, I feel pretty good." I turned to face him and rub his scruffy chin with the back of my fingers. "Really. Please stop worrying about me. I promise not to overdo it today, but I'm fine."

"Ok. I won't say a word." He looked me over, head to toe slowly. "Except you look...hot."

I laughed and felt it all the way in my stomach.

"Cain and Danny have got to stop teaching you lingo."

"What? You don't want me to think you're hot?"

"Oh, I do. It's just strange to hear you say it."

"How about gorgeous. Does that work for you?"

"Yes. Perfectly acceptable," I answered amusingly.

"Good. As long as you're happy." His smile was huge. "So, what's on your agenda for today, gorgeous?"

"Nothing. Absolutely nothing."

"Even better."

"What's on yours?"

"Well, we've bumped up the training sessions for everyone. Two hours of training instead of one, three days a week. I'm sure you can understand why. You, of course, don't get to practice yet, but in a week or so you need to start again."

"That's a good idea. And I'm looking forward to training actually. I did get to use a move that Miguel taught me at the facility."

"Did you?" he said but looked none too happy about it.

"Yes. I thought that was the point, to teach us to defend ourselves. Why are you upset?"

"It's different pretending in practice. When it's real, I don't want to think about you actually having to fight someone."

I sighed but knew enough to leave it alone.

"So, are you going to tell me what happened?" he asked meaningfully.

He was talking about the facility. He had waited and not asked me any questions about it, until now.

"Nope," I said firmly.

"I can handle it," he assured me, his hands on my waist flexing.

"Uh, no, you can't. You can't even handle me telling you I fought back, once. I'm not about to tell you what they did."

"I think it would be useful for us to know."

"Ask Billings. You can speculate as to what actually happened and what didn't. I'm not telling you anything specific."

His look said I was being stubborn and he was not pleased about it. I stood my ground.

"How did you hurt your head? It was something hard enough to cause a concussion. Do you remember what happened?"

"I remember the Lighter elbowed me into the window in the backseat of the car on the way to the facility. Then I woke up in the room."

"And then what?"

"I sat there, waiting and trying to block my thoughts. I sang 80's ballads."

He nodded but didn't smile like I'd wanted.

"Nobody came to talk to you?"

"Not for a long while. Then Daniel came in and gave me some water and a granola bar. He told me he'd help me all he could and that I should keep blanking my mind or singing. He blocked my thoughts for me while he was in the room for me."

"He did? How did you know he wasn't just saying he was?"

"When they came to talk to me way later, the other Lighter was mad. He said all the rebels they'd taken were blank and not taking the compulsion. He wanted to know why."

"Hmm." He stretched his neck to the side and I felt bad for putting him through so much lately. "Then what?"

"Nuhuh."

"Honey, I need to know-"

"You're just like Danny. You just want to know so you can be bitter and even more angry than you already are. I don't want to be the cause for someone else's hate."

"I hated them already, even before I met you. You're not changing anything."

"And I'm not telling you anything. I don't want to relive it. Please, stop."

He put his hands on his head and leaned it back to gaze at the ceiling, clearly frustrated and angry, maybe even a little at me. I thought it was probably healthy for us to finally have some kind of feeling other than crazy need for each other. Maybe I should do something to really piss him off, see how he'd react then.

I giggled a small chuckle at the thought. He always let me get away with everything. I couldn't picture him angry with me, unless I looked back on the time when Polly's compulsion made him hostile with me, but that didn't count. That wasn't really him.

"What's funny? I don't see anything funny about this," he said softly.

"It's not funny. I was thinking that I've never seen you angry at me before."

"I'm angry at them. I'm not angry with you. "

"Not even a little?" I quirked my eyebrow and dared him to lie to me again.

"Ok. Yes, I'm angry. I'm angry that you're being stubborn for no apparently good reason. You don't need to protect me, I'm a Keeper. I've dealt with Lighters for centuries. You aren't going to tell me anything I didn't already imagine anyway. I'm sure the things I thought were a lot worse. Especially since you're in one piece."

"I'm not trying to act superior. I just don't want to talk about it."

"You are so impossible," he groaned, took a deep breath and then placed his hands on my waist again. "Alright my little silent martyr, fine, but just so we're clear, I completely disagree and think you should be forced to tell us what happened to you. If for no other reason, research purposes."

"I agree with that and I acknowledge that you disagree...but I'm still not telling you. But I do love you."

"I love you, too, frustrating as you are." He hugged me and I felt his warmth seep into me and his anger creep away. "You really do look great," he whispered.

"Thank you. I feel great, even better now that I know I can fight with you and not succumb to your commands so easily anymore. I kinda like it that I can stand on my own," I said with a smirk.

"Let's not make it a habit, ok? I'm not thrilled with this discovery of yours." He cracked a playful smile. "I much prefer to order you around and you just do whatever I say."

"Your high handedness is impressive," I mused. "Don't worry, I promise to let you boss me around sometimes."

"What about right now, when I say that you've been standing up too long and you need to go relax for a while?"

"Yeah, I guess." I turned back to the counter and grabbed my mug. "My tea is cold now."

"I'll warm it. Please, go sit on the couch. I'll be there in a minute."

"Yes sir," I said and saluted with enthusiasm.

"That's more like it," he said amusingly satisfied.

I kissed him before I walked off. He released me quicker than I liked. Then I knew. I knew he didn't want to try to do too much before I got all healed up, to his standards. This was typical Merrick behavior.

"You're not gonna touch me for a week are you?" I said, letting him know I knew what he was doing.

He turned to look at me poignantly.

"Absolutely not."

I nodded, expecting this answer.

"We'll see about that," I countered.

"Sherry, you need time to heal-"

"Oh no. I'm going this way and not listening." I pointed toward the commons room. "In my book, you just issued me a challenge, buster. And I accept."

I turned without looking back, but not before I saw his obvious look of worry and then a small smile on his lips, no doubt imagining the possibilities of such a statement.

No Bloody Smooching
Chapter 6 - Cain

Things were quiet and boring, just the way we liked it around here. Sherry was recuperating nicely. Danny was helping Celeste grieve and she seemed to be taking it better than before. Lily was as happy as pie that everyone was back and she made her rounds, begging us all in turn to do all her favorite things.

And Lillian. We'd been wholly absorbed in each other; napping, playing with Lily, washing clothes, training, always together.

I had realized something. A very important something, but couldn't quite bring myself to tell her. I wasn't sure how it would be received. It was very unlike me to be so emotionally worked up over a girl or pretty much anything. I was usually laid back and nonchalant, but I couldn't be that way with L.

The thing I realized was that I loved her.

I know, it had only been a few weeks. I know I just got over Sherry. I seemed fickle and unstable and flippant, but I wasn't. I knew what I wanted and went after it. And I wanted Lillian more than I ever wanted Sherry. I could say that with full truthfulness.

Like I said, I couldn't read her as easily as I'd like, so I wasn't sure how she would take it. I had a feeling she may have felt the same but I didn't want to risk it.

So, instead, I told her everything but.

"Mmm, you smell so good," I told her, nuzzling her neck from behind at the training session. "How do you always smell so good?"

"Um, soap?" she said teasingly.

"No, it's not soap. It's something else. You purposely spray on something to drive me crazy. What is it? Spill."

"Jasmine."

"Oh, that's right. I remember Daniel talking about it. When he was sniffing your neck," I said sourly.

Daniel may have saved us, but he had a rotten start with Lillian when we first met him.

He'd tried to take Lillian to the Taker to become one of his girls. Then he'd tried to take her for himself, so he said. Then L offered him a proposition to save me and trade herself and he thought about taking it before he got a freak bout of conscience and saved our lives instead, killing two Lighters.

"Oh, don't be jealous of him. He didn't know what he was doing. He was just curious."

"Uhuh."

"I don't have that much jasmine perfume left actually. Won't be long until I'm back to smelling like any normal person. Then what'll you do?"

"You'll still smell good," I assured her.

She smiled and leaned back to kiss my lips and-

"Hey! I swear," Miguel shouted and glared at us, "I'm gonna post a sign on the door that says no bloody smooching once you cross that threshold."

"Sorry." I released L and moved beside her. "Continue."

"Now, Sherry is a prime example of why we need to do this and not kid around here. She was defenseless and caught off guard. We can't have that-"

"Uh, Miguel? I just thought you should know that I saw Sherry swinging out a few moves you taught her."

"What?" he asked, surprised.

"At the facility. I saw her practicing what you preach. She got loose a couple times, but was too weak to keep at it."

"Wow." He stopped and smiled. "I'm so proud," he said sincerely.

"Don't get too excited," Sherry said from the door and came in to stand with Merrick. She looked great, besides the huge bruise still on her face. All that rest had done her good. "It was only an enforcer. I didn't take down a Lighter or anything. And I didn't take down the enforcer either, just surprised him was all."

"I think you're missing the point, love," Miguel said and grinned at her. "Sometimes a seconds worth of surprise is all you need. And what are you doing here anyway? No practicing for you," he commanded.

"I'm just observing."

"Well go observe out of kick range."

She rolled her eyes and smiled tolerantly at him as she made her way over to the corner and sat down to lean against it.

Lily was chomping at the bit to go sit with her instead of practice but Merrick was firm. I knew he was thinking his girls needed to know how to defend themselves.

It was a full house today. The Keepers and Miguel were adamant about everyone training and apparently everyone had listened. Everyone was there except Danny and Celeste.

"Ok, so first things first. Partner up and let's work on some running-through strikes. I'd prefer you partner with a Keeper or someone who knows what they're doing if you don't. I've made some practice stakes out of old PVC pipe. Get one and start stabbing someone."

I grabbed two 'stakes' for L and me and we moved to the back corner to have room.

"Ok. You want to be the Lighter first?" I asked.

"I guess. It doesn't really matter does it? I'm gonna die anyway. I'll never stand a chance against you."

"Aw, don't get down in the dumps. We're just getting started."

"Fine." She raised her hand. "Lighter."

She watched me carefully as I ran her through over and over again in all sorts of positions and scenarios. She was intense about it. I had to say, it was hot.

"I totally feel like Buffy right now. All I need is a girly leather jacket," L said breathlessly.

"And some vampires. Don't forget that."

"Lighters qualify."

"I guess they do. So, your turn. Stab me."

She took a deep breath and got into the cutest 'staking' position, trying to look serious and tough. She turned and twisted to come around get me from behind, I stopped her. I started thinking maybe this wasn't so fair. I'd been in the military, had lots of hand to hand, she'd had none. Was it better to let her get some hits in? Or make her work for it so she understands how hard it would be in real life?

If this had been a man, I wouldn't have thought twice about it. I decided to not cheat her out of the experience. It would be better for her that way, safer for her to not get too excited and cocky. Plus, she'd probably know I let her and be upset with me.

She tried again and again with the same results. I tried to assure her that it took time, that she hadn't been to that many sessions and she'd get better. She got me in the arm once but that was out of sheer hysteria. She was so mad and frustrated she just started swinging just to hit anything.

I eventually just grabbed her, turned her and muzzled her neck playfully to tease her and hopefully calm her. She giggled and squirmed.

Then I told her the hit didn't count. She agreed and we started again.

When we were taking a breather, Sherry moseyed over.

"Hey. You guys look...tired."

"And sweaty. I don't think I've ever been this sweaty. Except on the tennis team," L said fixing her ponytail.

"You played tennis?" I asked, surprised.

Most preppy dance squad girls I knew weren't into other sports.

"Yes. And the track team and golf and debate. I was a busy girl all year round my four years of high school."

"Huh."

L in a tennis skirt...I cleared my throat.

"So, where's Danny and Celeste? His lazy butt shouldn't get out of this. I'm surprised Merrick hasn't gone to get him yet, actually," Sherry said and bit her lip, thinking.

What? Merrick didn't tell her about Margo? "Sherry, Danny is with Celeste."

"I figured that," she said with a 'duh' face.

"No, Celeste is...grieving. Danny is with her."

She made an 'o' with her mouth, but no sound came out.

"Margo. I'd forgotten. How selfish of me," she whispered with obvious distress.

"It's not selfish. You went through a lot."

"Merrick didn't tell me. I wonder why. I would've-"

"And that right there is why Merrick didn't tell you. You're no good to anybody if you're not well. You can't be everywhere and do everything. Danny had been with her, she's handling it. Get Merrick to tell you the story later. It's actually pretty amazing."

"Yeah, I will." She looked pained, but put on a smile and turned to L. "So, how's the training coming? Cain isn't letting you win is he?"

"No. He's whipping me at every turn and thoroughly enjoying it, I think," L said and poked me in the ribs.

"Hey! I'm taking it easy on you. I could be slamming your cute butt to the floor, you know."

"You wouldn't," she rebutted.

"Oh, I would," I said and winked at her.

She blushed and tucked her hair behind her ear making me smile.

The day I couldn't make her do that anymore would be a sad, sad day.

"Well, you looked good," Sherry said. "As Miguel would say 'nice follow through'," she said with a deep accent.

L laughed at her. "Thanks. Cain's a pretty good teacher."

"I bet. Well, I'm gonna go check on Celeste. I feel terrible that I haven't gone to see her yet."

"You were unconscious. I think you have an excuse," I said sarcastically.

"Funny," she said and smiled. "And I wasn't unconscious. Well, not for all of it."

"Still. It's a pretty good excuse. Besides, Danny has been with her every second, like I said," I said.

"Ok. I'll let you two get back to beating the crap out of each other."

"Uh, you mean a one sided beat down. I'm not exactly connecting hits here," Lillian said sullenly.

Sherry laughed and walked away, waving.

"Baby," I said sweetly, playing on her good side. "You are doing awesome. It just takes time. I was in the military for four years. You've only been at this...oh," I looked at my non-existent watch, "forty three minutes."

"Ok. Ok, I get it. I'm being a baby."

"No, you're not a baby." I wrapped my arms around her waist. "But you're my baby," I crooned over exaggeratedly.

"That's the sweetest and cheesiest thing you've ever said to me."

"You better get used to it."

"Why? Are you going to continue to strive for cheesiness?" she said and laughed.

"No. Because I'm not going anywhere."

She sobered and closed the small gap between us, wrapping her arms around my neck.

"Good," she whispered. "You are so sweet, Cain. I really-" She sighed. "I'm really glad I met you."

"I'm glad you met me, too. I'd miss you, even if I didn't know you."

She looked at me with her big blue eyes glistening. I started to apologize, but she smiled small, then grinned and shook her head, like she couldn't believe it. Then she pulled me down and kissed me. Her slim fingers on my neck tugged and pulled. She pressed against me and I forgot where I was.

What had I said? What did I do that was so great? I thought back, but couldn't think of it. Girls, I'd never understand them. But I didn't want to understand girls anymore...only one.

I pulled her tighter to me and heard her murmur her content. Then, I heard someone talking around us. No, they were yelling.

"Bloody h-" Miguel cut his curse off and looked Lily's way then back to us. "I said no smooching!" he yelled.

"Bite me, Aussie!" Lillian yelled without looking away from me. I laughed and she did, too. She spoke softly to me and I could feel her breath on my lips. "I think we need to have a talk about your being a gentleman."

I froze. Holy mother! How could she do this to me in the middle of training!

"L, we're gonna have to talk about the proper times to bring up such things," I said scowling, but she just giggled.

"I didn't say I wanted to jump your bones in the middle of the room with an audience, Cain. I said I wanted to talk about it. Later," she said clearly amused at my distress.

"Still. Not. Cool, L. What are you trying to do to me?"

"I'm sorry. Maybe you're right. Maybe we shouldn't talk about it at all-"

"Oh, we're gonna talk about it!" I said loudly and she smiled coyly at me. I knew what she was doing; reverse psychology. "Why you little minx."

She burst out laughing and I grabbed her around the waist. As we turned we saw Miguel glaring at us.

"Ok. Sorry. We're serious," I said.

"Yes. Serious," L said laughing.

He rolled his eyes and carried on with the lesson.

L grabbed my hand and laced our fingers. I rubbed the inside of her wrist with my thumb, feeling the softness there. She really was the softest woman I'd ever felt. I also felt her shiver. I turned to look at her and she had goose bumps on her arms. She looked up sheepishly and met my gaze. I smiled at her and she blushed again, tucking her hair behind her ear. I chuckled and tried to keep my eyes on Miguel.

Unfortunately, for him, he wasn't cute enough to keep my attention.

From Here To The Bush
Chapter 7 – Lillian

That night after a supper of noodle soup, Cain was begged to play guitar by the entertainment deprived bunch. I decided to wash some clothes but on my way to my room I saw Ryan and that girl that I still didn't know the name of. I slowed down, listening to the sounds of Cain's strumming behind me, and watched as the girl sitting right next to Ryan stared at the floor.

She was clearly distressed still. She refused to speak to anyone but Ryan and Billings because they had saved her. She looked young, maybe seventeen or eighteen. I knew she was terrified and there was no telling what the Lighters had done to her before we found her. I stopped and knelt down in front of them.

"Hey, Ryan."

"Hello, Lillian."

"So...how are things going?"

He looked down at her and back to me. His face would have been funny had the situation not been like it was. He was at a complete loss. He had no idea what to do with her, what to say, except let her cling to him because that seemed to keep her calm. He eventually shrugged.

"I don't know," he sighed. He took a deep breath and tried for normal. "So, I never got to speak to you about the facility. How was it in there?"

"It was...terrible. Daniel told us Sherry was one of the lucky ones."

He made a noise of disgust in the back of his throat and the girl looked up at me.

"You were there?" she asked, her voice scratchy from non-use. "At that place where they had us."

"Yes. I was with the ones who rescued you," I answered.

"Thanks," she muttered and lifted her knees and put her forehead against them.

I mouthed to Ryan 'What's her name?'

She told me it was Ellie. She hasn't spoken much, even to me, but from what I understand she was turned over to the Lighters by her two brothers. They were after the rebel reward money. She's only eighteen.

I closed my eyes and shook my head. What was this world coming to? I spoke my next words to her softly.

"I have some clothes you can have. We all kind of trade clothes anyway around here. Most of us didn't come here with much. I'm sure they'd be your size."

She looked up and at me with a wary expression.

"I don't have any clothes to trade."

"It doesn't matter," I said with a smile. "I'm sure you're ready to be out of those clothes. I can...uh, show you where the showers are and get some you some clean clothes while you clean up a bit." Her eyes went wide and her hand went straight to Ryan's sleeve, bunching her fist in the fabric, as if she didn't even realize she was doing it. I wondered what they had done to her to make her so scared. And why Ryan was the one she had claimed as her protector. "I'll bring you right back to Ryan when we're done. We'll be just down this hall." I pointed to show her.

She looked up at Ryan and he nodded and smiled as he said, "It's ok."

"Ok," she whispered.

I didn't touch her, I didn't think she'd like that, so I just led her slowly down the hall and prayed we didn't pass anyone, but we did. Miguel. He cast surprised eyes on us and then pasted on a friendly smile.

"Hello, ladies."

Ellie quickly looked down at the floor and sort of tried to blend with the wall.

"Miguel, this is Ellie."

"Ellie. Pretty name," he said softly and leaned down to try to see her face. "And how are you today?"

"Fine," she whispered and then peeked up at him from under her bangs. "You talk like that guy from Lost."

Miguel chuckled and nodded. I giggled, too.

"Yes, I guess I do. You watched Lost, did you?" She nodded slightly. "Me, too. Who was your favorite?"

"Hurley, of course," she said and gave him a subtle 'duh' look.

He laughed harder and nodded again.

"I think he's probably everyone's favorite."

She smiled at him and bit her lip.

"Say something really Australian."

He screwed up his lips and thought hard, or acted like he did for her benefit. Then he spoke with a way over exaggerated accent.

"G'day, mate. Let's head up to the boozer for a cold one and on the way we'll probably croak a croc or two."

She laughed and looked thoroughly pleased. She pushed her hair out of her face and lifted her chin a little.

"I'm Ellie." She extended her hand. "I'm sorry if I've been...weird. But I haven't had a very good experience with strangers lately."

He took her hand and shook it gently.

"Quite alright, Ellie. We tend to look a bit ruggish, but I promise you that this bunch of blokes and sheilas are the best lot you'll find from here to the bush."

"I have no idea what you just said, but it sounded fantastic," she said through a smile.

He chuckled and started to head up the hall.

"Good enough for me. See you later, ladies."

"Bye, Miguel," I said gratefully and he winked before turning.

"He's nice," she said.

"Yeah," I agreed as I directed her to the end of the hall where the showers were.

I told her where everything was, but she asked me to stay if I would, so I did. I turned as she undressed and then sat on the sink as she showered. She spoke to me over the rush and crash of water.

"So that Miguel is nice."

"Uhuh."

"I think he likes you," she said and I laughed sadly.

"I'm kind of taken."

"The lip ring one?" she questioned.

"Yep, the lip ring one. Cain."

"He's cute, too," she confessed softly.

"What about Ryan?" I asked. "You seem to like him."

"He's..." She peeked out the curtain at me and looked at me. "He was afraid to touch me."

"What?" I asked and stood to take a few steps closer.

"When Billings handed me over to him in the van...he was afraid to touch me. He was so careful with me that his hands barely touched me at all. He kept whispering in my ear that it was all ok. That he was there to help me, that he wouldn't let them hurt me anymore."

"Yeah. Ryan's pretty great like that. He's sweet."

"He is," she agreed and went back behind the curtain. "He's treated me the same ever since."

"Well, I know you've been scared but you don't have to be. We're just like you. We're all just surviving."

After some silence she sighed and said, "I know."

I let her finish and then gave her some jeans and a blue shirt to change into. She looked a million times better. She tussled her long chestnut hair and left it hanging in long waves down her back as we made our way back to the living room.

There were quite a few people there once we got there and she again seemed bashful and withdrawn but not as much as before. I realized she'd barely slept, barely eaten and hadn't showered at all since she'd been there. One down. So I took her straight to the kitchen. Ryan's eyes followed us all the way to the kitchen in fascination.

He really cared about her, but for some reason that seemed lost on him.

"Hey, Sherry," I called. She looked back and did a double take as she saw who I was coming with. "Can we get Ellie something to eat?"

"Sure," she said and quickly dumped a ladle full of noodle soup in a bowl and placed it on the table, directing Ellie to sit. "Hi. I'm Sherry."

"I remember you," Ellie said and started spooning the soup quickly. "You were the one they came to rescue."

"Yeah," she said softly. "I was. I'm glad we could get you, too."

"Me, too." She looked up at Sherry with wide eyes. "Did they do to you what they did to me?"

Sherry gulped and then crossed her arms over her chest in a very un-Sherry like move.

"Um...do you want some tea, too? I made some."

She turned to the fridge, avoiding the question and our gaze and it was strange for Sherry. Most people would need time to get over all she'd been through but Sherry usually just shrugged things off.

She got Ellie and me a glass and I saw Ryan come in and stand in the doorway, playing watch guard. Sherry took a deep loud breath as Ryan came in. He glanced at Ellie and smiled.

"Hey, you look better."

"Thanks," she said and looked up at him, smiling sweetly. "Thank you for helping me. I'm sorry I've been...strange."

"Not a problem," he said, waving her off. "I'm just glad you're here and that you're safe."

She nodded and took another bite of soup. Ryan looked at Sherry then and his face registered her look of discomfort.

"Are you ok?"

"Yeah. I'm fine," she told him, her voice small and flat.

He bent his head to see her face. She peeked up at him from under her lashes and smiled sadly at him. He held his arms out to her and she walked gladly into them.

I could hear him murmuring to her that it was all fine, that it was ok to feel strange after what she'd been through, that we were all here for her.

When I looked back to Ellie, her spoon had stopped mid-bite and she was looking at them with a perplexed expression. I waved to get her attention and mouthed 'It's ok' to her. Then 'Just friends'. That seemed to appease her somewhat as she started eating again, but she still glanced at them a couple more times. I'd need to explain the rules to her. That we were all family and everyone had each other's back. Especially Sherry. She was one of the original members of this group and everyone knew her and loved for the little mama she was to us. Ellie would just have to get used to that.

"I'm sorry," Sherry said as she swiped a loose curl from her neck and smiled bashfully at Ryan. "I'm a big baby."

"I remember someone telling me once that I was silly for saying I was a baby," he said and looked at her pointedly. "I think she was right about you, too."

"Ha, ha," she said and laughed at some private joke they apparently had. "Thanks, Ryan."

He nodded to her as she turned to leave and then he looked back at Ellie. I saw it. His whole face completely changed. He was her protector and her comforter. Maybe this stemmed from the fact that Calvin didn't really need him much anymore as a Keeper. But in his mind, and on his face, this girl was his now, he was her Keeper.

When she looked up and caught him watching her she smiled, but didn't look away. She was different with Ryan. He smiled too and sat in the chair next to hers, turning it to face her. They immediately started talking in low voices. He rubbed a hand down her back and asked her if the soup was good and if she felt better. She said she did, and I decided I was no longer needed there. So I left with a silent giggle at the new possibilities.

Love Implied
Chapter 8 – Merrick

I rolled over and inhaled the familiar vanilla that told me exactly where I was. I inhaled again deeper and longer, pulling the sweet smelling girl closer to me. I heard her giggle and it make me chuckle. It sounded low and on the verge of predatory even to my ears.

"You better watch it, mister," Sherry warned in a croon. "I remember someone saying that he was going to ignore me from here to eternity."

"I said until you heal, wife," I corrected and then groaned as she reached back and tugged at my hair. "Besides, we need to get up. The meeting is this morning and I want some coffee before that."

"Alright," she sang and rolled over while wrapping her bare leg around the covers. "I'm going to stay here for a bit longer and dream of the day when my husband wants me again."

"I want you, honey, I just..." I realized what she was doing as she rubbed her leg against mine. She warned me didn't she? "Sherry," I warned, but I still found myself running my hand down her leg.

"It's been days, Merrick. I think I can decide what's best for me," she said sternly and sat up giving me a strange look. She pulled me closer and I was just about to protest when someone knocked on the door.

"Guys, the meeting is about to start. Miguel wants to get going," Jeff said sounding somber.

"Ok," I answered back gruffly and turned to look at Sherry. "You got lucky."

"No, you did. Saved by the knock," she said softly and then wrapped her arms around my neck to kiss me. I could no sooner stop her than I could hurt her. She climbed onto my lap and kissed me with a forcefulness that belied her small frame. She tugged and pulled on me with urgency. When I finally gave into her and her small, sweet tongue swept into my mouth, she pulled back.

She bit her lip and gave me a small smile before pushing on my shoulders to stand and reaching for her discarded jeans. I grabbed her hand and gave her a look.

"What are you doing?"

"We have a meeting," she said as she pulled her hand easily from mine and tried to tame her locks.

"But you knew that before you kissed me," I countered in complete confusion.

"Yep," she quipped with a crooked smile that made me want to kiss her again. "Let's go, Finch."

"Wait, wait, wait." I stood too and guarded the door. She wasn't escaping from me. "So this is you pushing my buttons? You're just going to torture me until I give into you, is that it?"

"Yes," she whispered and moved forward to kiss my chin, "exactly."

"So you're a temptress now," I growled in frustration at the whole situation. She knew what she was doing to me, there was a meeting to go to and she was still recovering, but she looked pretty dang healthy and...able to me.

"You tell me. Is it working?" she replied in a sultry voice against the skin of neck. I heard my breath fight its way into my lungs before she bounced around me and swung the door open.

"Where are you going?"

"The meeting," she replied chipperly. "Come on."

"I think you're playing with fire, Sherry," I said as I tossed on a shirt and followed her out the door.

"Ooooh," she feigned fright as she walked backwards down the hall. "It's not so fun when someone else is in control of your body is it."

"What do you mean?" I asked in confusion.

"You." She stopped and stood looking up at me. "You're always so focused on my safety and healing and whatever else but you control everything for me. I can't even have a say in if I want to kiss my own husband."

"I'm not trying to control you," I said looking down at the sweet woman I loved more than my existence. "I just think sometimes you only do things because you think other people want you to."

"That doesn't make any sense. Especially with what we're talking about," she sulked.

"You don't want to kiss me and do *other* things just because you think I want you to?" I challenged.

"What? Do you think I don't enjoy it?" she said and laughed softly.

"I think when you're needing your rest, you just want to keep me happy and think you have to do these things to keep me satisfied." I pushed her gently to the wall and took her face in between my hands. "But you don't get it. I'm satisfied by just being with you. If we never did that again, I would still love you more than any other creature on the planet and I wouldn't feel unfulfilled."

"But what about me? The fact that you think I only want you to please *you* shows you don't know as much about me as you think you do."

"What?" I asked, baffled. "You're driving me crazy, baby."

"You drive me crazy, Merrick, in a good way. It's not just you. I want you, too, for my own reasons that frankly, at the risk of sounded selfish and shallow, don't have anything to do with you." I gave her a look that I hoped conveyed my utter confusion. "So this whole time you thought I only wanted to be with you to keep you happy? Really?"

"I don't know what I thought," I answered honestly.

"I wanted to make love to my husband this morning because I wanted you."

"It wasn't because you thought you were depriving me, because you've been gone and recovering? Not even a little?"

She laughed softly again and I felt my brow bunch in slight annoyance before she looked up at me, and then it all went away at the look on her face.

"You're so clueless," she whispered to herself. "You have no idea what you do to me. And the fact that you can still look at me as some kind of saint after all this time and everything that has happened to us makes me love you even more."

"You are a saint," I whispered back, but it was lost on her. Her face was bright and happy. She looked phenomenal, bruises and all. She was gorgeous and glowing and obviously fine. I worried too much, she was right. I needed to let the Keeper slide a little bit and let the husband take over. "I'm sorry. I didn't mean to be an ogre. It's just so hard to turn the protective mode off."

"I understand that. I'll never be mad at you for protecting me, but there are different things I need from you other than just protection sometimes," she breathed and bit her lip.

I nodded as I slowly descended on her, her mouth my destination. She smiled right before I touched her and it was the sweet, loving smile I've always known. She wasn't boasting that she won, she was just genuinely happy that I wanted to kiss her.

Her lips were just as inviting and eager as always. She wanted me...she just wanted *me*. It was an insane notion and I felt seriously slow on the jump to have misunderstood so much. I released her lips, but not her. She was so trusting and ready as she leaned against the wall where I pressed her, anxiously awaiting what I might have to say.

"I'm sorry that I'm just now understanding. I always just thought your love for me was a product of our circumstances or my protectiveness for you. I never really understand that it was just *me*."

Her face took on the look that I knew all too well as she recoiled and looked up at me devastated.

"You're just now figuring that out?" she said, her voice squeaked. "That part wasn't just implied, Merrick. I've told you a thousand times-"

"No, wait," I replied and once more took her face in between my hands. "I know you love me, ok, I just didn't understand the why. You love me for me. Just me, not for anything I do for you or have done."

"Of course." She let loose an exasperated sigh. "I can't believe you still think that-"

I cut her off with what she wanted. I lifted her and took advantage of the wall to hold her up to me as I used her want for my kisses to tell her everything my non-human mouth couldn't come up with. I heard her soft noise of surprise and contentment. She was light in my hands, but heavy on my heart. I finally got it. I pulled back just a little to speak.

"I get it now," I told her, my voice ragged with my revelation. "You love me just because I'm me. Not this body, not the fact that I'm a Keeper or the fact that I'm not."

"Duh," she said softly and smiled at me, refuting any sting that word may have induced.

"And I'm handsome and *extremely* charming and debonair."

She laughed out loud and shook her head at me. She continued to look at me and it made me hurt to feel the full force of the love that I'd never completely understood until then. I was someone's everything. And that scared me as much as it thrilled my human heart.

"You are all those things," she agreed, "but that is still not why I love you."

"I know," I answered truthfully and kissed her again because her lips seemed to be magnetic. I'd barely put a dent in the need I had for her when I heard a noise behind us.

We both turned to see Calvin, watching us with equal parts fascination and annoyance. I looked back to us and saw me, my hands on Sherry's legs and thighs as I pressed against the hall wall, her arms around my neck and both our faces flushed. I immediately put her feet to the floor and cleared my throat.

"What's up, Calvin? This isn't your hall," I said hoping we hadn't scarred his impressionable mind.

"I was going to get Lily for Marissa." He laughed and walked past us, calling over his shoulder. "Don't worry, Merrick. Mom told me all about the birds and bees. You haven't scarred my mind."

I gawked after him wondering how he'd read my mind so easily.

"Merrick," Sherry laughed and slid her palm down my cheek, "it's all over your face, babe."

"What is?"

"Embarrassment." She laughed again. "Come on." She pulled me to the commons room and we were greeted by a barrage of murmurings and conversations. "What's going on? What is this meeting about?"

"We need to go search for others." I saw her face change. "We talked about this, remember? Malachi isn't going to stop hunting them and they need to be aware if nothing else."

She smiled bravely before saying, "I know, I remember. It's ok."

"Ah, Merrick," Miguel said loudly and waved us forward to sit. "Now that everyone is here, let's get started."

We moved to sit against the back wall. Sherry ran to get us both a cup of coffee and sat beside me, her hand squeezed mine a little too tightly to be normal. I knew she was worried, but right then, there wasn't much I could do. And it was about to get worse.

"Now," Miguel began again, "most of you saw the news that day. Malachi is using every ploy to his advantage. He's using the people's need for food and shelter and money against them. There is a massive reward offered to those who turn in someone who is considered a rebel, though we don't know if he's actually giving them the money or not. Now we're lucky here." He held up his hand to Polly who was about to protest. "Compared to other people, we are bloody lucky. Others don't have this safe environment. Some are out there every day fighting wankers for food and abandoned places to stay. They don't have access to a telly and don't even know about the reward. They don't know they are being hunted now. We do, and it's our duty to go and try to help them, if nothing else to give them as heads up about the reward so that they have a fighting chance."

"I agree," Cain said loudly and stood up. "We saw what they did to those people at the facility." He glanced at the new girl sitting next to Ryan and then to Sherry. "We can't just sit back with the knowledge that we have of what's going on."

"But we'll be targets out there like that," Celeste chimed and hooked her arm through Danny's in a display of protection and possessive. Kay nodded her head in obvious agreement. It seemed the Keepers were split down the middle on this one.

"Can't be helped," Miguel shot back and turned the TV on, fidgeting with the rabbit ears. "The thing is, we have a hand up over the enemy. They don't know what we know. We'll be able to evade them quicker and get more people here if need be. Things are getting worse out there," he looked at Sherry sympathetically, "and sadly enough, our little rescue didn't help things atall."

"Sorry," she muttered, but he smiled and brushed off her apology with a wink. The news was on already and Miguel waved his hand to it as if proving a point. We listened.

"The rebels came in a deceptive and underhanded move. After posing as recruits for the enforcers and then destroying all the property and surrounding areas with homemade bombs they stole equipment, money and

vehicles from the facility. The enforcement officers present were all killed before even having a chance to fight back. The traitors who Malachi has worked so hard to rid us of were also released. Reports are not certain if this was a ploy to trick the enforcers; turning in a fake rebel, taking the reward money and then ambushing them. The brave soldiers who risk their lives to save us and construct peace in an otherwise un-peaceful world lost their lives. Estimated casualties are in the hundred. Efforts are being put into place to more aggressively search out these ruthless rebels. In an effort to thwart the new threat, Malachi has double the reward…"

Miguel slapped the button to turn the offending TV off and turned to look at us all. "See what I mean? Hundreds? Complete fabrication of what really happened to make us seem worse. The humans fear us too, now. They are not going to stop and things are not going to get better."

"What are we waiting for?" Cain spouted in his usual fashion.

"Told you he'd be all for it," Ryan said to Simon who scowled from the back wall.

"I'm in too," Billings announced loudly. "I wouldn't miss payback for all the corn in China."

"Good. We have to get a plan together," Jeff chimed in, ignoring Billings half joke, and stood. "No half cocked attempts, remember? This has to be all or nothing."

I squeezed Sherry's fingers in a soothing manner before standing. Danny stood too in response as I spoke.

"We'll need to get supplies gathered up. Look over the map of the area and see where and how far out we want to go. This will have to be covert. No traveling at night because it'll be too unsafe with Markers and car headlights. We'll move during the day and inconspicuously. And it'd be best….if we split up."

I felt the collective realization. No one wanted to do that, but they all knew I was right.

"Inconspicuous groups of five," Jeff agreed with a sigh. "It's the only way. We can leave on three or four day bouts and all be scheduled back at different times so as not to attract attention to the store."

"It'll work," Miguel replied and then moved towards the hall behind the stairs. "There was a whole but of atlases and maps in Trudy's old office. I'll get them laid out and we can have a war room."

"Great. Everyone that wants to come with us, come into the back office room and we'll work on a plan. I think the sooner the better. We can leave first thing in the morning."

My gut clenched at thinking of leaving Sherry so soon after we just got her back.

"That whole 'You're safer with me' bit isn't going to work this time is it?" Sherry asked me sadly as she stood, looking defeated.

"No, honey." I hugged her to me. "I hate to think about leaving you so soon."

"I'll be plenty occupied with Lily," she replied bravely. "And Calvin. There will be plenty to do here."

"Ok. I'm going to go with them to plan it all out."

She nodded and said, "Yes, go."

"I'm so proud of you," I whispered to her as I kissed her forehead.

"It would be selfish of me to try to keep you here."

It was my turn to nod.

"Sherry," Miguel called from the hall, "can you check and see if there's any supplies we can get or need? We can kill two birds with one stone."

"Ok," she agreed and then pulled me down to kiss me. "Go...plot."

"I love you, honey."

"I love you, honey," she repeated but it meant something a little different now because I knew exactly what she was implying. She loved me for me and no other reason.

A Well Stocked Pantry
Chapter 9 - Sherry

I watched him go and knew that what I said had been correct. There was no way to stop him without being selfish. I hated it, but there it was and I was determined to deal with it with grace and maturity, when really I just wanted to ball up and pout.

I passed Polly and Piper. They were whispering and watching me. I rolled my eyes at them and kept going down the hall to the empty rooms where we had been stocking food.

Polly caught up to me in the hall and said, "Is there something I can be doing?"

I looked at her in astonishment and replied, "Like what?"

"Anything. Everybody's just running around," she answered and swiped at her hair in a bored way. It was almost like she'd been made to ask me and hadn't really wanted to.

"Have you done the cleaning yet this week?"

"Nope."

"Well, that's a good place to start."

"You're not my warden," she barked.

"And you're not my prisoner, but you are assigned chores like everyone else."

"Whatever," she said and flipped her hair as she strutted away. Her ridiculous boots clacked all the way down the hall.

I huffed and wonder what the heck that had been about. I opened all nine pantry doors and peeked inside. They were all full. It struck me as awesome because it seemed that every week when they came back from food runs, the rooms got so much fuller. It seemed that they brought back more food than it looked like when they were unloading it.

And I was all neatly stacked and organized. I didn't let anyone else back here for fear of me never finding what I was looking for. I organized it all and I prepared most of the meals.

So I pushed the doors closed, happy with my assessment. As I'd said for weeks now that the pantries were full and smaller and less frequent food runs were needed.

When I turned I ran smack into Calvin's chest, with Franklin close behind him. He reached out to steady me and laughed.

"Easy there, Sherry. You'll break something running into people bigger than you."

"Ha, funny. Where you headed?"

"I was looking for you, actually."

"Ok," I said and waited.

"We, uh…" he glanced back at Frank and then back to me, "we wanted to see if we could go on the run with them this time."

"Why are you asking me?" I said and hated the thought of them going but knew that Merrick would never let them.

"Well, Merrick does everything you say, so we thought you could talk him into letting us go."

I burst out laughing. In fact, I laughed so hard that my side hurt. They looked at me like I was an insane person. I put my hand on Calvin's shoulder to steady myself before saying, "Come on, guys. You can ask for yourself, but even with my persuasion I guarantee that you won't be going. Sorry."

"Dang, Sherry. Please help us!" Calvin said vehemently as they trailed me down the hall. "It's just like the Service Draft back in the sixty's. It's not fair for us to be left out of the action when we can do some good." I stopped and looked at him, raising my eyebrow ever so slightly to indicate a question. He shrugged and said, "What? Marissa teaches us history."

I laughed again at his indignant tone, threw my arms around both of their shoulders and started down the hall once more.

"Sorry, boys. It's not my call, no matter what you believe."

"You're just saying that 'cause you don't want me to go."

"I don't want you to go," I agreed, "but I can't make someone let you either. Come on, stay with me and Lily. With all of them gone we'll need someone to be here with us to keep us safe...and entertained," I said trying to stifle a giggle.

"It's not fair though," he whined.

"I'm sorry that you feel that way. There are lots of things we're going through that isn't fair right now. It sucks, Calvin. I think you two know that more than anyone. You can't just be a kid in a world like this, but that is exactly what you are, and that's why you can't go."

"But the Lighters don't care if I'm a kid or not. They would kill me just the same."

I stopped in my tracks. It was heartbreaking. Not just his words and the truth that rang out behind them, but it was now our reality. Our kids knew death, hate, and devastation like we never even dreamed about as kids. Soon they may know even more: torture, pain, genocide...starvation. I shook my head to stop the thoughts and squeezed them both closer to me.

"Listen, we won't let that happen. That's why we're doing all this. We need to go out there and find others like us. They don't know the Lighters are hunting them like they are and there may be kids out there. We don't know who or what is out there. I've had enough of all of it and frankly," I was on a roll and it was getting louder, "I'm going to be worried enough about them all out there than having to worry about you two out there as well."

"Ok, sorry," Calvin replied as Frank sputtered behind him. "I guess it wouldn't hurt to stay here with you, especially after what they did to you." He stopped and grazed the toe of his shoe over the concrete floor over and over before looking up to my gaze again. "What did they do to you in that place, Sherry?"

"Nuhuh," I answered. "Come on, guys." I gripped their arms and pulled them with me down the hall again. I was the shortest of the bunch but I held in my sigh about it. "Why don't we stop all the heavy questions and get a snack, huh?"

"Sure," Calvin agreed. "What do we got?"

"I'm sure we can find something."

We made it to the kitchen just as the meeting in the back was over with. The plan must be in place...crap.

Ryan walked right to us and said, "Well, it looks like you'll have a chaperone, Sherry. Me." He grinned and ruffled Calvin's hair. "I'm staying behind."

"But why would you want that?" Calvin asked in a disgusted voice.

"Well, the people I care about most are going to be here so, I volunteered to stay behind. I didn't want to leave you here, kid."

"Oh," Calvin sang and crossed his scrawny arms, "I see. You didn't want to leave Ellie." He grinned at Ryan's shocked expression. "It's ok. I get it. She's cute."

"She is not," Ryan countered but stopped. "I mean, she is, but that's not why I-"

"Ryan," I interrupted, "you're playing right into his hands."

He glanced between us in an attempt to understand before he smiled a little and rubbed his neck as he said, "Oh, I see. You're joking with me."

"Speak for yourself, Sherry," Calvin called and then took off grinning as he ran with Franklin. "Ryan and Ellie sitting in a tree. K-i-s-s-i-n-g!"

"I didn't kiss her," Ryan told me like he'd gotten caught in the act or something.

"It's ok," I soothed. "He's just joking. It's a nursery rhyme.....sort of." I laughed but stopped once I saw how intrigued Ryan looked. "It would be ok if you kissed her, Ryan. I mean, if she wanted you to. You like her don't you?"

"I don't even know what that means," he told me and leaned back against the wall as if he'd fall over.

"Hey, Sherry," Josh called eagerly and slung his arm over my shoulder. "What's up? Ryan, dude, you look green," he observed.

"I don't know how to like someone," Ryan said as if Josh hadn't come up at all.

"You don't have to know how, Ryan," I told him. "It's not a job or something."

"Isn't it?"

"What?" Josh asked, but then a look of understanding passed over his face. "Ah. This is about that tasty morsel, Ellie."

"Josh!" I chastised through my laugh.

"Lady troubles, man. I've been there," Josh said wisely and nodded making me laugh more. "Let me give you some advice. I know you're an alien or whatever," he kept going, ignoring Ryan's scowl, "but the rules are the same for you. Number one, chicks dig it when you touch 'em. A little touch on the hand here, a little grazing your arm against hers there." Ryan's face took on an expression of revelation and Josh grinned. "Uhuh, see! You're already ahead of the game."

I just sat back and watched. I felt like I was getting a backstage pass into a guy's psyche and though I already had myself a man, it was still extremely fascinating. So I kept quiet and hoped my eavesdropping into why men acted the way they did wasn't noticed and I wouldn't be tossed out of enemy lines.

"So, number two, whether she is actually right or not, whatever she says, she's right. You got me?" I smirked and liked that one a lot . "And number three, and most important rule ever... respect, man. It's all about the respect."

Ryan nodded and rubbed his lip and chin in contemplation. I smiled at them both as we watched Ryan soak up the knowledge. Finally after a minute or so he said, "Ok, I understand all but one of those. I'm not sure what you mean by respect. I respect her, but why is that one the most important?"

Josh leaned forward and whispered something into Ryan's ear. His eyes bulged after a few seconds and he refuted whatever Josh had said, "No, I could never do that."

"I guarantee you, bro, in that body, you can."

"But I wouldn't-"

"Ok," I interrupted and pushed between them, "that's my cue."

I heard Josh laugh behind me, but Ryan was still in a tizzy. I laughed to myself as I made my way to my two loves, both of whom were waiting patiently for me.

"Lily bug," I crooned and she plopped into my lap as I sat on the floor beside them. "How was school?"

"5+4=9," she said and beamed.

"That's right. Very good."

"And I also know that I'm an ant!"

"What?" I laughed. "Well, you are kind of like an ant."

"Yep, I am."

I laughed again and looked at Merrick who'd been very quiet. He was waiting for me to freak out, I knew. I was going to try very hard to not do that, for his sake and mine.

"I'm ok," I told him. "When do you leave?"

"In the morning," he said solemnly. "We're going to pull out at different times and come back at different time so we're not attracting too much attention." He paused, but it was for stalling not effect. "Danny, me, Miguel, Celeste and Josh are on a team."

"Celeste is going?" I said, shocked.

"Yep," he answered but didn't seem like he was happy with it. "She wanted to go and convinced Danny that she would be useful with her gift. He didn't want to leave her behind."

"And Marissa is going too, right?" He nodded, but I already figured that she was going with Jeff.

"We'll only be gone three days the first time."

I gulped. Three days...

"Ok, well I guess I'll go get some supply kits started."

"How are the pantries looking?"

"Good. All nine are full," I announced. "I think we'll be fine for a while. Just focus on getting there and back not about anything else."

"I would help, but I promised Lily we'd do a puzzle or something tonight before supper," he said and looked down at her as she moved from my lap to his.

"It's ok. I can manage. You should spend some time with her before you go. Besides, I get you tonight, right?" I replied and dared him to refute my words.

"You couldn't beat me off with a stick," he said but it was soft and sad, the funny didn't even make itself known. I nodded and started to go but he grabbed my arm to stop me. He pulled me down roughly and kissed me, his urgency tangible and painful. I pushed back a little to look at him and he was almost shaking in his fury. I knew it wasn't directed at me. It just sucked that we had to deal with any of this. He didn't want to leave me and I didn't want him to risk his life. But neither could be avoided.

I kissed him once more before getting up. I grabbed a couple burlap bags from Mrs. Trudy's canning cabinet and made my way down the hall back to the pantry. I began to fill the bags with food enough for five people for three days, plus a little extra just in case.

I made sure to put the things I knew they liked most in the bags; creamed corn, spam, green beans. We would eat the beets here. I wanted them as happy and comfortable as they could be. My family would be out there in the thick of the Lighter's territory on a mission to save others. My hand shook thinking of the danger they'd be in. I gripped my fist tightly and refused to give into it, even for a second. I'd be strong, if for no one else but Merrick. He needed to know I was going to be ok without him so he could focus.

He needed to keep his eyes and mind on himself, on Danny and Celeste and the rest of them. He needed to bring them all home alive.

I'm A Wanderer
Chapter 10 - Cain

"So, like I was saying, it's really easy, you can just give them some math problems and sentences to practice with. That should be fine."

Marissa was explaining to Lillian about the school stuff for the kids. Marissa was coming with us and Lillian wasn't. And boy, she was not happy about it either.

"Ok, that's fine. I'm sure I can come up with something," Lillian answered, and though she was pissed at me, she was warm to Marissa.

"Great. Thank you so much for doing this. It'll be so much easier on the kids than having to play catch up when I get back."

"No problem."

We watched Marissa walk away and I waited for it as we stood in the alcove of darkness by the stairs. There it was; the glare.

"You, sir, don't get off so easy."

"Lovely," I crooned to get on her good side, but it was a no-go. I decided to change tactics. "Listen to me and listen good," I told her, all games aside. "I will never, ever put you in a dangerous situation that isn't needed. I know I took you to the club with me before, but that was a public place and I knew nothing bad would happen with all those people there to witness it. They were trying so hard to sway the human vote. This is different and I don't care if the Keepers said you could go with me or not, I wouldn't let you."

Her glare intensified as she said, "I'm so glad that you get to decide and dictate my actions for me."

"Lillian-"

"It's not fair that you have to go off and put yourself in danger just because you're a guy."

"It's not because I'm a guy, it's because I can handle myself. I was in the military. I've done things way worse than this, princess."

"Don't call me that," she sulked.

"And for the record, to further prove we aren't being sexists, Marissa and Celeste are coming, too."

"Then why can't I?" she yelled.

"Because you don't have a gift to help protect yourself!" I bellowed back, but quickly backpedaled and turned her so she'd be against the wall and I was on the outside. "Baby," I sighed and wished with everything in me that she would understand without my having to say the words. "I already told you," I said softly, "nothing is going to happen to me. I'll be fine. I'm not trying to boast or anything, but I can take down more Lighters than anyone in this joint put together," I said boastfully and grinned.

She smiled up at me and I was shocked at how easy she relented with, "Ok, fine." I must've been gawking because she added, "You would have thought it was odd for me to not put up some kind of fight, right?"

"Yep, I would have," I agreed with a relieved smile.

"I understand. Even though I may want to go with you, this is different, I know that. I want you to be completely focused on your trip. It sucks but…this whole thing sucks, so why should this be any different?"

"You," I bent and spoke into the skin of her neck, "are being pretty awesome right now." I kissed her collar bone. "I thought we were going to spend our whole last night together fighting."

"Not unless you want to," she goaded.

"I don't want to."

"Then who needs supper," she said flippantly and grabbed my hand to drag me with her.

"Where are we going?"

"I want to spend *all* my time with you before you leave."

I pulled her to a stop as her innuendo smacked me in the thinking part of my brain. "Whoa, hold the phone."

She laughed and yanked me forward again.

"I said I wanted to spend time with you, Cain, I didn't say that we were doing anything specific," she replied with a smirk.

"Ok, as long as we're clear."

She giggled some more and closed the door as we entered. I wasn't sure what I expected her to do now that we were there, but I didn't expect the sweet, tight, loving hug that she swept me into. She whispered her heavy words against my chest.

"Promise me you'll be careful."

"Of course."

"Say it," she commanded in her still whisper.

"I promise that I'll be careful and nothing will happen. I'll come back in three days."

"I know you will," she said with conviction and pulled me down to the floor with her. "Don't wake me up in the morning when you leave, ok?"

"Ok…but why?"

"Because I don't want to cry before you go," she admitted.

81

I lifted her chin to look into her face. She looked back at me and the unashamed look of love on her face hit me full force. Did she love me, too? I tucked her hair behind her ear just like the way she'd done a million times before. She rubbed her thumb over my lip ring before kissing me.

I had been worried before that she was going to try to do something rash with me because I was leaving. I would never have let her because it would have felt too much like a 'goodbye' instead of a 'come back'. But I should have known that she just wanted to be a snuggle bunny. I almost laughed, but I felt so...caught up in the sweetness of her.

I lay down with her, never breaking our lips. I hadn't slept in my room since...a long time. Since we got back from the club that time, I realized.

She needed me then and it felt like I needed her now. I needed to know she wasn't angry and she would be here, safe and warm and alive, when I returned. I'd never felt much like a soldier before. I was a machine. I didn't feel, I just operated. But with precious things at home waiting for me, it was harder to go. I'd never let her see that though. So I kissed her, and kissed her, and pressed her to me to feel her for the real thing she was. I kicked the door to tell them to shove off when someone knocked and said it was time for supper.

When someone came by later to tell us supper was done, I growled at them, making L laugh and press her lips together.

"Don't worry. Food is the last thing on my mind right now, Cain," she said sweetly and softly. Then she pulled me back down to her and I tried with every fiber in me to remember where my hands could travel.

Don't Cry Over Spilled Secrets
Chapter 11 - Lillian

I woke still snuggled against Cain. I looked at him closely, feeling strangely sentimental for such a time of day. He was a Neanderthal, a chauvinist, a gorilla when it came to me and my decisions. I smiled at the thought. Someone who was so adamant about my safety couldn't be all bad, right?

It had been a crazy few days. We had gotten Sherry back and gained a newbie, Ellie, who was just now starting to come back around to the land of the living. Margo had been dealt with, with surprisingly awe inspiring results. Merrick told us all about it, about how incredible it was. Danny and Celeste had retired right after understandably and not come out until afternoon the next day. They seemed fine now, though Celeste seemed less like her normal self and more like someone hell bent on revenge.

In times like this, I guess you needed that kind of drive sometimes.

Last night, Cain was relentless in his need to show me his affections, but not push me. I told him last night not to wake me up for his departure this morning, but I was wide awake. It was like my body knew he was leaving and there was no way it was going to miss it.

I crept out easily and smiled when he grabbed my pillow and said my name. Well, the nickname he made up for me, L. I loved it when he called me that.

I finger brushed my hair as I went down the hall and tried not to think about what was coming. Miguel met me as he burst from his door in a rush. I smiled at his eagerness to crack heads.

"The Lighters aren't going anywhere, Miguel. There's plenty of time."

He looked confused, but then laughed. Even his laugh had an accent. "Yeah, I admit I'm ready for some action. This sitting at home stuff isn't for me."

"Me either, but here I sit."

"I'm glad you'll be here," he replied. "At least I'll know you're safe and sound." He looked away at his admission. I stopped him and smiled, a friendly smile.

"Come back safe, ok? I'd hate it if we couldn't meet in the halls like this every day."

"Will do. You can't keep a good Aussie down," he joked. I laughed and hugged him. He accepted it easily, then released me and left with a wink in typical Miguel fashion.

Polly and Piper were friends again it seemed as they looked evil enough, no doubt plotting on the couch. They didn't even look my way as I passed them. They would be staying here with us. They couldn't be trusted to go out on the run. It was sad really.

In the kitchen, Sherry was up and making bottles of water. I decided to help since Merrick was nowhere to be seen yet. I wouldn't want to interrupt their goodbye.

"Need help?"

"I'm just finishing up actually, but thank you," she answered and when she turned I saw a bruise on her collar bone.

"Sherry, what happened?" I moved to touch the mark as she looked down at it, but then she flushed and covered it quickly.

"It's nothing," she insisted and her cheeks got even pinker as I understood and chuckled. She laughed too, pressing her lips together to stop the smile. "Merrick…gets a little carried away sometimes."

"No explanation needed." I waved a hand in flippancy. "I'm glad you guys had a…good time your last night."

She swatted me with a dish towel on my arm laughing and then smiled brightly as Merrick came up behind her.

"What's so funny?" he said to us, but he spoke low into her ear. I felt like I was eavesdropping so I turned to go. Neither one cared about me at all. I laughed as I watched her turn and he practically devoured her mouth right there in the middle of the kitchen as he lifted her up.

I sighed as I started back to my room. Cain needed to get up so he could get his things ready too, but when I got there he was gone. I peeked in the hall and decided I would try his room. He was there, bent over stuffing some clothes into a green duffel bag.

"Hey."

"Hey," he answered and stood up to tower over me. "I was about to come get you."

"You were?" I said suddenly solemn, knowing we had only minutes until he was leaving, and my voice practically gave that away.

"Yeah," he answered softly as he grabbed my hand and gently toyed with my fingers. "Don't be mad at me, ok? I wanted to do this another time, but seeing as how we escaped death at the facility, and know all of each other's secrets, and I'm leaving, it seems to fit the situation." I looked at him puzzled at what he was getting at. He didn't waste any time. He let my fingers go, held my face gently and spoke softly, but with conviction. "I am so crazy about you, L."

"Cain," I sighed his name and felt all my breath leave my body.

"I love you." He let me absorb that for a few torturous, silent seconds before going on. "Just know that I'm saying something to you that I've never said to another living soul. Not my parents, not my fiancé, nobody."

He leaned in and kissed me. He didn't wait for me to answer him. He doesn't seem like to type to want me to say it just because he did. He'd want me to say it when it was true for me. When he was certain about something, he just did it and dealt with the consequences.

He didn't know that I was in love him, too.

I kissed him back eagerly. I wrapped my arms around his neck, feeling his hands slide down from my face all the way to my hips. He was doing amazing things with his tongue as I broke off, before I got too breathless and couldn't speak to say what I *had* to say without another second going by.

I ran my hand over his head, scratching with my nails as I did it, over and over again to gather my courage. He groaned.

"You already got me, L. No persuading required."

"It's hilarious that you like that so much." He just smiled and closed his eyes as I continued to scratch and rub his scalp. Now or never. "I love you too, Cain," I whispered.

He opened his eyes as they snapped to mine, sea green and honest. He watched me closely for a few seconds.

"I didn't say it just so you would-"

"I know that, but I knew already. I was just too chicken to say it first."

He smiled slow and smug, looking thoroughly pleased and very much Cain.

"Really?" he said, his voice a happy growl.

"Yes...really."

He yanked me to him and pressed his face into my neck. "You're rattling my bones right now, L."

"I have no idea what that means, but it sounds good enough," I said through my giddy laughter.

"It means," he said suddenly serious and once more took my face in his hands, "that I am so incredibly happy with you. I don't think you realize what that means."

"I can guess," I answered back softly. "I love you," I said it again to make sure he got it.

"I'm gonna leave with that," he replied quickly and then pulled me to him, almost roughly. He held me close and still for at least a minute before looking up again. "I'll say it to you when I get back," he said, his voice grating and rough.

I nodded in understanding. This was not a goodbye.

He pulled me along with to him to the stairs. A devastated crowd was gathered there. This was it.

"My group is the first one to leave," Cain told me. I looked around and saw them already making their way up the stairs. "Don't worry. I'll make sure to keep them all in line," he joked.

"I'm sure you will, Sergeant."

"Don't you wrinkle that pretty nose with worry," he whispered into my hair. He'd said that to me once before and it almost broke my no-crying resolve.

"Ok," I said and cleared my throat before smiling at him. His ocean eyes never left mine. We heard Jeff saying it was time to go behind us and it was painful as his words lanced through my chest. Three days. I could make it for three days. This wasn't just stupid girly things though, this was worry. They would be out there for three days in danger. I was terrified for them.

I looked away to see them all saying their own goodbyes. Jeff was hugging Sherry, and Lily was practically forming a hug assembly line.

"Hey," Cain turned my face up to his. "I see a wrinkle," he said and tapped my nose.

"Nope." I gulped. "No wrinkle. I'm fine. Be careful, ok?"

"I will, promise."

He used his gentle fingers on my chin to lift me and bring me to him. I found myself winding my arms around him furiously, my hands bumping onto the bag on his back. He let it slide to the floor and engulfed me in his arms. With my feet off the floor I could do nothing but hold on and pray time would stand still. But it didn't and all too soon he was putting my feet back to the floor.

"Bye, my lovely," he whispered and then leaned down to retrieve his bag.

"Bye, sweetie pie," I whispered back.

He turned to go, letting our fingers hang on until the last second before they let go. I held my breath. I had to until he was out of sight. This just didn't make any sense. I was so crazy about this guy. I'd never been like this before. I had loved Michael, of course, but it wasn't like this. This was more than love, this was a need.

He followed Jeff and Marissa up the stairs and turned back once to smile and wink at me before disappearing. My breath still held, refusing to let me relax. I waited and the seconds ticked by. The pressure in my chest was so unbearable so I took a breath.

All it did was allow the tears to come. I wiped them away, thinking how stupid I was as I turned to go back to my room, when I felt a hard strong hand on mine.

I jerked around quickly to see him there. He pulled me to him and whispered in my ear, "I love you, too, L." I did one of those annoying half laugh/half cry things. He kissed me quickly and forcefully, reminding me that he could be sweet and cute, but at the heart, he was rough and rugged and all male. It was one of those fascinating things I loved about him.

He turned to go, smirking smugly at my inability to form words, and quickly ran to catch up with the rest of them. I touched my lip. I could still feel the imprint of his lip ring, or maybe it was all in my head. Either way, I found myself smiling and then caught myself.

No. No smiling until he walked back through that door.

Wooden Pony
Chapter 12 - Sherry

"Lily," Miguel said sweetly and lifted her, "I've got to run fast, but I wanted to give you this first." He handed her a little wooden carved pony that fit in her hand. She squealed and lifted it to her face to nuzzle it. "I made that for you."

"You did?" she whispered, enraptured in her awe of him.

"I sure did, little sheila," he told her and kissed her forehead before handing her off to Merrick. "You make sure to think of a good name for her while I'm gone, ok?"

"She'll miss you," Lily told him.

"Well, I'll miss you," he said and tweaked her nose before winking at me and turning to go.

"Be careful, Miguel," I told him and wrenched my necklace charm back and forth. "Come back, ok?"

"Will do," he confirmed and nodded.

"You're weaving too, Daddy?" Lily asked Merrick, but her eyes never left her wooden prize.

"Yeah, baby, I am," Merrick sighed his words and hugged her to him.

"I'll miss you. Can you bring back another watermelon?"

"I'll try real hard," he told her with a smile for her naiveté.

He let her down and she trotted her pony in the air towards the commons room. Then he turned to me.

I was never one to hide my feelings and though I knew it probably didn't make him feel any better about leaving, I couldn't stop the tears that decided to fall right then.

"I know," I groaned, "I know. I'm being silly."

I pulled him down and looked at his mark once more to make sure my cover-up job was still good. When I straightened again he looked pained, his lips twisted in a half frown.

"I'm sorry," he said roughly.

"It's ok. It can't be helped." I reached up and let him pull me to him. I wished I had the Keeper's mind talk at that moment so Merrick didn't have to hear the tears in my voice as I pleaded with him with everything in my soul. "Please, please be careful."

"Of course."

"Make sure you come back."

He pulled me back to look at him. His hand cupped my cheek in his way that was as loving as it was possessive.

"Always," he said firmly.

The tingles that had started months before at his very first touch were ever present. They traveled along with his touch across my cheek and down my neck. My everything was walking out the door. I sighed and breathed through it.

He lifted me once more and kissed me. His arms snaked around my waist as he squeezed and held me there. His stubble rubbed my cheek and it reminded me of things from last night; feverish hands, traveling lips, melding and hanging onto every second we had together. He'd been ferocious and I had been in a fevered scuttle. It was a magical combination for us and I couldn't stop the smile as I thought about the marks on my neck and other places. He'd never been very good at *not* making marks on me. It was funny, really.

But I liked it. It was strange. I liked having his marks on me, claiming me, possessing me. I was his.

"You've got to go," I whispered when he gave me a second to breathe.

"Yeah," he sighed against my forehead. "I love you. I'll be back before you know it."

"I love you," I croaked.

"Please don't cry after I'm gone. You know what it does to me."

"But you won't be here to see it," I joked and even tried to smile for him.

"But I'll know," he said ominously. "Remember everything Lily does while I'm gone. I'll want a full report when I get back."

I laughed and sniffed as I told him, "Oh, don't worry about that. I'm sure she will chat your ear off when you get back."

His loving fingers caressed my cheek and then reached down to run in the ends of my hair. When he leaned his forehead to mine he said, "I love you, baby, so much."

"I love you more."

"Not possible," he promised and kissed my forehead as he left with a sad smile. He waved to Lily and then with one last look at me he was gone with one just last word in my mind.

Always...

I smiled through my tears and then hugged Danny as he finally made his way out of their room.

"Be careful, brat."

"I will. I've gotta go or Merrick will leave me on purpose," he said quickly.

"Watch out for each other, Danny. Love ya."

"Love ya, shorty."

"We'll be fine, Sherry," Celeste assured me as I hugged her to me. "I'll make sure they both behave."

"I have no doubt," I said and laughed as she swatted his butt.

"Let's get moving, hottie," she said as she pushed him forward.

"Ok, ok," he laughed and called over his shoulder to me, "Bye, little sister. Don't worry so much."

"Like that's possible," I rebutted and then they too were gone.

"Bye, Sherry," Josh said from behind me and I turned into one of his all encompassing hugs. His Keeper, Racine, had a wicked case of the flu, and that was the only reason he was going without her right now. She was fevered, almost to the point of worry. "We'll all be together so what could go wrong?" he said trying to cheer me up, but I just felt worse. So not only could I lose one, but I could lose all of them. I smiled at him regardless though. "Make sure Ryan works on his lady skills while I'm gone," he said in jest and lifted an insinuating eyebrow.

I laughed as I said, "Oh sure. I'll get right on it."

He waved to everyone as they all wished him well in yells and goodbyes. He was the last one to leave…

I gulped at the utter empty feeling of the bunker.

I saw Lillian watching the stairs in a stupor. I slowly went her way and just before I reached her she jerked her attention to me.

"Hey," she said and cleared her throat. "They're all gone, huh?"

"Yep," I answered. "You ok?"

She nodded and gave me a contesting look.

"Are you?"

"Not really, but I don't have much choice."

"He said he loved me," she whispered and covered her lips with her fingers like she was remembering something. She smiled a little, but stopped herself.

"That's great, Lillian." I paused, but she stayed silent. "Do you love him?"

"Mmhhmm," she answered with a nod.

"Then what's the matter?" I asked softly.

"I just can't lose him. I always lose."

"You won't," I assured her and put my arm through hers. "Come on. Let's get Lily and make some cookies or something. Then I should probably take some soup to Racine."

"Ok," she agreed with a vigorous nod, eager to have something take her mind off things.

"We don't have much in the way of cookie stuff, but we have flour and sugar."

"Sugar cookies are my favorite."

We passed Ryan and Ellie who were playing cards on the floor behind the couch. She was trying to teach him to play to Spades. They were laughing and he was animated. I even saw him smirk once as he pulled the end of her hair playfully. It was curious behavior. He had no notion to go on the run with them at all and was perfectly happy to stay here with his two charges.

Katie and Sky were in the rocker as we went by. Katie was fighting a yawn and Sky was about to wail away, I could tell.

"Here," I told her with a smile, "let me take her for a while."

"Thank you, Sherry," she said as she handed her off gently.

"It's ok. Go do whatever you need to do." I looked down at Sky who was fascinated by the taste of my hair. "We'll be fine."

Lillian followed me to the kitchen and we both laughed when Sky burped loudly.

"There's no way to cover that one up as lady-like," I laughed. Lillian continued to watch Sky even as she dumped ingredients in a bowl. "You want to hold her?"

"Nah," she said and shook her head. "I just love babies. Michael didn't want any."

"What?" I asked completely shocked by that. "Why not?"

"He said he wanted to wait, that he wasn't ready; that he might not ever be ready." She smiled sadly. "I was devastated by that, but now, I think it was probably a blessing." She came closer and rubbed Sky's cheek before the baby promptly gnawed on her finger. We laughed, but Lillian still said, "Can you imagine having to keep this little one safe? The worry would eat me alive."

I thought about that. It was true but I still felt that little ache for it, the little itch that never quite went away. Being told you couldn't have something made you want it more. I didn't think the want would ever go away, however irrational it was.

Lily marched in, making her horse gallop and neigh, before she looked at me. She pursed her lips and scrunched her nose in disapproval.

"What you doin' with that baby?"

I tried to stifle my laugh as I said, "I'm holding Sky for Katie. Do you want to see her?"

"No, thank you," she said haughtily and marched right back out of the kitchen.

We couldn't help it as Lillian and I laughed in fits that we desperately needed.

Roof Under Foot
Chapter 13 - Merrick

"Sherry packed up way too much food," Danny was saying but I was barely listening. "Dude," he said and waited for me to look at him in the mirror. He and Celeste were smushed together with Josh, who was clearly not happy with the seating arrangement, in the back. Miguel sat next to me up front. "The sullen look is not working for ya."

"Bite me," I muttered and went back to sulking and driving. Our group was to take the west side of the outskirts of town. We'd spend as much daylight as possible looking through abandoned houses and buildings. Look for any signs that someone may be there, even if they didn't want to be found.

"I know I have no room to talk, because my girl is with me," he continued and I gave him a look to agree with that, "but still. You know she's safe there, nothing will happen to her. I feel better about her being there. I wish *someone* else had stayed behind as well."

"Me, too," Kay sulked from the trunk space. She was the smallest person to fit back there and she swatted her red hair away from her face as it blew everywhere from a tiny hole in the soft top.

Danny gave Celeste a poignant look and she stuck her tongue out at him before saying, "You can use me on this run and you know it. I can find people, and though I'm not sure if I can find people I don't know yet, I think this is a perfect opportunity to test that."

Miguel leaned over in the seat and whispered loudly, "Are they going to be like this the whole time?"

"No doubt," I answered.

"Bugger," he groaned and leaned back into his seat. I heard him mutter, "I'd rather be fed to a Marker."

I held in my chuckle. We were minutes away from the first place on the map to search. We'd test Celeste's gift theory soon.

As we turned into the first building I pulled all the way into the back. The Jeep's brakes squeaked loudly echoing off the walls. I cringed, but it didn't matter. We wanted them to know we were here so hopefully they didn't jump the gun, literally.

"Alright, let me do the talking, please," I told them and gave Celeste a look to make sure she understood.

"Of course! Why do I get the look and no one else?" she said and scrunched her nose.

"Babe," Danny said sarcastically and lifted his eyebrow with meaning. "Come on."

"Ok, fine. Whatever," she said and pushed Miguel's seat back. "Let's go, bush man."

"Watch it, sheila," Miguel growled and opened the door. "You're stuck with me for three days so let's not start off on the wrong foot."

"Miguel, in those shoes, you're always on the wrong foot," she said and laughed, leaning on Danny like it was hilarious. I sighed and waved Miguel off who was inhaling for a rebuttal.

"Alright guys. Leave all the stuff here and let's go," I told them. I knew right then that this whole operation was probably going to be more of a pain than it was worth. I was away from my girls and if something good didn't come of this run, I was going to be one unhappy Keeper.

"So, should I try now?" Celeste said and I was pleased that she sounded serious now.

"Please."

She kneeled on the ground, just like that day in front of the Mayor's Manor. Her eyes took on that greenish freaky look. Her mouth opened slightly and though her breaths were steady, she looked a little peaked, like she was exerting herself.

"I'm sorry," she finally said and her eyes went back to their color. "I guess I have to focus on someone specific. I'm getting nothing."

"It's alright," I told her at the same time that Danny said, "It's ok, babe."

"I don't see anything either," Josh supplied and shook his head to clear his vision. "All I see is wall after wall. That doesn't mean that someone isn't in there though. It's just too much to see through."

"Well, we go in like the good old days. Blind," Miguel said and checked his knife in his boot and his stake in his waistband before straightening and leading the way. "Let's get this show on the road."

"I swear, Miguel," Celeste said as she tripped over the doorway and kicked it in retaliation. "Your accent is so much more pronounced when you're itching for violence."

"As it should be," he answered and looked around the worn and weathered warehouse. He looked at me. "Should we just ring the bell?" he said sarcastically.

"I'm afraid we're just winging it."

"Great," he drug out as he eyed the massive creaky doorway. "I'll let my coconut be on the chopping block first, since I don't have a pretty little sheila waiting for me."

"Neither do I," Josh muttered behind me, almost startling me because he'd been so quiet.

"Aw, Miguel," Celeste chimed. "You want me to search in my mind for you a lovely little sheila?" she goaded.

"Oh, boy," Danny replied.

"Alright, everyone, let's muzzle it so I can think," Miguel growled.

He looked around as we all stood in the doorway. It was wide open, but that didn't mean anything either way. It was a very likely possibility that we would search for days and find nothing. I almost growled at the thought as we inched our way inside, but it didn't take long before we heard a crunch behind us.

My fingers automatically went to the stake in my back pocket. With Miguel and me flanking the group we stood silently waiting for something to indicate what we had heard: friend or foe?

"What was that?" Celeste hissed as Kay pulled her tighter to her just and Danny did the same thing.

"Quiet," Miguel barked, which was silly given the word he had just said. "Hello?" he called. "We aren't here to hurt you."

The silence was too eerie, too telling. It reeked of trouble. I motioned them back to the doorway until we could regroup and maybe grab more weapons. My actions were futile as two Lighters dropped down from the roof right in front of the doorway.

"Mmm, Keeper," one of them acknowledged with a nod and a grunt. Then he looked at Kay and grinned. "And Keeper. What a surprise."

"Lighters right out of the gate," Miguel mused beside me and switched his stake from one hand to the other. "And I was beginning to think my lucky rabbit's foot had failed me."

As I began to think strategy, one of the Lighters walked straight to Danny, his gait lazy and languid as if he had all the time in the world. I balked and blurred to him, but Danny held his hand up. He easily handed the Lighter a slim stake and I watched as he walked back to his comrade and staked him right through his stunned chest. The lightning burst through his chest and the crackle in the air had barely gone away before the Lighter then staked himself in a blur. Another burst of lighting burst forth upward, taking out the rickety ceiling and a huge chunk of the wall.

We all turned to Danny. He shrugged.

"I figured I'd make it easy on you, Keeper-o-mine. Sorry, Miguel, I know you wanted to bust heads."

"That wasn't much fun," Josh said and laughed at Miguel's expression.

"It *was* rather anti-climatic," Miguel sulked and I almost laughed.

"Yeah, dude," Josh said and slapped Miguel's arm. "Why'd we even come along? We're outdated models now."

"Well, it was just-" Danny started, but there was a loud groan.

We all stopped and looked around. The groan was strained and metallic. It got louder and I was clueless, but Miguel must've understood.

"The building's coming down. Move!"

We moved, but it wasn't fast enough. I could have blurred and made it, but I would have had to leave someone behind. So I stayed behind too, blurring my way to Danny out of instinct instead, and as we all watched the ceiling collapsed around the massive hole already in the structurally unsound ceiling from the lightning. We leapt back and though we were out of danger, we were covered in dust and pieces of wood and metal. Our way out was blocked. The doorway was smashed and covered in large chucks of debris too big to move with our hands.

As Celeste muttered as Kay helped to brush her off, I took the opportunity to address my Special, after looking him over to make sure he was alright first, of course.

"You know that was all on you, pal."

"What?" he screeched. "I saved us from the Lighters!"

"Yep, just to trap us instead," Josh said, but he laughed and pulled a big chunk of something from Celeste's hair. "Dude, we're screwed now."

"I'm sure there's another way..." he stopped his explanation when we all turned to see we were in a box. No doors, no windows, no stairs. It was a holding containment of some kind and we were now stuck. "Oh."

"Yeah, oh," Celeste said in a grunt, but then softened. "But, it wasn't entirely your fault, babe."

"Ok, fine. Maybe I should have lured them outside first. I thought I was helping. What do you want me to say?"

"Well," Miguel drawled, "I don't really think 'woops' quite covers it here, mate."

"Woops," Danny rebutted sarcastically. With his arms crossed, he said, "Seems like it works just fine to me."

Simon Says
Chapter 14 - Cain

"Simon, man, come on. Somehow, I have survived for many years without you hanging on my heels."

"That is not true!" he answered vehemently. "I've watched you every day since you were a baby. If you had ever been in real danger, I would have come for you, even in the war."

"Touché, but I still want you to sit in the car and wait. I'll scout and then give you guys the go ahead, ok? That body of yours is breakable, you know."

"I'm not too keen on this idea either, Cain," Jeff turned traitor and spouted.

"Whatever, turncoat, I'm the only one here trained for things like this."

"Cain has his sonic hands....boomy thing," Marissa said and I nodded to my unlikely ally. "He'll be fine."

"Yeah," Billings chimed in, "he'll be fine with his hot hands or whatever. Let the Marine go first."

"For the sake of argument," I explained, "let's call them Magic Fingers." I grinned, but no one smiled but Marissa, who was hiding it from Jeff. "Guys, I'm gonna go so crazy out here if y'all don't simmer down. Chill, mellow, chillax, veg, something. I can't handle all this alpha male bull crap the whole time, ok?"

"This is about me keeping you safe, no matter how useless you think I am," Simon said with an edge. "You can keep all your alpha male talk and your idioms to yourself."

"Ah," I laughed, "looky at Simon, playing professor."

"Cain," he said in exasperation.

"I'm just joshing you, man." I punched his shoulder lightly. "You've got to lighten up."

"I'll *lighten up* when we are back in the bunker."

"Alright, I'm going to move on inside. I'd prefer you all wait for me to check first, but if you must come," everyone piled out with gusto, "then...come on," I sighed.

"This is the whole point in bringing a team with us," Jeff said as he passed me, towing Marissa behind him. "Strength in numbers."

"Or," Billings replied happily, "it could be the weakness is the loud footsteps of the many." He stopped and stuck his hands in his pockets when everyone glared at him but me. "Depending...on how you look at it."

"Billings has a point," I said.

"Sadly, not a good enough one," Simon rebutted gruffly. "We stay together, end of discussion."

"Fine. Simon says lead the way," I replied and swept my arm wide for him to do just that.

He looked at me in confusion before shrugging, no doubt just brushing my sarcasm off as unnecessary. I did not get people who couldn't appreciate a little sarcasm.

"So, it looks deserted, but we better tread lightly just in case," Jeff said and took up the front lead. From the looks of things he'd coined himself the leader of the troupe. That was a-okay with me. I was a Sergeant no more and had no inclinations to pick back up the stars.

"Great. And I'm guessing you want to lead the way."

"Despite what you believe, Cain," Jeff answered easily, his voice steady, "you are still the more breakable of the two. It's better for a Keeper to go first, always." He started to walk on, but then stopped and barely turned to me. "Besides, you don't want me to have to go back and tell Lillian that you didn't make it, do you?"

"Low blow, man," I growled at him for even mentioning her name. I was trying to put on my game face, harden myself up for a fight, and he was bringing up the one thing that made me crumble?

"It's true."

"Regardless," I barked back.

"Let's go."

I followed, scowling at his back. Maybe I needed to rethink this whole not-in-charge thing because taking orders sucked.

I bit on my lip ring. Something I'd always done before a mission or fight was pinch or scratch myself to get alert and pissed. When I pulled it or irritated it, it made me agitated. It seemed to bring me an edge of pain that I needed to want to hurt someone. I also used to hum when I cleaned my guns and polished my boots. It was a running joke in my barracks that I was a psycho because of it. But for some reason that I was unaware of, Nirvana made me want to hurt people. Hey, whatever works to get the job done, right?

Billings bumped my arm.

"Hey. So, the old guy is your Keeper right? And Jeff is a Keeper and Marissa is a..."

"Muse," I provided."

"Yes. Muse. Why did we get stuck with all the crazies and the other group only got one?"

"They have five," I told him. "The only one without power is Miguel."

"Really? I can't keep track. I forgot some of you... Specials," he drug out the word, "have powers, too."

"Watch it, pal. I'm one of those Specials," I said and bumped back his arm.

"I know. That's ok. I'm really curious about it all, actually. How did you know you were a Special?"

"Simon showed up and told me," I answered steadily.

"And you just believed him?"

"Well, no. It took some persuasion. But when he spoke into my mind, that was pretty much all I needed."

"Oh, yeah. I forgot about that, too," he grumbled.

"Dude, you've got to get over this whole grudge against the Keepers. The Lighters were feeding you horse manure and you were eating it up like Sunday dinner."

"You are way too descriptive, man."

"Just saying," I reasoned even as I continued to look around for signs of life.

"Horse manure or not, the Keepers weren't exactly honest either."

"When?"

"Well, when I showed up for one. Not one of them made themselves known to me until you outed them."

"I didn't out them," I argued and lowered my voice so the ones ahead of us couldn't hear. "If you had come down the chute and the first thing anyone said was, 'Hey man, I'm a Keeper, can I take your gun for you?' You'd have run for the hills before I could even stop you."

"Probably," he conceded. "I'm just saying, you say that the Lighters are deceitful and shifty, but I've heard stories, man. I mean even Merrick had to kidnap Sherry and lie to Danny to get them to go with him."

"For good reason! Same reason we let you settle in and get comfortable before we told you. Could you imagine Sherry being told by some guy, her ex-boyfriend no less, 'I'm an alien or angel or whatever and I've come to help you. Pretty please come with me underground?' No way, man. Sometimes you have to stretch a lie a little bit to see the truth underneath."

He was silent for a second before he muttered, "Did you just make that up?"

"I did," I said and smirked proudly. "Like it?"

"You are something else, Cain."

"Hey, slowpokes! Let's get going," Jeff called and then put Marissa behind him as they flanked the door.

He rapped slowly and lightly on the big wooden door. It was an old abandoned house. Merrick's group took the business district. We took the side with mostly houses on the outskirts. In honesty, I was glad we got this. We'd probably see more action, I figured.

No one answered so Jeff tried the knob. Locked.

"Kick it in, Chuck," Billings told him eagerly.

"What?" Jeff asked. "Who?"

I laughed as Billings said, "How can you not know who Chuck Norris is?"

"Um, I've been somewhere else, and since the Lighters came I haven't had time to dig into earth's pop culture. Chuck Norris had his own Keeper, I'm sure," Jeff sneered sarcastically.

"Seriously?" Billings replied in excitement. "You really think he had one? He could still be alive somewhere. We could track him down-"

"Really?" I said incredulously. "We're really having this conversation?"

"Chuck would be a vital asset," Billings sulked. "He does all of his own stunts and everything."

I didn't know whether to laugh or kick him for being an idiot, so I just said, "This isn't Zombieland, ok? We aren't going to run into Hollywood and land ourselves into Bill Murray's mansion."

"Bill Murray," he mused. "Think about all the people who could still be alive out there somewhere. I bet we could find Chuck if we looked hard enough."

Marissa was laughing into her fist and Jeff and Simon were positively clueless.

"Ok," I stopped him, "first off, we need to eat soon because Billings is going into delusions." I heard his disgruntled 'hey' but kept going. "Secondly, move."

I kicked the door open for them and it gave way surprisingly easy. But the wood was rotted and my foot landed on the other side all by itself. I grunted in annoyance. This was the most ridiculous, unorganized mission I'd ever been on.

Jeff smashed the wood around my leg the rest of the way with his boot and the door fell loudly to the floor inside the house. We waited for a second. I had to hold out my hand to Billings who was trying to make a break inside.

"Don't you know anything about entering enemy territory?" I asked and pushed him back a little. "Don't ever enter head first. That's how you end up headless."

"Hey, I know that," he argued, his tone indignant. "I've seen plenty of cop shows."

Marissa was no longer containing her laughter. I peeked back and even saw her wiping her eyes. Jeff looked at her funny, not understanding what was so hilarious. I almost wanted to sit there and explain it all out to him. How this was so utterly ridiculous, just so he'd understand and know why my eyes were rolling every eight seconds, but there was no time.

I'd just have to bear this burden of idiocy myself. So after I checked the entrance I dragged the idiot through the door with me.

"Hello?" I called and heard nothing. I sniffed and almost gagged. "It's rank."

"If it's empty," Jeff started, "we should go ahead and move on. By the next place it'll be dark and we can bunk down for the night."

"Agreed. I'll head upstairs."

"With me," Simon said and pushed in a blur to move in front of me. I gawked at him. He'd never moved fast like the other's before. I realized there was plenty I didn't know about my old Keeper.

I followed him upstairs and we began to search the rooms, Simon first each time. The further we got the more I knew what we were getting closer to. I started to warn Simon, but he already knew. He nodded and had the look of a solemn man. We ventured on anyway, like we had to see it with our eyes.

Even with me expecting it and being a military man, a hard-nosed jerk, a guy who'd seen death and used a gun more than I'd used a hairbrush…I gasped at what I saw.

There on the bed in the master bedroom was a middle aged couple and two small children. They were all lying on their sides, spooned together with their hands entwined in front of them, all had on pajamas. It had been a while since they died and though the window was open slightly to let out the stink, it was still rancid. Their skin was wrinkled and a pale gray from death.

A bottle of something was sitting on the nightstand and a single sheet of paper lay on the bed next to them. My fingers trembled as I reached for it and read it aloud because I couldn't seem to stop myself.

Demons,

We died on our own, but were not alone. You tried to take us, use us, but we were one step ahead. We refuse to be your puppets. Judgment shall come and it will not be swift for you. My only regret is that we won't be alive to see your demise. Rot in hell while we rest in peace.

-John, Cathy, Ike, Sarah and our Ron,
whom you took from us already…

"Oh…my…" Simon said behind me. "Brave souls," he whispered in reverence.

"They committed suicide," I muttered and though to me their death was honorable, even with the children there on the bed with them to spare them the horrors, it still hit too close to home for me. My own mother's suicide was something I'd never completely worked out. In fact, the shrink at the base said I was borderline incompetent and I was almost sent home for mental instability when I got the call. But I pulled my crap together back then and I could do it now, too.

"They weren't affected by the Lighter speak," I mused as I looked at the father's hasty scribbled words. "They knew exactly what the Lighters were."

"It would seem that you're correct. Strange. I'm very curious about what happened here."

"Doesn't matter now."

I set the letter right back where I'd gotten it gently. I hoped the Lighter bastard who stepped into this house knew how to read. He'd be reading what was coming for him and I'd make sure of it if it was the last thing I did.

Judgment was coming.

Hell was waiting.

Hell Is Waiting
Chapter 15 - Sherry

We'd barely gotten Lily into bed when someone was knocking on the hatch door. I bolted up in surprise from the couch. People didn't just knock on our door. No one was in the store right now. In fact, we hadn't even figured out the whole store situation yet with Margo gone and all. We were no longer allowed to sell food except finishing up our inventory. We could only sell gas and maps and things like that.

So who was knocking on our door?

Max and I looked at each other a second before he blurred to the stairs. Ryan was right behind him. Lillian and Ellie came and stood beside me as we waited to see who had paid us a visit.

I wondered if Max would say, "Who is it?" but he just grabbed a stake, unbolted the door and opened it in one quick motion. Then he growled and his hand holding the stake snapped forward. I couldn't see who it was, but assumed it wasn't someone good. Meaning it was a Lighter.

But Ryan stopped him with a hand on his forearm and a, "Wait, brother."

"Wait for what? Ryan, what's wrong with you," he said and struggled against him.

"This is the Lighter who helped us at the facility."

"Daniel," Lillian said softly and ran towards them. I followed.

There he was; dirty, disgusting, his clothes a mangled and torn mess. And he was watching Max's stake with wary eyes.

"Move, Max. Let him in!" Lillian insisted.

"He's a Lighter, Lillian. Have you lost your senses?"

"He's hurt," she said and pushed Max away, but he caught her by the arm and moved her behind him.

"What has gotten into you?" he asked her and then looked to Ryan. "Ryan-" he started.

"It's true, Max. He helped us," Ryan explained. "Daniel, how did you find us?"

"I..." he looked at Lillian guiltily, "I followed you that day."

"See!" Max insisted. "A tame Lighter is still a Lighter."

"No, let him in," Lillian pleaded. "He's hurt and dirty."

"He's not a puppy, Lillian," he scolded. "You can't just bring a Lighter in from the cold."

"Daniel," Ryan tried again. He seemed to be the only level headed one operating. "Why did you come?"

"I can no longer work at the facilities. My cover is no more. They figured it out, they didn't know it was me, but they became very suspicious. I had to leave before they found me out."

"You didn't answer my question," he said quietly.

"I came because...I was invited," Daniel told him and looked at Lillian, then at me. "Does the offer still stand?"

"No!" Max boomed and looked at Lillian and I sternly. "Don't even think about it. What in the worlds has gotten into you two?"

"Merrick was the one who invited him, Max," I rebutted.

"Well Merrick isn't here now, so no is my answer."

"Max," Ryan said and his eyes moved and bulged slightly as he looked at him. They were fighting in their heads. You could tell who was talking because their head moved slightly with the vehemence of their words.

"He's a Lighter, Ryan!" Max bellowed. "A Lighter! The very opposite of us. I don't care what he did, he's not coming in here." He thought for a second. "As a matter of fact, we have to kill him."

He moved to push the stake through Daniel's belly. We all moved forward, but there was no stopping the swiftness of a Keeper on a mission. Except another Keeper. Ryan and Max were locked in a never ending battle of arms and wills. I heard Ellie's small gasp and looked to see her covering her lips with her fingers in clear distress.

I needed to intervene.

"Max," I said softly and went to stand next to them. They both strained against the other in a silent and strangely still fight. "He saved me, Max. He saved Lillian and Cain. He would have turned us in already if he was going to."

Max looked at me and I saw him soften the smallest bit, but he still scowled at me as he said, "Look, I'm not Merrick. I'm not going to just give you whatever you want because you pout at me."

"I'm not pouting. I'm asking," I said steadily.

"This is on you," he said, but still didn't let Ryan go. Or maybe it was the other way around.

"Understood."

He took a deep breath and looked at Ryan, who removed his hands and the stake. Max swept his arm wide with a sardonic twist to his lips for Daniel to enter. Daniel, the most polite Lighter I knew, thanked him, but Max just scoffed and stomped off. But not before yelling over his shoulder, "All on you!"

Daniel, Lillian, Ryan and I stood at the stairs awkwardly. Finally Daniel spoke.

"I didn't mean to cause trouble. I told you before that I would not be accepted."

"It's fine," I answered. "Max is old school," I said, but forgot and changed it to something more simple. "He hasn't…acclimated like some of the other Keepers have to our way of thinking."

"So you said you got caught?" Lillian asked getting right down to business. "What happened?"

"Well," Daniel drawled like he wasn't sure…or didn't want to say. He lifted his shirt and showed us a massive gash on his side. Lillian gasped and knelt to look at it. "Normally, my skin would have healed by now. I don't understand it, but I had to kill my brother who gave me this. If I can't heal, I have no idea how I would keep that from them."

I glanced at Ryan. He was gaping at Daniel's wound like it was a bomb.

"Wait," I stopped Daniel. "You're not…spurting light like the others do, from your wound."

He looked at me pointedly and nodded grimly. "I know."

"What could that mean?" I asked him as I went to the cabinet and got some gauze and tape.

"I can not conjure a response for that."

I almost smiled at his formal tone and language. Lillian held her hand out for the supplies and didn't even look at me. Again, I wanted to smile. Oh, boy…the boys were not going to like this when they got home.

"What the…" Max said and we looked up. He was white as a ghost. "How is that possible?"

"I don't-"

Max wasn't giving him any room to talk. He marched right up to him to examine himself. "It went clean through." He looked up at Daniel's face. "You were run through."

Daniel nodded. "Yes, he found me sneaking water bottles. We fought. I lost until...I didn't lose anymore. He died when I ran him through. I didn't."

"What does this mean?" I asked Max.

"Your guess is as good as mine."

Then Lily walked in.

"Hi!" I heard brightly behind me. We all turned and Lily was standing there with her doll; innocent and oblivious.

"Lily, get back!" Max barked and I looked at him funny. He looked at Daniel and then back at me. "I have no idea what this means, Sherry. Are you willing to risk it?"

I huffed, but before I could say anything either way, Lily came forward and grabbed my hand.

"Hi," she said to Daniel.

"Hello."

It was then that I finally looked up to his face. He was fully involved in the Lily trance; full blown, no way out, tractor beam. I pressed my lips together to stop the smile. Max was in no mood for anything above the line of disgruntled.

"Does that hurt?" Lily asked and scrunched her nose at his stomach.

"It does. Yes," he answered cautiously and a little stiffly.

"You should put a band-aid on it. Mommy has plenty," she said and tugged on my hand. She then moved her head and eyes in an impatient gesture. "Get him a band-aid, Mommy."

"Honey, he needs a little bit more than just a band-aid."

"Ooooooooh," she said like it was a light bulb kind of revelation. Then, "Well, we can help him."

"How?" I asked, but immediately felt chagrinned for doing so. Lily however walked right up to him. Max started to stop her but I held my hand out. For some strange reason...I needed to see this out. She crooked her finger to beckon him down to her. He went without hesitation to his knees in front of her. He held his side out of pain, but the grimace was replaced with a small surprised smile as she took his face in between her small alabaster hands.

"I see you in there," she said to him softly. I gasped a little, not knowing what to make of it all. She looked back at me. "It's ok, Mommy. He's not a bad man. I can help him."

She reached her finger to his face again, agonizingly slow. She touched the end of his nose with one finger and we all held our breath and waited. Then Daniel grunted and his face turned red from strain. He fell to the ground in a forward drop and didn't even try to catch himself as his face and head smashed into the floor. Lillian was there in a second and looked up at Lily curiously.

"Lily," I said and bent down to look at her. "Why did you do that to him?" I asked softly. "I thought you said he wasn't bad."

"Just wait," she said and giggled a little like I was being silly. I was being terrified is what I was. I glanced up at Max and Ryan, but all they could do was watch, fascinated. Then Daniel's coughing subsided slowly. He began to take deep breaths as he rolled over to his back. And when he did, we all gasped in horror.

And shock.

And relief.

Not only was Daniel's stomach healed of all traces of his wound, but his skin was a normal human healthy color and his black eyes had softened into a silver. He sat up and looked at her. He looked so human, it was unreal. I mean he still had insanely dark hair and all. You could tell he was a Lighter, no doubt, but you could also tell there was something different about him. And when he spoke, his voice was wrapped with richness and gratitude.

"Thank you, little one."

"You're welcome, Daniel."

"How did you know my given name?" he said on a breath.

"I just do," she answered calmly. The air was crackly with tension.

"Lily, what did you do?" Ryan asked in awe.

"Nothing," Max said with surety. "She didn't do that. He healed himself like all Lighters do. Maybe it took a little longer than normal. It was just a coincidence."

"I don't agree, brother," Ryan said as his eyes bounced between Daniel and Lily. "I think our Lily has made herself a new friend."

"Yeah!" Lily said loudly and grabbed Daniel's hand. "Do you know how to play Spoons?"

"Uh...."

"Lily, we need to talk to Daniel and it's your naptime," I interrupted.

After some persuasion, I got her to go to bed with the promise that Daniel would be there when she woke. When I came out of her room, Lillian and Daniel were speaking in low tones as Ryan and Max glared at each other and spoke in Keeper form. I sat between Ellie and Lillian.

"Please, stay," Lillian was saying as they sat opposite each other on the couches. "Max is just protective. He'll come around like the rest of them."

"I will not be the wedge in your line. You need to be a collected unit, together, as one. I will only make you weak in their indecision of what to do with me."

105

"Did you not see what just happened?" she asked a little hysterically. "Lily just healed you!" She glanced at me and then back to him. "We didn't know she could do that, but she did. She even said it, she said...she saw you in there, which means she knew you were a good person. Stay. That's the best way to be redeemed."

"Why do wish for me to stay so badly?" he asked softly and inched forward as if to hear her response better.

Max stormed off behind us in a blur and Ryan huffed, causing Ellie to look at him. He looked over and waved away our gazes. "He'll be fine. Just needs to cool off. For Daniel to show up the first day that the others left is just...bad timing. Sorry," he said to Daniel and I smiled at him hoping to convey my thanks. He was trying with Daniel, just as Merrick had.

Of course oblivious Ryan had no clue what my smile was for.

"What?"

I shook my head at him and turned to see Ellie watching me. She didn't seem mad, but she didn't exactly look happy either. I smiled at her, too, and she kind of returned it before getting up and making her way to Ryan. He smiled at her in an *I'm completely oblivious* kind of way.

But even I could see as they walked away together that Ryan would not the one making the first move in that relationship. Hmm. Maybe Ryan needed a little nudge.

Menace
Chapter 16 - Malachi

So...the humans, after all the incentives I'd given, all the rules put into place and punishments outlined, were still rebelling.

"Whatever happened to following the crown to thy death?" I asked no one in particular. "Whatever happened to the good of the many outweigh the good of the few? Don't they know it's not good for the ones we find when they rebel like this? Don't they know it's the other ones that suffer?"

I looked down into her sweet, oval, pale, human face. She was begging me silently with her eyes. She was so desperate I could practically taste it in the air. I narrowed my eyes at her and she whimpered, looking away.

"Please, my...Lord," she said awkwardly and I almost wanted to laugh. She didn't actually believe that nor did she want to call me by that name. She was just trying to save her own neck, no matter how futile the effort.

"Quiet," I said gently. See, humans were programmed to respond to certain tones and implications. Regardless of what word was said, if it was said in the right way, the humans guard would automatically be lowered. I could feel her rapidly beating pulse under my fingertips slowing. She wasn't conceding to her death. No...no. She was tricking herself into believing that there was a way out. I waited for it. Wait for it....wait for it....

"My Lord, I'll do anything you want."

There it is! I smiled to myself, boasting a skill I'd always possessed, letting my disgust for the human's predictability slide for a moment.

"Yes, I agree that you would."

"I'll...I can be your girl if you like," she croaked and it sounded like she gagged on the words.

"Oh," I laughed, "don't sound so thrilled about it."

"I'll do anything-"

"Silence."

I looked to one of the many minions running the mansion and held my hand out. I did so much fret about getting my hands bloody on her already bloody body. In this century, it was impossible to find a good shirt. I'd ruined many a cuff with blood splatters. So I placed the robe that the minion gave me, placing it on myself in a flourish. I raised my palm and let her see my light showing through. She gawked at it silently, wide eyed and even though she knew this would be the instrument of her death, she was fascinated.

"Beautiful isn't it?" I murmured and glanced at my palm. So ordinary, so plain, yet so utterly vicious in its stealth.

"What is that? What are you? You're going to kill me?" she whispered her questions in a hollow rush.

"Why not?"

"I'm not a rebel! Please. I didn't do anything wrong."

"Moot," I said evenly. "I have to set an example. Sadly, you are just the means to the end. Sorry," I said and laughed at how stupid and insignificant that word sounded.

I pulled her to me, placing her in my arms gently; the trembling in her body giving me my own shivers of delight. I lay my hand on her chest, but her words stopped me.

"Why? Why do I have to die?"

"Because I follow tradition," I told her and smiled. "Call me sentimental."

Then I pulled her life force to me. My palm tingled as she jerked and screamed, but was unable to evade me. I held tight and let it flow into me. I sighed and even heard myself moan. I licked my lips and savored the human's life. She filled me. Some humans were different than others for some reason. They tasted and felt different as they entered my body. This human was exceptionally delectable.

All too soon, she was on empty and I was full...for the moment.

I dropped her ashen, dead body to the floor and immediately disrobed. It was a hot maroon thing that was very ceremonial, but necessary. I took a deep breath, my lungs pulsing with new life. I threw the robe to a minion. It clung to his back as he leaned down to remove her body from the room.

I swiped my hands through my hair and stopped mid-swipe. I cursed loudly and one of the minions came to bow at my feet as he said, "What is it that you require, sir?"

"I got her blood on my sleeve," I sulked and removed the shirt. Human blood was disgusting and after my boys took care of the humans in interrogation, then they were given to me. And they were always wet and bloody. Maybe I should rethink the arrangement.

"I'll get you another, a clean one."

"You do that."

He ran off. Literally, he ran. My good little minion. I turned to the other two who were left in the room.

"Well, I'm already soiled. Bring in another."

As they dragged in another human, a male who wept more than the female had, I rubbed my chest against my hands in anticipation.

One of the humans asked me if I was a vampire once. I had laughed at him and his stupidity. I told him that I was not a vampire. He asked what the difference between the two was. I explained that a vampire could get his fill, and that I was a never ending basin. His eyes were round as lemons and it made me smile. He didn't scream when I took his life like the others. It was as if he understood there was no stopping his end.

No, I was not a vampire. And I wasn't after a measly meal. I was after all that there was on this planet. And I was *going* to have it all.

Perpetual Misunderstanding
Chapter 17 - Lillian

"Well, we can find you a room. You can take a shower, too. Have you eaten? Do Lighters.....eat?" Sherry asked him.

"We do," Daniel answered. "Our bodies are as human as yours."

"Ok. Are you hungry? Would you like something?"

"I don't want to trouble you-"

Sherry touched his hand and he stopped.

"You fed me, remember? It's the least I can do. Besides," she stood, "it's kind of my thing here. I have some pea soup ready. Not the most desirable thing, but-"

"That would be acceptable. Thank you, Sherry."

She smiled and went to the kitchen. The girl practically lived in there.

I turned back to Daniel and almost gasped at his closeness. He'd inched forward some more. He seemed concerned and edgy.

"What's the matter?" I asked.

"I just...can not comprehend that I am here."

"Well, you are."

"You did not answer my question," he said quietly.

"What question?"

"Why do you wish for me to stay?"

"Because it's not safe out there for you now."

"I can fend for myself."

I looked at his side and grimaced as I replied, "You sure about that?"

"This," he palmed his side, "was merely a miscalculation."

"A pretty big miscalculation. You could have died."

"But I did not."

"But you could have!" I yelled. He didn't recoil at my tone. In fact, he inched closer.

"You are very upset," he observed.

"I am."

"But why? You act as though you are invested in my welfare."

"I am...I...don't want to see you get hurt."

He inched further still. I realized he was now kneeling on the floor in front of me. I should stop him. I shouldn't let him get any closer. But there I sat.

"Lillian," he said my name in a soft growl, "my chest hurts."

"It does? Where? What-"

"My human heart," he answered. "It beats uncontrollably."

Ohhhh...dang. I gasped slightly as he took my hand and put it over his shirt front.

"Why?" he asked. "Why is it doing that?"

I gulped and said, "I don't know. They beat fast for lots of reasons."

He moved closer, his free arm going beside me on the couch. He inhaled deeply.

"You still smell of...Jasmine." I could only nod. "All human females do not smell that way," he mused.

"No," I agreed. "I put it on."

"So you smell this way on purpose."

"Yes, I guess so." I decided to change the subject. "Aren't you curious about what Lily did to you?"

"Very. She's...precious looking. My body instantly wanted to protect her."

"Yeah," I said and smiled. "Everybody is like that with her."

"Is everyone like that with you?"

"No, why?"

"Because that's exactly how I feel about you," he said, his voice an awe filled whisper, "except worse. My need to make sure you are safe is doubled over more than once in comparison." His hand moved and I let him touch my cheek. I shut my eyes and felt his sigh against my face. I opened my eyes and he looked like a half-drugged man. "You are the light in a dark place. You are the water to my drought. You are everything I never knew existed and everything I wanted all at the same time."

"Oh..."

"This body...my body, very much wants to...put my mouth to yours."

I was shocked into silence. I'd never had someone say those kinds of things with such conviction before. Oh...he was leaning forward. I couldn't let him kiss me. No...no...

"No," I whispered and when I spoke, my lip touched his with the barest brush. He was that close.

"Lillian," he groaned. His eyes opened and he watched me. "Please."

"I can't let you," I told him. "I'm with Cain." He seemed confused. "We are...together. I love him. You only kiss a person that you're with... like that."

"I've seen many people kiss that were not in love."

"Yes, but not while they are with someone else."

"But Cain isn't here right now with you," he reasoned and I realized that he really didn't understand. He wasn't trying to talk me into it. He was just genuinely clueless.

"But I love him. And I'd never betray him."

111

There was a pause. A pause that I knew was full of understanding.

"So…your heart beats this fast…for him," he said finally.

"Yes."

"And not for this body, mine."

"It doesn't matter about your body, Daniel. It's about you, who you are. That body is yours now. You decide what you do with it and what to feel. I'm sorry. It's not that I don't…like you. It's just that Cain is very important to me and I was with him first. I don't want you to leave. I want you to stay here and be safe but, you can't kiss me."

"I can not put my lips on yours," he hedged with a slight grimace, "ever."

I shook my head as an answer. He looked crushed and confused. He wanted to kiss me, didn't even know what kissing was really, and he was confused at the rejection and the want to do it. I felt about as useful as a teacher with no class.

I tried for another way to explain.

"For humans, we find one person who we want to be with in every way. Cain is that person for me. And he trusts me," I added.

"I think I understand." His grimace intensified and he sat back on his heels though he kept my hand trapped to his chest. "I'm sorry. I didn't mean to offend you."

"You didn't," I assured. "I'm fine. And I want to be your friend. We can figure out all this stuff together, alright?"

"If you suggest it so."

"Can I…can I have my hand back now?" I asked softly.

"Oh," he said and looked down, "I'm sorry." He took my hand from his chest and held it in his hands. He turned it over and over in observation. "Your skin is very delicate."

"Most girls are," I said easily.

"I don't believe you. I think you are soft and sweet smelling because you are you," he said but it was gentle, like he was just making an observation and nothing else. Sherry came back then with a bowl tucked in her hands and he released my hand as he stood abruptly.

"Thank you."

"No problem," she said and eyed me kind of funny. Had she seen his little love display?

"So," he eyed the bowl in his hands, "this is pea soup."

"It is," she answered. "It's pretty good, but it's also all we've got so…"

"No, I am most appreciative. Thank you for allowing me to stay and feeding me. I will try ardently not to be a burden. I will address your Merrick when he returns and guarantee him that I will do all I can to help your cause and your people."

"Thank you, Daniel." He continued to stand there, as if awaiting instructions. "At ease," she said and started to laugh at her joke, but he actually spread his legs in an easy stance and one hand went behind his back. She balked. "No, Daniel. We are not your superiors here. That's not how we do things. If you want to eat, eat. When you want to sleep, sleep. If you want to leave, leave. We won't stop you and we won't keep you here against your will. You are your own now; you're free."

"I don't know what that means, either."

Though Sherry didn't know what he was talking about with the 'either' she still got the gist. There was lots that Daniel didn't understand.

"Well, we'll make sure you understand then. I'll make it my mission."

"I am your mission?"

"Absolutely. So, go on and eat. Then we'll get you settled into a room."

"Ok," he replied and walked slowly to the stairs. He sat on the edge and glanced at her as he took a sip of soup from his spoon. His eyes flashed a little and the corner of his mouth lifted in a wanna-be smile. Then he plowed through it.

Sherry turned to me and put her hands on her hips. Her short self looked flustered and every bit the mother hen she was pegged to be. "He kissed you?" she hissed.

Yikes…

Lousy Situation
Chapter 18 - Merrick

"Well, we may as well hunker down for the night," Miguel said, but didn't move to do so.

"Screw that, man," Josh replied. "I'm not tired. And I think I can lift little Miss Keeper here up into this air conditioning shaft." He threw some chunks of wood and a sheet of metal to the side. "Right here." He stood up on a cinder block and held his out for her. "Come on, Kay. You'll fit perfectly."

"You want me to climb in there?" she squeaked. I looked at her. Kay wasn't scared of anything and right then, she sounded the most human I'd ever heard.

"Yeah. You climb through and make sure it's clear. If it is, you can call to us and we'll come through, too. Or you can look for another way out."

"Ok," she said and smoothed her hair. "Of course, yeah."

"Wait," Miguel said and you could tell he was about to blast the whole thing. "What can Kay do once she gets up there? No offense, but you're not exactly built for fighting, if you get my drift."

She turned to look at him and I knew. Crap, Miguel.

"I am a Keeper," she said, her voice shrill and demanding and I stood back to enjoy the show. "I am a guardian and have been so for thousands of years. I was the Keeper for soldiers and blacksmiths and good men and women of worth. I was Keeper to Joan of Arcadia for goodness sakes!" Miguel's eyes got wide and he leaned back and she came forward. She poked his arm with her finger. "So don't you dare think for one second that I can't handle some human endeavor just because I'm in this body. Climbing through a vent is nothing compared to what I've been through."

"Ok, ok. Jeez," he groaned and rubbed his arm. "Is everybody smoking the wiffy when I'm not looking or what?"

Danny and Celeste laughed, then Josh, then me and even Kay. We were wound tight, it was true. Kay gave him an apologetic smile and then accepted Josh's hand to lift her to the vent. Kay was the slimmest and slightest person of the bunch and he lifted her easily. He had to put his hands on her rear to hold her up. He grinned and winked at Miguel as he said, "Been working out, Kay?"

"Watch it," I growled and he laughed, not a bit scared. I rubbed my neck and tried to think. If this didn't work, we'd have to find another way out.

"I think I've got the latch," Kay groaned as she strained. "Just a little...more."

Josh hoisted her higher, she flipped the switch and the door swung open easily. She grabbed the inside ledge and wiggled her way inside with Josh's help. She leaned back in to say, "Celeste, stay with Danny."

"Duh," Celeste muttered.

"So I'll see if I can get out. And then we'll figure a way to get out the rest of you."

"We're fine here," I told her. "Guard your way, sister."

"And you, brother."

And then she scampered through the tunnel. We could hear her and then we couldn't. I knew she was fine though. Kay was just as fierce as the rest of us.

"What does that mean?" Josh asked. "Guard your way?"

"Guard you in all your ways," I answered. "It's what Keepers say to one another. It means be safe and do your job, basically."

"And you're all related?"

"No, why?"

"You called her sister, she called you brother."

"We are sisters and brothers in our kind. We are not related in the sense that you are referring to, though."

"So, how do you procreate?" he asked and I saw Miguel and Danny's ears turn our way.

"We don't," I answered and gave him a look that said not to touch that subject.

"Are you aliens or angels?" he asked some more as he looked into big bins and tubs that were in the middle of the room.

"I am neither of those human words."

"Dude, you are way cryptic right now."

"I am what I am. I'm not a word that your human mind can come up with or comprehend. Just call me guardian or Keeper or better yet, Merrick, and that'll be fine."

He thought about that for a minute, his jaw working back and forth. Then he finally said, "Racine's gonna be seriously pissed that I left when she comes out of her flu coma."

"Yep," I agreed. "She probably will be. If you were my Special, I'd be seriously pissed," I said and gave Danny a pre-emptive look. He laughed and shook his head.

"So, Keepers can die like everybody else can? Like she could die from the flu?"

"Yes," I answered. "We are human for all intents and purposes."

"Huh," he muttered. "That sucks."

"Are you worried about her?"

"Kinda." He stuck his hands in his pockets. "She's a nice lady."

"Hmm. Well, she'll probably be fine. Ok," I looked around, "let's help Kay out and try to see if maybe there's a trap door or something somewhere."

"Yeah," Miguel said and immediately started to rummage, eager for something to do.

"So," Josh asked as he tossed some debris aside and felt along the walls, "if you can't get your freak on to make little Keepers, then how are there so many of you?"

"Freak on?" Miguel asked. "That's all you've got?"

"Hey, I found-"

I turned to Josh when his voice cut off and he was nowhere to be seen. I blurred to where he'd been and he was gone. When I felt along the wall, it gave under my hand in a large square right at my waist level. I pushed it and leaned in to see that it was chute. A laundry chute. Dang. That's what those bins and tubs had been. This was some kind of dyeing plant. I called down to him, but heard nothing.

"He slid down," I told them.

"I'm going after him then," Miguel said and attempted to move me.

"We don't know where that leads," I told him.

"To the laundry room," he said sarcastically.

"Ha ha. We have no idea how far it goes or to where-"

"Hey!" Josh yelled and the echo in the chute hurt my ears it was so loud. "Hey!"

"Josh!"

"Yeah. I found a way out. There's stairs down here, come on down!"

"Bugger," Miguel said. "That kid's getting on my last nerve, but at least he found a way out. Let's roll."

"But what about Kay?"

"Here." He took a piece of paper and pen from his pocket and wrote "We're down here" on it. "See, we'll stick this is door of the chute. Problem solved, mate."

"You just happen to have a pen and paper in your pocket?" He shrugged. "Alright, I guess that'll do. Danny and Celeste, come on."

Miguel climbed down the chute with no qualms at all and even squealed on the way down...like it was fun. Humans.

"I can't leave Kay," Celeste complained and then I showed her the note. "Ok, but if something happens we're coming back for her."

"Of course. I'm not one to leave someone behind."

"Let me go first, babe," Danny told her. "Then I can catch you."

"Aw, you're so sweet, baby," she said through a sigh and I took a breath to keep from grumbling.

"Ok, let's a move on. Go, Danny," I urged.

He went through and then Celeste got up in the chute mouth. She looked back at me and smiled.

"Don't be scared, Keeper."

"Thanks, Celeste," I said dryly, her laughter carrying up to me as she let go and shot down the chute. I settled myself in the hole and let the edge of the door catch the note so it would stay. Then I let go and hoped that Kay would find us and that this was a way out.

When I reached the bottom, they were all standing around gawking at something behind them. I looked around Josh to see crates. Crates and crates marked as guns and explosives…and can goods. I felt my heart pitter-patter in response. In was like a beacon or light was shining on them with angels singing in the background.

But where did they come from? Who did they belong to? Was this someone's hideout after all and we'd destroyed it, albeit unintentionally? It had to belong to someone and the Lighters wouldn't keep things like that here.

I suddenly had a very bad feeling about it all and a desire to get out that place.

"Guys, this isn't good. Let's go."

"What?" Josh said. "We can't just leave this stuff. We can use it!"

"And how would we get it back to the store? Jeep's full and this stuff belongs to someone. We'd be taking their stuff that they've saved and who knows who they fought for it and it wouldn't be right."

"Are you taking the piss?" Miguel reasoned, in his strange roundabout way of saying 'Are you for real?'. "Where are they? Maybe they left in a dash and couldn't carry it all or something."

"It wouldn't be right. We're leaving it," I said harder to make sure they understood I wasn't looking for a discussion. "Now, come on. Let's put these stairs to use that Josh was bragging about."

"What luck," Josh mused as he began to take the steps two at a time. "I was feeling along, saw the chute behind the wall, pushed a little too hard I guess and wham!" he yelled and slapped his hands together, "straight down the chute." He opened the door at the top and it welcomed us into a hallway that went up a few stories. He grinned back at us. "You can all thank me later for saving your backsides."

"Oh, we'll get right on that," Celeste said and giggled as Danny lifted her onto his back to take the stairs. I took up the rear of the group and once again found myself hoping this led to somewhere safe and no more trouble was to be had.

When I got through the door I listened to Celeste and Danny gabbing about nothing as we scaled the steps.

The stairs were made of rickety wood that groaned and pressed under our weight. A split second before I told Danny to put Celeste down, that I didn't think the wood could hold them both like that, he fell. They both did. They went straight through a step that gave way under their weight. I blurred up to them and grabbed Danny's hand as it passed the last inch of wood. He somehow managed to snag her hand out of the air as she fell, too. They dangled three stories up above the concrete floor we'd just been on at the bottom of the laundry chute.

"Hold on," I told him, though I knew it was stupid to say that to people in these situations. What else could they do but hang on?

My conscience buzzed loud and alert in my ears for my charge, but I could still hear Celeste whimpering and crying beneath me though I couldn't see her face. I was too far down myself, having stopped my descent down with them by grabbing a piece of a step in one hand and hooking my foot under the ledge of a step below me. Even with my Keeper strength, I wasn't going to be able to just pull them out when I couldn't even pull myself out. And Kay wasn't there to help me. Crap.

"Help me, Josh," Miguel said behind me. "If we can pull Merrick up then we can get-"

"No," I told him. "Danny won't be able to hold Celeste while you jerk me and him up like that."

"Ok, then," Miguel said easily and launched himself off the rail of the steps. Before I could think of what he'd just done, he was dangling beside me by one arm. He had a hand on one step and reached the other out. "Come on, Celeste."

"I can't," she barely breathed, but it carried in the air. "I can't, I'll fall."

"Look at me," he told her. "Look at me." Danny was grunting and I couldn't see Celeste still, but I guess she looked at Miguel because he went on. "Good on ya, good on ya. I'll get you, I promise. I won't let go. Come on. Reach for me, Celeste."

"I...."

"Go, baby," Danny pleaded with her. "It's ok. Go."

I saw her slender arm reach out, but wasn't close enough. She confirmed my thoughts when she said, "I can't reach."

"Let's swing her," Danny suggested. "I'll swing her your way."

"No," I said. "What if Miguel misses? I can hold on all day if I need to until we figure something else out."

"But I can't," he groaned low in a hiss meant for me. "She's slipping. Come on, Miguel. On three, I'll swing her your way. Celeste just reach out and take his hand and let go of mine at the same time, ok?"

"I don't know if I can," she said hysterically.

"Yes, you can. Do it, babe. Miguel, you better catch her or so help me," he growled. Miguel nodded. "Now," Danny said and then counted as he and I swung her back and forth. It made me sick to watch it; their bodies swaying over a concrete slab that would mean their death. I prayed this would work. When he got to three he swung her hard, grunting, and as soon as Miguel had her hand, Danny let go. She screamed, but Miguel had her. Danny lay limp in my hand and muttered, over and over, "That was so close. Too frigging close."

"It's all right, Danny," I told him as I looked over at Celeste. Miguel was just then pulling her up into his arms and she clung to him as he shhed her and tried to calm her. He held her close as he reached out and caught the edge of the steps with his foot. He told her to reach up and grab the railing. She did, but her hands were shaking so badly I was worried about her ability to hold on. But she did. She pulled herself up and then we did the same thing with Danny. I swung him to Miguel and he gripped his hand and then guided him to the edge.

Celeste and Danny didn't embrace like I expected. He pulled her hand up the stairs and then pushed her butt to keep going as he bent down to help Josh pull me out.

"Go on, Celeste. Get off the stairs."

"But-"

"Go," he said with more edge. She went. I think we all knew he was too rattled. Once I was upright and we made it to the top of the stairs, he pulled her to him and exhaled loudly, burying his face in her hair.

"Gah…Celeste, that was so close."

"It's ok," she answered, her voice shaking as much as her fingers that were wrapped in his shirt.

"It almost wasn't. I almost dropped you." He whispered the rest. "I was so close to losing you."

"I know," she croaked and looked up at him. "I was so close to letting go."

"What?" he said harshly. "Why?"

"So I wouldn't drag you down with me."

"That's so-," he said angrily, but stopped. He looked as haunted as I'd ever seen him. He pulled her face up and kissed her roughly holding her jaw in his hand.

Miguel and Josh and I trudged up the hall ahead of them, giving them a minute of privacy. I rubbed my upper arm. It felt tired and sore from holding them in the hole that long. I hope I hadn't pulled anything. But I'd do it again in a heartbeat.

When I reached the end of the hall, there was no door. I looked all over and found a trap door in the ceiling. I used the string and the stairs came down easily. When I got to the top of the small ladder and pushed on the door, it wouldn't budge. I pushed hard with my shoulder and it inched a little and groaned, but no good. I yelled for Miguel and he squeezed in next to me. Together we pushed the thing until it went all the way over. It had some sort of…debris on the door. And all around us. I was confused for two point five seconds before I was as raging mad as a prodded bull.

119

"What the …" Josh muttered as he came up behind us.

"I'll. Be. Stuffed." Miguel was hopping mad. He barked from behind me, "Bloody hell!"

"What's all the yelling about?" Danny said. "Did you find a…way…" He helped Celeste up and they both stood, looking disgusted and upset. "You mean Celeste almost died and we're right back where we started? It was all for nothing?"

"Looks that way," Miguel said and kicked some blocks with his foot.

"I'm sorry," Josh said and rubbed his head with his hands back and forth. "If I hadn't fallen down that-"

"It's fine, Josh," Celeste said softly and sniffed. "We'll find a way out. Besides, we're still waiting for Kay."

"Here!" Kay called. "I'm back."

We all ran over to the vent where she was. She was filthy.

"What happened to you?" I asked.

"Oh, just some dirt and soot. The vent does lead to outside, but it's way too high to do anything with. But I found an old big chimney that leads to the roof. And that leads to a ladder to the ground. Josh, build some steps with the blocks and let's get going. It's getting darker out there." She looked at Celeste. "What's wrong?"

I wasn't sure how she knew, but she did.

Celeste tried several times to start. "Nothing," she finally said. Kay gave her a look that said 'bull crap', but she went ahead and slid back into the vent anyway.

"So," Josh started, "she found a way out and if we had just waited here, none of that would have happened."

"Yep," Miguel said and took a deep breath. "No sense in throwing a wobbly about it now. Let's just get out of this bloody building before we all cark it."

Danny took Celeste to the vent and hoisted her up, even as Josh was making a step for them. She climbed in and turned to him. He asked Josh to give him a hand up. With Josh's hand as a stirrup he bolted him up and Danny landed easily. He urged Celeste on and I watched them go, then went to help Josh so they rest of us could get up.

Everyone was extremely ready to leave this place.

Come on, Chuck
Chapter 20 - Cain

We had searched the other place and found nothing. It was almost dark and though the skies were clear now, they wouldn't be for long. We pulled into the last house of the night to check and then we'd bunker down in. It was a house I could see myself living in; big slanted roofs and a long porch, gorgeously girly in all the right places yet classy. I imagined taking Lillian to a house like this and her loving it. I smiled, but I saw Simon looking at me funny so I stopped that real quick like.

"We'll stay here if it checks out all right," Simon was saying, but he hadn't even finished his sentence when I saw headlights behind us in the driveway. Then yellow and green flashing lights. Well, dang.

"Enforcers," I told them.

Simon turned white as a ghost, if that's what ghosts looked like. I bit my lip ring and beat a rhythm on the steering wheel.

"Alright, Billings. Hop out," I said finally.

"Gotcha," he spouted and got out eagerly. "Everybody else, sit tight."

We came together at the back of the van and made our way to the car. The two officers stepped out with an air of authority and arrogance that followed them and I was ready for it. I was ready to fight something.

One of them was short, one was tall, both pudgy and balding where it hurt their looks the most. This was too easy.

"What can we do for you, officers?" I asked and crossed my arms.

"Hey," one of them muttered. "Didn't you used to work as an enforcer?"

"I still do and I'm your superior," Billings barked. "Now Cain here asked you a question, answer him."

"Well, we, uh…" They looked at each other and then back to us. "We have to pull anyone over who enters the tainted territories."

"I'm with him. He's thinking about joining. I'm just showing him the ropes," Billings told him.

"You're not in uniform," one of them said and looked behind us to the van. "And you've got others with you. Are they recruits, too?"

"Yep."

The enforcer's hand went to his belt…to the gun. He apparently wasn't buying it. I kicked his arm, making the gun go flying out of his hand into the bushes. He cursed and looked at me stunned just as I put him in a headlock and

121

made him go to sleep. Merrick and I had done this several times on our runs together. It made me wonder how they were doing.

Billings was working on the other enforcer and though he took a little longer, Billings still got the job done. With both enforcers down and all the commotion, everyone got out of the car.

"Problem solved," I said and brushed my hands off. I took one of them by the arm and dragged him into the bushes so no one would see him just in case they passed by. Billings did the same.

Then another one stepped out of the back seat of their car. Only he wasn't an enforcer, he was a Lighter.

Crap.

"Quite a show," it muttered. Then he smiled, and it was pure evil.

"Glad you enjoyed it," I said and felt Simon beside me as he moved to my side.

"Keepers," it muttered some more, "it's been too long."

"Not long enough," Simon said loudly and steadily.

"You know, I haven't seen a single Keeper since I've been back to this planet. It's a real treat to have two at once. Two kills with one shot. And a Muse?" He whistled. "Pretty little Muse, too. Just my luck."

There's just one of them. We can take him and get the heck out of here before any more...

When Jeff stopped I looked back up and saw why. Four more Lighters had made an appearance; from where, I didn't know, but there they stood.

Five of us and five of them.

"Billings, got your stake?" I asked low.

"Yep, boss."

"Good," I replied and then lifted my hands. I'd only ever done it that once at the Mayor's Manor. I never practiced it with the others, using work as my excuse. When the reality of it was that I hated it. I hated having power. I hated having responsibility for something like that. In my opinion, people shouldn't have this kind of power all to themselves. But it was mine, and nothing was gonna stop me from using it now.

As I felt the power come, just like before as it was summoned to my palms in flash of heat and tingles, I let it loose on the enemy. The release was a boom of air and command. They cowered to it against their will as they flung through the air. I felt a deep boned satisfaction at smacking the cocky smiles off their faces, no matter if it was with a power that I didn't enjoy.

I immediately started barking orders to Billings and Simon. We were all armed. We needed to ambush them before they could regroup. We ran, the Keepers blurred and as soon as they stood back up from the ground and started to come at us, we were on them in a flurry.

Marissa slapped one in the face, apparently telling him to lie down, while Jeff staked him. I had to wonder if the lightning would call other Lighters. The next one was wise and ducked back to avoid her hands. Mine grinned at me like he was having fun, so I kicked him in the face with a roundhouse. He looked shocked that I'd moved that quickly as he peeled back around. So I grinned this time.

He came at me and man, they were strong and quick. But not unbeatable. The last time we'd fought Lighters, it was just like this; equal numbers and very little weapons. Lighters didn't usually use weapons, which was strange. You would think that they'd wise up to technology and gain an upper hand, but I wasn't complaining as I jabbed my palm into his nose. I felt the crunch of his bones and the blood that flowed down his face startled him as he looked at his hands. I used that lapse of awareness and pulled the stake - I preferred to use the headless iron gold clubs myself - and rammed it through his chest.

The following burst of lightning that sprung from his chest was so forceful, it knocked me on my butt, but I still watched it in awe. I looked back to see Billings wasn't faring as well. His Lighter was winning and laughing about it.

I got up and ran forward to stop him just as the Lighter got a hold on Billings arm…and snapped it like a piece of celery on Grandma's veggie platter. While he howled and carried on the Lighter was distracted so I stabbed him in the back, just like the traitor they accused me of being.

I was ready for the lightning this time and pushed against the cold wind. When it stopped, I realized it was over. Billings was knelt on the ground, holding his arm and cursing over and over.

"Let me see it," I told him. He held it out and yelped when it swayed. It hung there like dead weight. "Dude, that's gross."

"Ah," I heard Marissa groan behind me. She covered her mouth and looked at Billings' stumpy limb with disgust. "I'm gonna be sick." Then she tripped and stumbled to the bushes and up-chucked the perfectly good lunch Sherry packed us. Poor gal.

"Are you alright, sweetie?" Jeff asked and rubbed her back. She pushed him off, muttering that she was fine, she didn't want him to see that.

I turned back to Billings. Simon had shrugged out of his over shirt and was helping to wrap Billings' arm with it. Billings winced when Simon tied the arms of his shirt and pulled it tight.

"It's fine. I'll be fine," he told Simon and then looked at me. "Thanks, boss man. I would be broken in a few more places if not for you."

123

"That's true," I replied and rubbed my lip thoughtfully causing him to scoff and give me a droll look. "Miguel's gonna have to add you to his beginners class when we get back. You're a little rusty there, enforcer."

"Physical fitness wasn't exactly on the daily agenda back at the enforcer's camp, ok?" he said defensively. "Cut me a break will you?" He held up his arm. "I'm an injured man."

"Yeah..." I looked at it and grimaced as blood dripped for the makeshift bandage. "It's not very aesthetically pleasing to look at is it?"

"Bite me," he grumbled. I laughed and helped him up.

"Come on, Chuck," I joked. "Let's get you in the van."

"Hardy har har."

"You two are very hard to keep up with," Simon muttered as he helped me put Billings in the back seat. "I can barely think let alone process what you two are constantly yakking about."

"It's a skill, for sure," I rebutted sarcastically.

Simon sighed and shook his head. He made his way to the other side of the van and we heard him yell, "Let's go. I'm too old for this."

We laughed. I looked at Billings and told him, "Well, Simon says let's get going."

"Where to now, boss?"

"We should probably take you home, Billings. I think that arm takes precedence over looking for homeless rebels."

"I agree," Jeff chimed. Marissa was leaning on his shoulder, looking green and spent. "Plus, Marissa isn't feeling well."

"I don't agree," Billings argued. "I'll be fine. My arm's not going anywhere. It'll be there when we finally get home. Just throw me a couple Ibuprofen and I'll be good as new."

"Oh," Jeff said loudly, "is that what Chuck would do?"

I laughed so hard. Billings, too, so hard he snorted.

"Jeff made a funny!" I told him. "I'm proud of you, man."

Marissa agreed saying, "Yeah, that was a good one."

"I have my moments," Jeff spouted and smiled out the window.

"Ok. So compromise," I suggested. "We go home, but hit a few spots on the way. Are we a go?"

"Go," Billings said hastily.

"Go," Jeff said.

"Go, I guess," Simon answered begrudged.

"Go it is. Simon says," I joked and Simon's brow lifted to me in the mirror in utter confusion and loss.

Caught Red Handed
Chapter 21 - Sherry

"What were you thinking?" I asked softly. "Cain is out there and-"

"I didn't kiss him," she said and turned red. "He tried...but I didn't let him."

I sighed in relief. The last thing Cain needed right now was another woman cheating on him.

"I'm sorry. I know it's none of my business, but Cain is like family to me. I don't want to see him get hurt, again."

"I'm glad he's got you looking out for him, Sherry," she said dryly.

"I said I know it's none of my bus-"

"No, no. It's fine." She chuckled to herself about something. "I really am glad. I never thought that it was possible to just be a friend with a guy before." She shook her head and swallowed. I wondered if she was thinking about Mitchell. "I have no idea what I would have done if Mitchell hadn't come for us and brought us to you. If we were stuck out there all by ourselves... I know I freak when Cain's gone, but this is good. This is right and we have to do this. We have to help the ones who have no one else. Mitchell won't have died in vain."

"Of course he didn't," I told her. "None of them did. We're gonna get them, I don't doubt it." I felt my jaw tighten thinking of Mrs. Trudy. "Merrick, Cain, Miguel, Jeff - they won't let Malachi win."

"So..." She looked at me closely. "What do you think about what Lily did?"

"I have no idea." I rubbed my heart charm in between my fingers. There was an ache deep in me. One of happiness and the possibilities of Lily and one of sadness that a child could have such power. "I don't know what to think, really. I wish Merrick were here. He would know what to do."

"Doubt it," she spouted. "He's probably just as clueless as Max and Ryan." I wondered if people would treat her different now, like they had with Marissa. Scared to touch her... It must have been on my face what I was thinking because Lillian touched my arm and said, "Don't worry. Lily is still the same sweet little girl she was when you put her to bed."

"I know. I just...she was so calm and giddy about it all. It was a little creepy," I admitted.

"Yeah," she agreed and twisted her lips as she wrapped her hair around her ear with her fingers.

"Acceptable sustenance," Daniel said as he came up behind Lillian. "Thank you, Sherry."

"Um…Thanks? I guess?" I muttered.

"Did I say something wrong?"

"No," I laughed. "No, it's just gonna take some getting used to; you being so proper."

"Proper," he mused. "Proper is bad I assume. I will try hard to not be so…" He sighed. "I don't understand what that means. I don't understand what anything means anymore," he growled, his silver eyes flashing a black for a split second before going back. I inched back at seeing it and he noticed. "I'm sorry. Please don't be frightened of me. It's just so much to learn, so fast. I feel more like an outsider and someone who doesn't belong more than I ever thought possible," he said sadly.

It was still weird to see a Lighter so emotional.

"I know. And like I said, I'll help you."

"And I appreciate it. I think I'd…like to go to my room now if that is acceptable."

"Sure," I said and looked at Lillian. I was about to ask her take him to one of the empty rooms down the hall, but the way Daniel was watching her and the way she was avoiding his gaze showed me there was going to be some tension, albeit misunderstood and unintentional tension, between the two for a while. So I volunteered. "Come on."

We made it about eight steps when we ran into Ryan and Ellie. Really we didn't run into them, more like casually spying. Ryan had Ellie haphazardly cornered by the record player. She was toying with the buttons of his shirt and he was having trouble deciding what to look at; her face or her fingers working his buttons.

She smiled as she talked to him about something I couldn't hear. He nodded and continued to watch her. Then her eyes started to tear up a bit and she bit her lip. He leaned closer, his hand tentatively coming up, letting his finger sweep under her eye. She looked about as amazed as someone who was completely wrapped up in hero worship could be.

And when she moved in to hug him around his middle, he wrapped his arms around her without anymore hesitation. I thought at first, that he was still misunderstanding. That he thought she was just being 'friendly', which I knew was not so. But as he leaned back a little, he let his hand come to her cheek, his thumb swept over her lips as he felt them for probably the first time.

She was going to kiss him, I could see it in her eyes. But as she raised up to meet him, she peeked over his shoulder and saw us coming. She ducked back and smothered her face in his chest again.

Dang. I felt bad for ruining his moment, but go Ryan!

Daniel made a noise to get my attention. I realized we'd almost slowed to a crawl while I was being nosy. He followed me, but then stopped. His eyes went black again. He rubbed them as if he knew they had but didn't understand it. Then he stopped dead and looked at me with an odd expression.

"They are here."

"Who? What-"

"My brothers. Go. Hide everyone in a back room."

"Daniel," I said in sudden hysterics at his implication. "What are you going to do?"

"I will hold them off. My eyes..." he drifted off and Lillian made her way swiftly to us. "The others won't be able to tell something is different with me. I'll send them off, they won't know you're here."

"You're putting yourself up for bait?" she asked.

"No. I am one of them as far as they are concerned. I'll tell them I already assessed the place. That it is clean and there is no need to stay further. I'll get them to go away."

"You're putting yourself in danger," she argued.

"I am a Lighter, Lillian," he said harshly. It was the first time I'd heard him get upset and speak anything but softly. "I am what they are. I have been for thousands of years." He grit his teeth and gripped her arm gently, in complete contrast to each other. "Please go in the back room. If you are safe then it doesn't matter what happens to me."

"What if they kill you? What if they find out about you?"

"It'll be worth it."

"No, it won't."

He pulled her close, his nose almost touching hers. He closed his eyes and put an arm around her waist to pull her to him. He inhaled deeply and intimately from her neck, his nose skimming the skin. He whispered anguished words to her.

"You are the thing that brought me out of the darkness. Please don't take that away from me. I have no idea why your spell is so strong on me, but I wouldn't change it. Please, go to the safe place with the rest of them and let me do what I was made to do." He pulled back a little and I sucked in a breath - so did she - when he kissed her cheek. "I kill things and deceive. I always have and I'll do it now, for you. Go."

"Be, careful. Please." She gripped his shirt. "Brave and stupid are sometimes the same thing. Do you understand?"

"Yes. Go."

She stumbled to me and let me tow her. I yelled for Max and Ryan and gave them a quick run through. They met him at the stairs. I pushed Lillian to the back hallway, towards the stock room, and ran to get Lily out of bed. When I came back through the commons rooms with her still sleeping in my arms, Ryan, Kathy and Max were guarding the stairs with stakes in hand. Ellie was there, too. Daniel was already gone.

"It's ok, Sherry. We've got this," Ryan told me and nodded towards the stairs for me to go. "Ellie, go with them."

"Wait," she pleaded and kissed his cheek. His mouth opened in surprise. "I'll go if you promise to be careful, as cliché as that sounds."

"I promise. Go with Sherry and wait for me to come get you." He looked at me pleadingly.

I nodded as I took her arm and made my way to the back room with the others. When I got there, everyone else was already there.

"What's happening?" Kate asked. "What's going on?"

"Lighters are here," I told her and she squeaked in response.

I shhed and rocked Lily even though she slept soundly in my arms. It was amazing. I realized that I ran in there and lifted her from her pallet as if she were a bag of feathers instead of flesh and bone. Normally, I struggled and groaned against her weight, but my body knew she was in danger and it gave me the boost of adrenaline or something to make it happen.

Like that tale about the mother being able to lift a car off her kid if she had to because her motherly instincts kicked in and gave her what she needed to literally move mountains. Motherly instincts...

I bit my lip and took a deep breath squeezing me eyes. Pull yourself together, Sherry, you have things to do. I looked around and saw that everyone was scared. No one spoke at all, we just listened.

I asked Lillian if she'd hold Lily and she took her numbly and blankly, but held her as if she were a doll as she stared at the wall. The Keepers, Ann and Patrick, stood by the door to the back room and guarded us. They looked at the ceiling as if they could see and understand everything that might be going on. I realized, they were probably just waiting for a signal or sign from Ryan and Max.

I went over to the bed where Racine was laying. She looked awful still, but I noticed her fever had broken when I touched her cheek. She was freezing as a matter of fact. I pulled the blanket up to her chin and turned to go back to Lillian, but stopped. We all did.

There was a loud boom and a slam above us. It rumbled our ceiling, dust and bits of particle board sprinkled us. Then it happened again and Ann and Patrick tensed, slamming the door and locking it. They stood with their stakes and waited.

Oh, God, no.

They were waiting for them to come to us. They knew something we didn't and we're getting ready for trouble.

The Lighters were inside.

Irony
Chapter 22 - Daniel

As I swung my fist to connect with my brother's jaw I was struck by the irony and inconsistency of this situation. I could sense my brothers, but could no longer hear them in my head. There would be no more pretending to be one of them, those days were gone. And I didn't see into the human's minds either. I could no longer see and hear their thoughts and I was more than alright with that.

It felt like a complete release and rearranging of my mind and whole being when that little human touched me and healed me. She did something to me, changed me, in a way that was all encompassing. And I would be forever grateful to her for that.

She had reached something in me that only Lillian had touched before, once, in the very beginning. It was a part of the humanity that this body once carried. That was the only reason I could have to explain the change in me. With Lillian, when I smelled her that day and she was so willing to sacrifice herself to save her comrades…it was a slow pulling and turning to something else. It took me a few moments to understand what I was feeling for the first time.

Regret.

Utter regret for putting that look on her face. Lillian had been scared and borderline terrified and to know that I and I alone made her that way was a slap of the cruelest kind.

But when little Lily healed me it was like lightning, and not the end-of-me kind. This was the good kind. The kind that doesn't destroy and dissipate, but alters and changes completely. I was a different person now. I was a human, but with super human strength. Lillian made me see just how human I wanted to be and I was determined that I could make her proud. That she wouldn't want to be with me or let this body be intimate the way it craved was devastating and heartbreaking, but that was inconsequential now. Her safety was more than living, thinking or breathing. She was the center of my universe and I didn't understand it at all. It just was.

All of the humans under this ground were a volatile and strangely knit together group. They were not blood kin to each other, but they all acted as though they were truly invested in each other. Not just their safety, but their happiness.

I drove the human object, an umbrella I believe it was called, through my brother's stomach and let the blinding lightning consume him, it was strange to me how I felt no remorse. In fact, it felt like a mission of a different kind had been seared to my soul. Protect Lily, my little healer, protect the humans under my feet at this moment, protect Lillian at all cost and do what was necessary to make her acceptably satisfied - or happy, whatever they called it.

First, I would end my brothers who dared put her in harm, then I would find her Cain. And I would tell him that she was somehow my everything and though she had chosen him instead of me, if he wanted to continue to exist on this earth he better make certain that she never came to harm, ever. Or I'd find him and he would know a very intimate knowledge of hell.

But all those thoughts flew away as one of my brothers went to the door behind me. The two Keepers were ready, I knew, but still I panicked. And that moment of human panic cost me a jab to my newly healed side. I caught my breath and finished the last brother remaining. When I turned back around, the one that got away was already inside the bunker door.

Well Ain't That Something
Chapter 23 - Merrick

"Will you bloody go already! I'm tired of looking at your arse," Miguel yelled and pushed whoever was in front of him. I heard Josh 'oomph' so that answered that question.

"Watch it, Aussie," he growled back. "I can't go if the person in front of me won't go."

We'd been slowly squeezing and crawling through that vent for almost twenty minutes now. Kay was right, I fit, but it was really tight. And I wasn't the only one. Every two minutes Miguel was banging his head or shoulders and muttering all kinds of interesting words. Some I understood, so I did not. Some I would have punched him for saying had Sherry been here.

"Here's the end!" Kay yelled and the echo carried it to me.

"Finally," Miguel grumbled. "If I had to spend one more minute down here, I was going to have to shoot someone."

We inched our way until Kay got up. I heard her in my mind. Trouble.

Guys with guns, Merrick. They're making us come out.

Got it.

I stiffened myself for a fight. I let Miguel go and then blurred to the surface only to find Miguel in the clutches of a redhead. Her hair was in big curls down to her backside and her green shorts were Celeste short. She was what the humans called a firecracker, I could tell that right off, as she held a knife to Miguel's neck so easily while she gripped a fistful of his hair. She even smiled as she did it.

But it wasn't her, nor the other guy standing around waiting for us, that I really saw. No, there was only one who had my full attention.

"Pastor?"

He glanced at me sharply, pointed and shook his finger like he was trying to figure me out.

"I remember you. I can't place your name, but you're that Keeper. I married you and that little gal a while back."

"Yes, sir."

133

"Well, I'll be," he replied and smiled. "Let him go, Rylee," he said to the redhead holding Miguel without looking at her. "Let him go," he said a little louder like he knew that she hadn't already just from knowing her.

She growled - actually growled - and threw her knife back into its sheath on her hip, her precision and speed that of someone who'd done it way too many times already.

"Pastor Berns, right?" I hedged.

"Just call me Pastor Bob, everybody does."

"Ok, Pastor Bob, what are you doing?"

"Correction. What are *you* doing? You're on my turf now, son."

"I beg your pardon?"

"This is my house, so to speak. You came crawling out of that vent, which means you were inside, which means it was you who destroyed the joint. Am I right in my assumptions?"

Leave it to Josh to be completely inappropriate.

"Well you know what they say about assumptions-"

"Josh," I barked, "not now. Pastor *Bob*, we had a run in with Lighters here, that's what happened to the place. It was... unfortunate, but unavoidable."

"Funny, we haven't had any problems with Lighters until you came," the redhead said sarcastically. "I smell a rat."

"Leave it to the redhead to be irrational," Miguel said and she glared at him. He grinned and winked at her which made her eyes round and her breaths through her nostrils were loud and aggravated. I decided to diffuse the bomb.

I stepped in front of Miguel and hoped he got the message to shut up.

"Listen. We're sorry about the place. We didn't mean to cause trouble. We came here looking for others. We were trying to warn anyone we could find the Malachi is starting a reward program. You'll be hunted. This isn't just about hiding anymore."

"We are well aware of the rewards. We have a man on the inside."

"So do we. Several, in fact." Or at least I still hoped Daniel was on our side. And that Cain and Billings were alright.

"So," he mused, "you're just out here to warn us. That's it? You didn't come looking for supplies or food or shelter. Or women?"

"Women?" Miguel asked.

"This is my daughter, Rylee," he said and pulled her to his side. "I've had several people try to buy her from me. Don't act like you're all so innocent that you don't know what I'm talking about."

"That's disgusting," Celeste muttered. "We don't have people like that in our group."

"And just how many are in your group?" he asked me.

"A lot," I told him. "More than anyone else I'm sure. We've kind of got a little collection going. We take strays, Specials and Keepers, and recently, enforcers, too."

"Enforcers!" Rylee barked.

"What do you mean?" Pastor Bob asked. "You're harboring an enforcer?"

"Nope, we converted one. No pun intended, pastor."

To my surprise, he laughed. Rylee looked up at him disgruntled and then glared at Miguel some more who glared right back at her.

"Well ain't that something?"

I wasn't sure what to say as we all just stood there. So I asked my most itching question.

"You said you wouldn't get involved. I remember you telling me that. What are you doing now?"

"Well, those devils took my Patty from me," he said and him and Rylee shared a look.

"I'm sorry," I said and he nodded in acknowledgment.

"It was over something that made no sense to me; politics and nonsense. It was then I knew I could no longer sit on the sidelines, I had to pick a side. I just wish I'd done it when Patty was still alive. Once that happened, I knew the only thing to do was get Rylee here and go into hiding. So that's what we did. We met Jethro here on the road."

"Not that *I* needed to be protected," she said indignantly and crossed her arms. I realized then how young she was. She couldn't be more than early twenties.

"Of course not, darling," he said dryly. She gave him a look that said she knew it, too. He chuckled at her and then turned back to me. "So…the questions is …what do we do with you now?"

"You have to *do* something with us?" I asked.

"Well, you destroyed our place, intentional or not, and though you said you didn't take anything, I can't imagine that to be true. Not with what we're packing."

"We saw your crates," I told him. His eyes focused a little at that. "We left it all right where we found it."

"How did you find your way to the basement?"

"Laundry chute," Josh said blandly. "That was fun."

"And the stairs were more fun," Celeste said and cringed into Danny's side.

"You used the stairs?" the other man said from behind him. "I'm surprised you even made it out at all. Why didn't you use the elevator?"

I heard Celeste gasp and moved on. What was done was done and there was no point in dwelling so I said, "Ok, let's get back to the part where you think you have to handle us. We can make it out of here just fine on our own."

"And what about us!" the man roared. "Where are we supposed to live now?"

"With us if you like. We have plenty of room."

"Where?" Pastor Bob asked cautiously.

"Outskirts."

"Where?" he asked again.

"Outskirts," I repeated. "Deep outskirts. I'll show you if you want to come with us, but I won't just tell you."

"No offense," Josh broke in, "preacher man, but we ain't had the best of luck lately."

"That applies to us all I think," he replied softly. "Do you understand how hard it is these days to just trust people and know that their intentions are good without any proof?

"Yes, sir," I said, "I do. You can trust me. If there was a way to prove it I would, but for now, you haven't been hurt by our hands and your stuff is intact downstairs. I think that's as much proof as you can have right now."

"True," he answered. "Very true. Well..." He looked back at Rylee and Jethro. They all shrugged, albeit unhappily. "I guess we can join you. But we're not going to be grunts in your army, you hear? We can take care of ourselves and carry our own. We give as much as we take."

"We are all in this together as far as any of us are concerned. There won't be any ranks."

"Good," Rylee said and bumped Miguel's shoulder as she passed him. "Because I ain't taking orders."

He made the profound mistake of grabbing her arm. It was all downhill from there. She twisted his arm under and then flipped him over her back. I looked at Pastor Bob, but he just watched. It even looked like he was smiling a little. Miguel got up like a shot and went to grab her arm again. She jabbed his shin with a swift side kick and then swung a kick to his knee back to put him flat on his back, once more.

He stopped and just looked at her with awe filled and embarrassed eyes with a side of chagrin and anger. He didn't move as she leaned over him, her hair falling in a fiery cascade over her shoulders.

"Don't touch me, ever."

"I'm a black belt," he growled. "No one has put me on my back in years."

"If there was something more than a black belt, that'd be me. Try to keep up, why don't you." She offered her hand to help him up. He debated, almost too long, on whether to take it or not. Then with a begrudged sigh he took it. When she had him half off the ground, she let go. He fell back to his butt with a thud and glared a new rage at her. She laughed a genuine and happy burst of joy as she walked off.

Danny and Celeste were laughing, too, but he turned his gaze to them without getting up. They followed Rylee, trying to keep the chuckles down.

"Looks like you got some competition, Aussie," Josh jested. "Hot competition."

"Young man-" Pastor Bob started, but I cut in.

"Josh, get going. Sorry, Pastor. He's just...that's just Josh. He didn't mean anything by it."

"Hey, when you-" Josh started, but I gave him a look and he backed down with hands raised. "Ok, ok. All I was going to say was I wished I'd met you guys sooner." He went to stand over Miguel who still refused to get up. "Especially you, Aussie. You are a hoot and a half, my friend."

"I'm so glad," Miguel said and got up, brushing off his jeans. "Tell that to the redhead with the biceps."

"She'll come around. They all love that accent, man. You know it's true."

"It hasn't helped me out so far," Miguel said quietly.

"It'll happen, man. I have a seventh sense about these things."

"There's only five senses, Josh," Miguel spouted and spoke slow to goad him, "or don't they teach you biology in Missouri?"

"Oh, they taught me Biology alright. That's where my extra two senses come in," he said and grinned. Then he winked at us, like we were all in on his joke, and followed the rest of them.

I ran my hand through my hair, at a loss to explain anything further. Pastor Bob was just going to have to get used to it or take to fighting his own battles.

Because in our group, the battle of jokes, wits, and wills never stopped.

Botched
Chapter 24 - Cain

"Maybe we should take him to a hospital instead of home. It looks pretty bad," Jeff said low over my shoulder.

"You don't think Miguel can fix him up?"

"Maybe, but we're already in town. It makes sense."

"Maybe we can get Marissa checked out, too. She hasn't been right for a while."

"No," he said quickly. "They'll know she's a Muse if you run into Lighters."

"Ok. Well…" I looked back at Billings. He was snow white and grimacing. I clicked my tongue. "Ok. It's probably not the smartest thing; stopping at a place like that with a van full of Keepers and Muses, but…"

"Since when are we smart," he said and clapped my shoulder as he laughed. "Better safe than sorry. If that arm got infected or the bones misaligned when we set it, we'd have no way to fix him, you know?"

"You're right."

"A broken arm doesn't mean incompetent or deaf," Billings grumbled and sat up straighter, wincing. "I can make up my own mind whether I want to go to a hospital or not."

"And?" I asked. "What's the big decision, Mister Competent?"

"Hospital. Pronto."

Jeff rolled his eyes with me and he leaned back in his seat as I took the next turn towards the Community General.

"I'm not in love with this plan," Simon chimed.

"I have no doubt about that, Simon, but it can't be helped. Billings is all botched up."

I kept glancing back. Marissa still didn't look good. She'd been out of it for a while now. Right now she was sitting on Jeff's lap. She looked fragile and small against his chest, which wasn't like Marissa in the slightest. Her normally olive Asian skin looked even paler compared to his creamed coffee. His big dark hands moved on her arms, her neck, her face. He was trying his best to soothe her as she leaned on him and groaned every few minutes.

I wondered what was up with her. Throwing up sucks, but this seemed like more than that.

138

So I pulled in, parked the van. I got out and looked all over to see if anything looked out of the ordinary. It was pretty deserted. So I opened the door, took Billings' good arm and threw it over my shoulder as I said, "It's almost dark, let's get cracking."

"Cain, be careful, please," Simon pleaded.

"Simon, come on. You make me feel like I'm a soldier hell bent on a suicide mission. This is just simple facts. Broken arm equals hospital. Nothing else to do."

"Just be careful," he repeated in exasperation.

I nodded to him and half carried Billings' groaning butt inside. The nurse took one look at us and scrambled up. She looked concerned but also eager for something to cure her boredom. "Broken arm," I told her.

"I'll get him in to see the doctor immediately."

"And I have one more patient in the car." I slammed Billings into a chair and he glared at me. "Be right back."

She nodded and I made my way back outside.

"I cased the lobby," I told Jeff when I opened the sliding door. "It's clear and quiet. I can take her in."

"No," he growled and gripped her tighter.

"Dude, she looks terrible. And she's barely even able to hold up her head. After all that throwing up she's been doing and all… Let me take her. I'll stay with her the whole time."

"I'll come," he conceded after a few moments of intense thought.

"That's a no-go. I'll take her. They can't sense me and she is in no position to hurt them. They wouldn't risk exposing themselves for that, but for a Keeper, I'm sure they would. Besides, there's no Lighters in there." I held my arms out for her like a child. "Hand her over. I will not leave her side, I swear it, but she needs to see a doctor."

He grabbed my shirt collar and said harshly, "I've never harmed a human before, but if you let her out of your sight, you will be my first."

"I dig."

"What? Speak English!" he barked and I understood that there would be no sarcasm for this situation.

"I understand. I will stay with her. All they need to do is hydrate her and figure out what's wrong. It's probably the flu or something."

"I think she used too much power when she helped Margo and Celeste. She hasn't been the same ever since," he said sadly and looked down at her like he was anguished about it.

"Well, I'll leave that part out when I explain her symptoms," I said and went to take her. He let me. She clung to me which, like I said, surprised me because Marissa was hardheaded and strong and independent. She didn't lean on people.

Her soft arms went around my neck and she hung on as I made my way inside the building with her.

"Now what's wrong with this one?"

"Sick for days. She's been throwing up and stuff," I told the nurse.

"Is she pregnant?"

I scoffed, "No. She's been...she's just been sick."

She gave me a look. I had no way to explain anything further, so I just let her think what she wanted.

"Well, bring her back here."

She indicated for me to place her on the table. I thought about what Jeff said and even though I knew I could take him, I still wasn't in the mood to piss off the Keeper. He was so clearly whipped by the gal in my arms.

I smiled as I said, "I'll just keep her if that's ok."

"It's not actually. How are we supposed to help her if you won't put her down?"

"It'll have to be ok, because I'm not putting her down 'til the Doc comes."

"Whatever," she muttered and left without another word.

I sat in the waiting chair and positioned her on my lap better. I looked down at Marissa and muttered, "That old lady thinks I'm whipped."

"Yep, she does," Marissa said and smiled a ghost of a smile.

"Hey, you," I said softly. "You still with us?"

"Barely," she whispered sarcastically. "I feel like death."

"No offense, but you *look* like death, too."

"Funny," she muttered and barely peeked her eyes open. She put her hand on my cheek. "You're so funny, baby."

"Sorry, I ain't your baby. He's outside in the van worrying like an insane person."

"Mmfffppgmm," she mumbled and snuggled her face into my neck. "Ffrrpppmmm."

"Sounds good to me," I told her and almost laughed.

Then her face took on a sad expression, then pained, then terrified. She looked up at me, but she wasn't seeing me.

"Jeff. Oh, I'm so sorry. I didn't mean to. It was an accident."

"What was? What's the matter?"

"I didn't mean to. Please don't be angry," she begged and pulled me closer.

"I'm not angry," I played along. "What's the matter?"

"Kiss me. Just kiss me and it'll be ok," she said and though the girl was sick as a dog and barely awake, her strong arms pulled me down and planted one on me.

I tried to extricate her, but she gripped me tightly. When I finally managed to pull her away she cried. She burst into a million pieces and I was sorry right off.

"I'm sorry," I told her and pulled her face close and hugged her. Anything to get her to stop crying like that, so devastated and heartbroken. "Hey, hey listen. I'm not angry, it's ok."

"You hate me," she said and sniffled . "You hate me now."

"I don't, I promise. It's ok," I soothed and ran my hand up and down her freezing arm. "I'm a-okay, Marissa. We're good. Please don't bawl like your dog died."

"You won't even call me sweetie anymore!" she sobbed like that was evidence of something. Ah, man, what in the world was going on?

"Sweetie, hey, please don't cry. You know what it does to me. Come on, please?"

"You still love me?" she sniffled again.

"Of course I love you, sweetie. Everything's alright," I told her just as the doctor came in. "Doctor's here so you'll feel better soon."

"Whoa," he said as he looked at her. "We have a seriously dehydrated woman. What happened?"

"She's just been sick for days. Throwing up and stuff."

He leaned his head out the door and told someone to come and start an IV. He came back and I was surprised he didn't try to take her from me. He moved his rolling stool over to us and started with her pulse, then her eyes and tongue.

"She's very dehydrated," he said again then motioned me up as he stepped back. "Come and lay her on the table. You don't have to let go," he said quickly, "just lay her down so we can get some fluids in her. Then we'll see what's making her so sick."

A different nurse came as I got up and smiled at me warmly. She hummed as she did the IV and it was a little unnerving, but oddly comforting. Marissa didn't let my arm go. I knew in her mind it was Jeff's arm. She needed it so I let her use me. Poor girl was sick out of her mind.

"Uuuhg," Marissa groaned as the nurse worked her phlebotomy on her. "Baby, it hurts."

"It's ok," I told her. "A few more minutes and you're gonna be good as new."

She eased me down to her slowly and pressed her face into my neck again. I imagined she did this often with Jeff. I smiled at that sly dog. Taming Marissa had been a feat, I was certain, but if anyone could do it, it was Jeff. She kissed my jaw and murmured something into my skin.

"What, babe?" I asked quietly.

"Please don't hate me," she said and kissed my jaw again. "Please," she begged. "I need you. I love you..."

141

I was beginning to wonder what she was going on about. She was genuinely worried. This wasn't just about her incoherent babble anymore. She was really scared that Jeff was going to find out something. Was she really sick, like with a disease or something and hadn't told him?

"I could never hate you. What are you so worried about?"

"I…I…" she tried, but stopped. I knew it was her own doing not the sleep she was pretending to be in. Hmmm.

"There," the nurse chimed cheerily and thumped a couple bags hooked up to her IV line. "All done."

"I'll check on you in few minutes," the doctor said as they both left. I nodded and looked back at Marissa.

I rubbed her hair and was relieved when she sighed, the tightness in her body and shoulders releasing. Her grip lessoned, too, and I knew she was already feeling a little better.

I stayed right there for a while and thought about how different she felt from Lillian. Lillian's hair was fluffy and soft with its curls. Marissa's was straight as it could be, a thick, black curtain. Her bangs were stuck to her forehead a little from sweat. A cold sweat.

"Right as rain yet?" I asked.

"Not yet, but better," she answered and rolled to her side. She glanced up at me and I knew that she knew who I was this time. She squeezed my arm and looked a little chagrinned. "Thanks, Cain." She cleared her throat a couple times. "That wasn't Jeff with me in here earlier, was it?"

"Nope," I replied and grinned.

"I'm sorry," she said and laughed sadly. "I was half out of my mind. I didn't mean to kiss you."

"Not a problem."

"I'm sorry, really. Just forget everything I said and did, ok?"

"Not likely, but it'll be our secret," I whispered.

"Thanks," she whispered back and closed her eyes. "I hate feeling like this."

"Yeah…about that. What's going on with you?"

"Nothing. I just hate being sick."

"Yeah, but why are you sick? Jeff thinks it's because of what you did to Margo."

"It's not," she insisted.

"Well then what is it?"

"Nothing. It's ok. Thank you for coming in with me. And staying with me."

"Go on, say it," I told her in humor and moved my hand in a 'go ahead' motion.

"Am I supposed to say that you're awesome or something?"

142

"That'll do."

She laughed and shook her head. "You are awesome. Thank you. Don't tell Jeff I kissed you or he'll cut your head off in your sleep."

"No problem there," I dragged out in agreement. "That Keeper has a mean streak as long as the Mississippi."

"A protective streak," she corrected and smiled. "It's so strange. I always thought I wasn't into the Alpha male type. I hated to be told what to do or…whatever, but with Jeff, it's different. He makes me feel safe and fragile even though I'm not really either of those things anymore."

"No, you're not, but you should be. That's the whole point." I thought about Lillian. "You all should be safe and home and cozy." I smiled so that I wouldn't grimace at her with my thoughts. "But then you and old Jeffy wouldn't be bungalow buddies, now would you?"

"Nope, we sure wouldn't," she agreed and then laughed at something she was thinking about. "I would still be a skirt suit wearing school counselor and still hoping that idiot Football coach was going to ask me out one day." She giggled. "I was such a sap. And now I'm an even bigger sap about Jeff, I think. He's just my…whole world. That's crazy, right?"

"Not crazy." I flexed my fingers that were still on her scalp. "Not crazy at all."

We sat in companionable silence and waited for the Doctor to return. It didn't take long, and he was accompanied by the nurse. "And how are we feeling now?"

"So much better. In fact, I think I'm ready to go," Marissa said and sat up slowly, but the nurse held her down as she readied to take her blood.

"Whoa, hold it, hotshot. We haven't even looked you over yet."

"I'm ok, really." She hissed and winced as the needle eased into her skin. "Just had a bad couple of days, that's all."

"Still-"

She pulled her arm away from the nurse who sputtered about having only half a tube, but Marissa was done. There'd be no getting it from her now.

"I came in with free will and I'm going out with it, too," she argued. I could have argued with her about that, but figured the situation didn't really call for it. Plus, she was kind of right. We needed to high-tail it. "I feel so much better. Thank you."

"How's our friend?" I asked before he could start in on her.

"He's fine. Arm was a clean break. Though I'm confused about how it could have happened. He said you were…fighting Lighters?"

I choked and Marissa gasped. What the hell, Billings?

"Did you give him something?" I asked.

"Of course. He was groaning and complaining about the pain and wouldn't even let my nurse look at him hardly. When she went to take his blood he threw a fit, so I gave him a slight sedative-"

"Ah," I said like I knew what I was talking about. "He gets really loopy. We were actually sparring is how it happened. We're both in the enforcers and he was hurt at an impromptu training session." I leaned forward and whispered loudly. "He runs off at the mouth a lot. He had it coming."

"I see," he said and went to the door. "Well, his arm is set and he should be fine. As far as you, Marissa," he said looking at her chart, "I can't make you stay, but I really wish you would, for some tests."

"I appreciate it, but I'm fine now. We really should go," she told him and took my hand, leaving me no choice but to help her so we could go.

"Ok, then. Drink lots of fluids when you get home and rest." Marissa nodded and as the doctor left he stopped in the hall. "Ah, here are some of your recruits I believe," he said to someone. I stiffened. This wouldn't be good, I knew it. Sure enough, a frigging Lighter came to stand by him in the hall. I squeezed Marissa's arm to remind her to be calm. His face hardened as he looked at Marissa, then at me. He smiled a fake congeniality as the doctor asked him about something they must've been discussing earlier.

How stupid was I to think we'd actually get through this unscathed? Jeff was going to kill me.

"So, I'll see you at the facility tomorrow for physicals. Goodnight," the doctor said and took his leave.

"Goodnight, doctor," the Lighter said evenly, his eyes locked on us. "Well, well. What have we here?"

"Just a little fever. She was dehydrated, but feeling much better now," I said and tried not to look any different. "And our friend broke his arm. It's been a long night," I said and helped Marissa across the room. The hall would be better than being cornered in a little room.

"Not so fast. She doesn't look so good. I think she should stay here for tonight," he said slowly. Crap. He was trying to compel me. "Take her back to the bed and lay her down. I think you both should stay." He'd know I was immune if I didn't obey him.

Double crap.

"Uh…" I looked at Marissa and hoped she'd forgive me for what I was about to do. "Sorry, chief, that's a no-go." I threw Marissa behind me to the bed and rammed the Lighter into the wall behind him. He put up a good fight, I'll tell you the God's honest truth. He kicked my feet out from under me and when I was flat on my back he tried to take my head off with his big booted foot. I moved just in time and glared at him.

He kept at me, not giving me any time to regroup. I felt my eye pound and sting under his fist more than once, but I couldn't stop. I looked around for something to stake him with.

Then an idea shot into my head like the lightning I wished would shoot from his chest.

I swung open a door marked 'Stairwell' and ducked just as he swung. The Lighter was then in my spot in front of the stairwell, so I lifted my hands and let the power come to them. The sonic boom blasted from my palms to him and he toppled down, flipping and rolling all the way. I slammed the door shut and pushed a crash cart in front of it. I knew it wouldn't stop him, I just wanted it to slow him down.

I ran into the room and helped Marissa, who had already gotten back to the door by herself, and we made a hasty getaway down the hall. We passed a few nurses and doctors who gave us a strange look, but ultimately left us alone.

We reached the front desk and found Billings checking out. He was all casted and slung up...and he was high as a kite in May.

"Guuuuuys!" he slurred and laughed as the nurse rolled her eyes and pointed for him to sign the paper. And Marissa was barely able to hang on to me anymore as she struggled against her own legs. So I slung hers arms around my shoulder and held her close as I made my way to Billings.

"Gotta fly, Billings. Now."

"Are you two together now? Cuz Jeff's gonna be pisssssssed."

Then he laughed like a hyena and almost toppled over. Crap. So I yanked his arm, the bad one, and watched him wince. He growled at me and grabbed my collar. "What the...the hell was that for?"

"Get your crap together. We have to fly, now. You dig me? Now."

"Ok, ok." He was still high, but a little more lucid. Pain would do that to you. I thanked the nurse and left anyway even as she was yelling at me about Marissa's paperwork. Billings stumbled after me and then I heard the alarm. At least we made it outside first. I saw Jeff's head pop up as he heard the alarm and then he jumped into the front seat and started the van, yelling at Simon to open the door.

We climbed in and Jeff gunned it.

"What happened? Are you ok?"

"I'm fine," Marissa said. "I feel better, really."

"Then why was Cain practically carrying you out?"

"They gave her fluids, but we left before the blood results came back. A Lighter came to pay us a visit. Wasn't that sweet?"

Jeff's eyes shot between Marissa's in the rearview mirror and the road. She looked better, yes it was true, but she was nowhere near well. I reached over into

145

one of the bags and gave her a sandwich. The homemade bread was falling apart, but it didn't matter.

She shook her head at it and I pushed it closer to her along with a bottle of water. "Eat it. You have nothing in your system but salt water. You're not gonna feel better until you get your sugar level up."

"But I'm not hungry."

"This isn't about being hungry. It's about doing what your body needs. Eat it."

She took it, but she wasn't happy about it. She ate slowly, which I encouraged. Jeff said he wanted to stop and I could drive, but I said no. They weren't just going to let us go if they found us and they were probably looking for us right then. We needed to keep going and get as far away as possible.

"We can't go home tonight though, just in case they're following us. Pull into an abandoned place in a while and we'll sleep there for tonight."

He nodded. Marissa finished off her sandwich and started nodding off on the floor beside me. I pulled her to me and leaned back, letting her head rest on my shoulder. She didn't fight me which proved to me how exhausted she was. I was about to doze off myself.

I glanced up at Jeff, certain I would be see his scowl of annoyance at my holding his girl. He had the alpha-male thing down pat, but instead I saw gratitude.

Thank you, Cain. Seriously.

I nodded and closed my eyes. The breath that blew from my body was of relief and a little gratitude myself. I was pretty darn grateful for my family. Now that I had one for myself, a real one, I knew exactly what it looked like.

Last Straw
Chapter 25 - Sherry

"What's going on out there?" Ann nor Patrick answered me. I fumed and stood, putting a sleeping Lily on the bed with Racine. I refused to be treated like a child stuck in a fire drill. I yelled in a harsh whisper, "What's going on?"

Patrick glanced my way once and said, "Be quiet so they won't know that we're down here. It seems that your Lighter was telling the truth. He's fighting them, but one slipped inside. Ryan is handling him."

"Ryan," Ellie whispered from behind me. "No."

"He's a Keeper, Ellie," I told her without looking her way. "He knows what to do. Ryan's pretty awesome like that."

"But what if he-"

"Don't say it!" someone hissed. I looked back. Margaret. "Don't whisper the words of death and bring it all on us."

"I just...I need to go. I can't just sit here and wait like some-"

"Like some what?" I turned to the hateful Keeper and glared at her in the darkened corner. I knew Piper could see me. There she sat with Polly, old friends again. And her Keeper butt was just sitting there in the corner while her brothers and sisters worked to protect the door. "Like some human? What? Do you have something to say, Sherry? You can't take care of yourself, always getting into trouble and having to have people come save you, so I really don't think you get to look at me so judgmentally for sitting here and doing what this human body was made for; to be weak and vulnerable and selfish. So that's what I'm doing."

Gah, I can not stand you, I thought. I saw Lillian glance up sharply and Piper's eyes narrowed. She said, "Well, I'm not crazy about you either, human."

I must have said that out loud. Oh, well, it was out and it was true and everyone knew it. I guess it was time for a little Piper cameo. Polly only ever spoke to me to ask about chores and then left in a huff. They'd both been awfully quiet and reserved lately, keeping to themselves. Fine by me.

I turned back around and listened some more. I looked us all over. Frank, Calvin and Lana were in the corner and he was signing to her what was going on. Paul and Katie with Sky were on the opposite side by the door. Margaret and Pap were huddled on the loveseat. Pap was actually snoring a little from his siesta. I wanted to be angry with him, but he was older and just...strange sometimes.

I kept listening. I was utterly calm, but utterly terrified. It was weird, like my body didn't know how to act. There weren't any noises outside or upstairs, but that didn't mean anything. Lighters and Keepers both were quick and light on their feet, especially when they fought. I was still scared of out of mind for them.

"We can't just sit down here and wait," I told him.

"We have to keep you safe," Ann argued.

"But you should be out there helping Ryan and Max," I said, trying another tactic. "We shouldn't just stand down here knowing that they are fighting up there."

"They're fine," Ann barked. "We have everything under control. Just sit down and wait until we tell you that the coast is clear."

Oh, no, she didn't. What was wrong with her?

I looked back at Lillian and she had that 'Uhoh. What are you gonna do?' look. What was I going to do? What could I do? It wasn't like I could fight anyone, but I hated feeling useless. And worse still, if Ann and Patrick were using us as an excuse not to help Ryan and Max....what if something happened to them? I couldn't do it. Though I was scared out of my mind that something would happen to someone...

It was the last straw.

Unfortunately, before I got to play hero, there was a bang on the door. I pulled Lily to me from the bed and decided right then to do something drastic. I had a feeling come over me, a paralyzing and debilitating fear. I had to save Lily. I didn't know what was coming, but I knew it wasn't Ryan or Max.

I hefted her up and ran through the people, who were now alert and on edge, and placed her in the closet floor. She still slept soundly and I hoped she kept at it. I shut the door quietly and went to stand next to Ann. The door broke apart into pieces, throwing me into someone behind me. I shook my rattled head, wincing at the pain in the back of it. I reached my hand back and it came back bloody. I gasped, but realized it wasn't my blood.

I peeked back and saw that it was Paul who I had smashed into. His nose was broken and he was out cold. Poor guy. I was then lifted and dragged out of the door by a cold hand on my arm. I looked up to see that I wasn't the only one being dragged or pushed. Oh no.

Ryan and Max were still fighting Lighters and so was Daniel. It appeared to be an ambush. I scratched the one who was holding me and squinted as the light burst out of his skin trough his wounds. He hissed and slapped me, but it barely registered as I rolled, got up and took off running up the stairs. I had to do something and it seemed that the best thing was to lure them out of the bunker.

"I'm going to sound the alarm to alert the others," I yelled. We didn't have an alarm per say, but I hoped the Lighters didn't hear the lie in my voice.

Maybe if I ran, they'd follow me. It worked.

But then I was facing three Lighters and nowhere to go and nothing to stake them with. Shoot, I hadn't really thought this through. But I got what I wanted didn't I? I always wanted to go and meet the Lighters head on when they tried to cause problems. Here I was and not a clue of what to do. And I was shaking with terror.

"I remember your face," one of them said.

"I just have one of those faces," I said and I made a backwards retreat in the snow covered ground behind the store. It was hot just a few days ago, but now it was snowing in a soft trickle. They all inched forward and encircled me.

"No, you look… Ah! Crandle's girl. The human, Sherry."

"In the flesh," I said and looked around.

"Wow. Look at you. You've really let yourself go."

"You'd be singing lightning if I had a stake right now, buddy," I said, part bravery, part anger.

They all laughed. I was used to it. They all trumped me in size and height, and the fact that there were three of them all without a conscience or care didn't help my situation in the slightest. My bravado slipping and the door banging closed on the store back in the wind were gulp inducing occurrences. This was it for me.

But Lily was safe, for now in a closet, and Merrick and Danny were off on a run. So were Cain and Jeff. My loves were all safe. I closed my eyes. I didn't want to see the look of satisfaction on their faces as they ended me. I felt a cold palm on my arm. I peeked to see, unable to stop myself, and saw Calvin behind them. He had his hands up and ready to go. They were aglow and eager for usefulness. I took a deep breath out of sheer self preservation. Like I knew that the flaming licks that were about to consume the Lighters around me would suck up all the oxygen.

Calvin extended his hands to the unknowing Lighters and the first two in front went up in flames of red and orange and yellow. They bellowed and the lightning seemed extra cold for some reason. I shivered and then realized that the one who insulted me still had his hand on my arm.

Calvin stepped forward and that's when I saw Frank behind him. He was holding a stake, though he had no knowledge of how to use it, he was defending Calvin's back, which was better than nothing. My boys.

"Let her go, monster. It's over for you," Calvin said in a surprisingly steady voice.

"That right? Over, huh? Well, what about this one?" he said and pulled me closer to him. "You going to let this one go with me?"

"Not a chance."

"How do you plan to stop me, boy? Do you plan to singe your lady friend as well?"

"Nope," he said and grinned, "but I won't have to."

149

I heard the Lighter's swift intake of breath before he burned up in a lightning strike. Then I was enveloped in arms that warmed and comforted like no other. I turned to find my Keeper.

"You're early," I squeaked and let him lift me in a hug that took my feet from the ground. Behind him were Josh and Miguel and Danny, Celeste and a few new additions…the pastor? "You brought me some recruits," I joked.

He leaned back and took my mouth with his. I loved how he was all business when it came to my safety, my comfort and my lips. He squeezed me as he showed me that he was angry and worried and relieved all at once. I'd get an I-can't-let-you-out-of-my-sight lecture later, for sure. And I'd welcome it.

He sighed against my lips and then said, "You always have to test my heart, don't you?"

I laughed, though it was sad and full of truth. I nodded.

"Where's Lily?" he said in a harsh whisper.

"I hid her inside," I answered then remembered. "There might be more Lighters inside still." He kissed me once more roughly and took off running, his boots making deep gashes in the snow. He turned and yelled over his shoulder, "Stay right there!"

I yelled back, "Daniel's in there, too! Don't stake him!"

Danny came and pulled me into a rough hug that was long and hard. Celeste stood behind him looking more solemn than usual. I started to question them, but didn't get a chance to.

Miguel and Josh ran after Merrick as he blurred, but they didn't make it very far before the ones on the inside came out to meet us. And they had prisoners. The two Lighters who came out had Lillian gripped in one of their arms and Ellie in the other. How had they gotten past Ryan and Max with…ah. I saw they both had something in their hands planted into the girl's backs to keep them cooperating and to keep anyone from pulling a stunt. The rest of our group piled out of the back door, eyeing the Lighters with weariness and wariness.

Racine wobbled out, pale and sickly still, but she was standing. Josh immediately made his way to her and pulled an arm around her back to help her stand. She looked at him a bit shocked but ultimately, grateful and happy. As Merrick had said the Keeper and Special relationship was tricky and for the two to make it work was definitely a good thing.

Merrick blurred himself back to me and Danny, and put an arm around me as he stood half in front of me. The protectiveness coming off him was as tangible as the malice coming off the two Lighters. I gripped and rubbed his arm to tell him to calm down.

I am so tired of having to protect you, Sherry.

150

I gulped and nodded. Of course, that sucked. I always seemed to be in trouble or someone did. It was all we could do be safe anymore-

He lifted my face and shook his head. "Really? That's the conclusion you jump to?"

"I didn't say anything."

"But I could see it on your face. I didn't mean it like that. I meant, I'm tired of *having* to protect you because there always seems to be a reason to. We can't ever have a moment's peace and I don't want this life for you. I will always protect you with a willing and open heart. Don't ever think otherwise." I nodded and even though we were in the middle of the yard with Lighters and everyone else, he kissed me hard and deep to make sure I absolutely understood him.

Gah, I loved him.

"Now," he started and turned back to the threat, "stay behind me the entire time, Sherry Elizabeth, or you *will* be in trouble."

I snickered at his back. He was such a guy. But then the Lighter's rant reached all our ears, even though he was speaking normally. Freaky like that.

"I will ram this…" he glanced at the object in Lillian's back, "human tool through her lungs and end her life in a second if anyone tries anything funny."

Where the heck was Daniel? Where were Ryan and Max? If I didn't know better, it looked like they bailed. The Lighters they were fighting were right here in front of us now and they hadn't come out with everyone else.

"What do you want?" Merrick asked.

"I want you to wait for back-up to arrive. When they come, we'll take you all into custody and you'll be processed through the enforcement facility. Well, not all of you," he said eying Merrick with distain. "The world has no use for Keepers, so I think we'll just dispose of you here."

"That won't happen," I almost growled and then realized I'd once again said it out loud. I peeked and saw that I had in fact said it out loud as the Lighter laughed, his black soulless eyes glowing with humor.

"Feisty," he muttered. "I like that. Maybe I'll keep you for myself."

Merrick jerked and growled at him, making the Lighter laugh harder.

"And, now I've found the one that you're attached to. So gullible! I know exactly who to use against you."

Merrick's arm tightened on me a little. I stayed quiet and so did he. What was the use of with fighting wits with Lighters?

Then a thought hit me. Lily…she could heal. I'd almost forgotten. I hated to think of using her that way. It hurt my chest to even conceive it, but we may not have another choice. I glanced over my family and saw them all sullen and

151

defeated looking. Even sick Racine was here. The only ones missing were Lily, Piper and Polly.

I threw my gaze to Danny and gave him a look. A look that said 'What the heck are just standing there for. Compel them, idiot.'

He got an 'Oh yeah' look causing me to roll my eyes and watch it all unfold. The one with the stake to Lillian's back suddenly tossed the thing behind him. A screwdriver. Lillian got the hint as the Lighter looked around for the source of the trickery; she ran. He chased, but Merrick was faster. He blurred from me to the Lighter like a shot and as they collided, sand and snow kicked up all around them. Racine jumped into the fray too, though Josh yelled at her to stop. The other Lighter looked panicked.

Panicky Lighters was a new sight for me. They were usually so calm and cold.

He held on tight to Ellie and dragged her backwards. When she tripped and fell he continued to drag her backwards by her hair and shirt collar. I searched for what to do, but saw out of the corner of my eye, Danny. He stepped forward and looked at the Lighter. He concentrated hard and then grimaced before settling on a frown. The Lighter though, grinned. He looked down at Ellie and then back up to Danny. He pulled her up and hugged her to him, almost like she was important and precious.

Danny's mouth opened and he breathed faster. Celeste tried to come and help, but he pushed her back behind him. Danny was acting pretty strange and Celeste hadn't jacked him for pushing her around? What in the world?

"You know, don't you?" the Lighter asked Danny. "You know what this means? What she is?"

I was clueless, but Danny didn't seem to be. The Lighter started to back further away, Ellie whimpering in his arms. Danny bolted forward a bit and yelled to someone, "Don't let him leave with her!"

It was almost dark, but as I glanced up I saw that Daniel, Ryan and Max were descending upon the Lighter from the roof in a falling glide. There was a burst of lightning off to the side so I knew that Merrick and Racine had taken their Lighter out in the snowbowl.

I glanced back to see Daniel wrench Ellie from the Lighter's grasp, tossing her behind him as he went for the demon. Ryan blurred and grabbed her up, crushing her to him. She clung to him and cried as they stood and held on to each other for dear life.

Daniel and the Lighter didn't last long together. Daniel had the Lighter on the ground and was looking for something to stake him with. He yelled for Merrick to throw him his stake as Max looked for one, too.

I screamed as I saw it, but I was too late to help. The Lighter on the ground had reached under him. With the screwdriver in his hand and a whip of his inhuman wrist he sliced it through the air at Ellie. Her eyes bulged, but she didn't make a sound as the screwdriver sunk into her back.

Stabbed In The Back
Chapter 26 - Merrick

Ryan's eyes grew with unbelief as Ellie fell on him. He helped her to the ground and held her in his lap, the realization of what happened hit him.

I watched, anguished for him, as he roared into the air his anger and hatred for the demon, who just smiled in triumph with his bloody lip.

"If I can't have her, no one can," he said quietly, but once again it reached all ears. As I tossed Daniel my stake he plunged it into the Lighter's chest and leaned back to avoid the lightning that blared through the sky.

"We need to get these people inside," he barked as he grabbed Lillian's arm and started to tow her. "The Markers will have seen that and they'll come for you all."

"Wait," Sherry said, "one of them said there was back-up coming. What if there's more on the way?"

"There is more on the way," he concurred, "but that can't be helped. We'll be waiting for them and take them out. We'll be ready. Inside now."

Ryan held a broken and bleeding, but still alive Ellie in his arms as I helped him stand. Keepers didn't need help physically. He could have lifted Ellie as if she were nothing, but he was in shock. Sherry put her arm around his lower back and urged him inside with me with human murmurs and words of encouragement and hope. We could take her to the room in the back and see what the damage was.

I really hoped she was ok, for her sake, but also for Ryan's. He had been on a fine line of depression and melancholy before Ellie came. His mind had been a tangled weave of desperation to be useful, to be needed and his want to go home. He and Simon both had thoughts flitting through their heads about it constantly. Though Simon's were bitter, Ryan's were longing.

As we all piled inside the bunker door, a snow dusted Miguel took over the Ellie situation and I was grateful to him for it.

"Bring her in the back. I'll check her out there," he told Ryan, who zombied his way where Miguel led.

I pulled Sherry along with me, refusing to let her out of my sight for a moment. We'd have to have another talk later. As much as I needed to do these things and be away, I couldn't leave her anymore. This wasn't working. The old 'You're safer with me rule' needed to go back into effect.

"Where's Lily?"

"Here." She went to the small closet and right there still sleeping in the floor was Lily, with her doll and hair a cute mess. I sagged in relief. She had slept through the whole thing, thank God. I pulled Sherry down to sit on my lap as I sat on the floor next to the closet. I needed to be near my girls right then.

"What happened? Why are you back early? Not that I'm complaining," Sherry asked. I glanced over and saw Ryan place Ellie down on her side and sit next to her, stroking her hair.

"We had an accident," I told her gently and watched her predictable face fall in upset. "It's ok, we're fine, but…anyway, we decided to come home after we found the pastor and his daughter."

"I thought that was him," she mused and inched forward a little. I bent to accommodate her. "I'm so glad you're ok. Thank you for bringing Danny back safely." I must've made a face because she knew right off that something had happened. "What? Please just tell me and don't make me beg it out of you. Did something happen with Danny?"

There was no way I was telling her that I not only did I almost lose her brother, but Celeste, too. I looked to see Miguel working on Ellie, knowing there was nothing we could do there. So I did what I always did to distract her. I kissed her good and hard. Such a hardship, I know.

She resisted for a split second with a small push to my shoulder, but easily relented and melted against me. The little noises she made, small grunts and sighs of relief and satisfaction almost did me in. I was a drowning man and Sherry was the shore. She was the moonlight and I, a shadow in her glow. I was a fish that enjoyed the pain of her hook. She was my everything.

I pulled her closer to me on my lap and enjoyed her intake of breath. She was still stunned that I wanted her, that I needed her always, that she was what I breathed.

I didn't know what else it would take to make her see that without her, I was nothing. Of course, true or not, she would say the same about me.

I ran my fingers through her hair, down her neck to her collar bone. I coasted my thumb over his skin there, getting dizzy with the knowledge that she was still mine. Her skin - soft, supple, and shivering under my touch - was the thing I most wanted to remember if I were to perish. The feel of it was the last thing I wanted to feel if this world kicked me out.

I pulled back, barely, loving her harsh short breaths of love and longing on my neck. I totally understood the male mind now. It was in our system and brain waves to protect, care for, and…conquer our female. I smiled a secret smile to myself, knowing that I had done just that. But she had conquered me as well.

But the reason I was suddenly having this revelation came back to mind. We were huddled on the floor because we'd once again been attacked.

"I'm so glad you're ok," I told her. "I don't know what happened, we'll talk about it later, but I'm so relieved that we came home." That brought a thought I didn't want to think. What if we hadn't come home when we did? "And Calvin, he was outside when I came. It looked like he was defending you."

"He was. He saved me. I ran outside to draw them off when they got in-"

"You what?" I asked, my voice betraying me. Just the thought, let alone the actual act, of Sherry sacrificing herself made me hurt all over. "You did what?"

"I had to," she said and didn't even try to deny it. She couldn't lie and we both knew it. "I'm useless, Merrick. I'm small and defenseless and the only way I could see to help was to be a diversion. They were inside! So I got them to follow me. It worked. If I hadn't, we'd have still all been in the bunker with them and I have no idea what would have happened."

"That's it," I said. "You can't be apart from me again."

She laughed softly and shook her head. Her small, cold hand coming to rest on my cheek as she said, "I knew you were gonna say that. I love you."

"I love you," I said, but it came out a desperate growl. Ah, I didn't know how to just be a human man and I didn't know how to be a Keeper anymore either. One side of me was screaming irrationally and angry and the other side was fighting for logic and a way to make the situation work. The Keeper in me wanted to lock her up in our room and never let her leave. The man in me knew that this war of the worlds was far from over and it was naïve to think that any one person was safe and able to just sit back and watch it all happen around them.

I had no frigging idea what to do anymore.

"Merrick, look at me." I did as she commanded without a second's thought. "I know you're freaking out and struggling with everything. I know something happened while you were gone that you don't want to tell me. I know that you want to lock me and Lily in a safe place and keep us there. But, baby, that's just not possible. I worry about you so much while you're gone and though my first instinct is to say 'No, just stay here with me', I know that's not possible. I was terrified for you, I always am, but I tried to think about the people you were helping. What if you hadn't come for me and Danny?" I shook my head to tell her that was an impossibility. "I know, but what if you weren't his Keeper?" That thought hurt worse than the other. The thought of Sherry and Danny not being in my life cut me to my core. "If you hadn't saved us then I have no idea where we'd be. And how many people out there feel that way? Just…lost. I'm so proud of you for doing that and the fact that you brought home some new people with you just proves to me that you're amazing. You always do what you set out to," she said, her eyes watering. "You're so good and big hearted."

I framed her face and looked at her closely as I said, "There's no way I wouldn't have come for you in the beginning and there's no way I won't come back for you now. Honey, why are you crying?" I asked softly.

"Because I just love you," she muttered and sniffed. When she looked back up to me, her eyes had a glassy film. "One day this will all be over right? And we'll get to go and live in that house that you talked about? You'll be here always, and won't ever leave me."

"Never, ever," I told her. "And one day this will be over, baby. It has to be." One way or another…

"Daddy," a voice said full of sleepiness. A voice that held my heart as much as the strangely vulnerable and open wounded girl on my lap did.

Sherry was worrying me. She always tried to be so strong and optimistic for us all. She'd only ever really broken down once, after Crandle took the kids and she blamed herself. And now that Lily was awake she was pulling herself back together and smiling at our little girl. But I wasn't buying it. I pulled her face up with a finger under her chin.

"It'll be ok, baby. We'll be ok."

"Don't, Merrick. Please let it go," she pleaded, her voice quivering.

"I want to make sure you understand that no matter what happens, we'll be together. I don't know what's gotten you so shaken up, but I won't let anything happen to you. Or Lily. You're my whole world-"

That was it. What I had been waiting for and expecting happened. She broke down and closed her eyes as she shook silently, like she had something to be ashamed about. I pulled her to me and she sagged against me in defeat. She reached to grip Lily's hands, pulling her into our embrace as well. As I felt my collar start to soak, she lifted her head and looked me right in the face.

"I'm sorry." I shook my head, but she kept going. "I haven't felt right ever since I got back from the enforcement facility. I'm so afraid. What if they got you or Lily or Danny? To think about you in there and them doing those things to you just makes me…" I felt my face go hard.

She still refused to tell me what they had done to her, but if she was this worried about it, and was breaking down over her worry, then it must be worse than I thought. But I let that go and went back to her.

"I won't let them hurt you or Lily ever again. And I won't be taken by them either. I had no idea you were struggling over this so much."

Her face was blank and haunted as she said, "I had Lily here and they were beating on the door. I didn't know what to do. The only thing that I could think of was what if they got her and took her? What would they do to her?" She burst wide open again, her tears big and falling. "And then I wondered if you'd ever speak to me again for letting something happen to her. So I hid her in the closet, it's the only thing I could come up with to keep her safe. But oh....if something had happened to her... Merrick, I don't think I can..." She stopped her rant and looked down at Lily. She mouthed 'I don't think I can do this.'

Lily was gazing at Sherry with concern and I even saw her rubbing Sherry's arm. I was floored. Both of my girls were fretting and crying over each other. I was so in love with them both. I grabbed my chest to stop the ache and pulled them to me. They both clung to me like I was their whole world. That was exactly the way I wanted it. I whispered in Sherry's ear, "You don't have to do anything, Sherry. You're already doing it, baby." She leaned back at looked at me confused. "You don't think every mother out there would freak in that situation? But you handled it. She's alive, she's fine, in fact better than fine because you thought and acted fast, she didn't even have to see a thing."

"Are you talkin' 'bout me?" Lily spouted but I had to finish with Sherry.

"I am so proud of you for being level-headed and caring enough about her to do what had to be done. For the love of all, you lured the Lighters to follow you outside away from Lily and everyone else." She sniffed her annoyance at my praise. "Seriously. I know it was scary...at the facility and here tonight. It doesn't make you weak to be scared. Courage comes from being scared and doing what needs to be done anyway. And you are the most courageous woman I have ever have the pleasure of knowing."

She scoffed a laugh, "You don't know anybody. That's not a very fair assessment."

"Still true."

She put a hand on the back of my neck and pulled me to lean against her forehead. "Oh, my....I love you so much, Merrick."

"I know. And I've never been more grateful of anything in my whole existence. Lily, come here, baby."

She huddled in with us and we just breathed a sigh together of release and need for a human touch that was filled with love for one another. When we heard a grunt we turned to see that Miguel had just removed the screwdriver from Ellie's back. She was screaming silently, mouth wide. Ryan looked on and caressed her hair to calm her, but it was no use. Miguel cursed and put another needle into her arm. He glanced at Ryan, "Sorry, mate. I thought I gave her enough to knock her out."

In seconds she was falling back down to the mattress, eyes fluttering. As I looked back to my girls, I felt guilty. All the pain and suffering around us...it seemed almost wrong to be so happy.

Human And Anti-Rebelliony
Chapter 27 - Cain

I woke to the annoying sun sweeping itself across my face. I peeked up and saw that we were still in the van. It was early still and freezing. I felt a warm body next to me and immediately pulled her closer on instinct. Then I remember that it wasn't Lillian with us, it was Marissa. My eyes opened wide.

Marissa was curled up next to me, using my arm as a pillow. There was a coat spread out on top of us. Jeff was leaning against the back seat upright, watching us.

"Dude, did you sleep?" I asked and kind of wanted to pull my arm out from under her, but she was so peaceful and looked so much better than the day before, I just couldn't.

"Nope. It started snowing so I kept turning on and off the van for the heat. I stayed up all night to keep watch. Simon tried to do shifts but...he passed out."

I looked over to see Billings and Simon lying back to back on their sides. They were symmetrical, both using their hands as pillows and the legs out to the side as far away from the other guy as possible. I chuckled and then looked back to Jeff. He was watching Marissa's hand. I looked down. It was twisted up in my shirt collar.

"Why didn't you take Marissa from me?" I asked.

"She was sleeping, I didn't want to wake her. Plus, if she was with me I'd have fallen asleep, too. She has that peaceful effect on me," he said and sneered as he looked at us.

"I didn't mean for her to sleep on me. Sorry."

"It's ok. It kind of pissed me off to watch you two snuggle all night and it helped me stay awake."

"I said, I'm sorry-"

"And I said, it's fine. I needed to stay awake. I've never watched her sleep for so long like that." He half smiled. "She makes little noises, and she kept saying something about chocolate, and she was wrapping her hands in your shirt. I bet she does that to me when I'm asleep, too."

"I'm sure she does."

He shook his head sadly and after a long pause he said, "I'd give anything to be a human right now."

"What? Why?"

159

"Because you can do things for her that I can't. I couldn't even take her into the doctor last night, because of what I am. I'm a liability to her."

"She's a Muse. The Lighters detect her just like they can detect you. And they despise her just as much if not more than you."

"Is that supposed to make me feel better?" he asked in annoyance.

"I'm saying that you are pretty equal on the spectrum. You're both supernatural beings who love each other. So what…you're not from this planet. Who cares? Marissa doesn't and she's the one that matters right? Besides, you guys have the whole ebony and ivory thing down."

Ok, I was already over the Dr. Phil session.

He looked confused at first, but ultimately just shrugged and said, "I guess. But I just hate it that I can't take care of her the way that she deserves."

"You were doing a pretty good job of that when I tried to take her from you. A human man couldn't do any better, trust me." I pointed to my chest. "I am one."

"But she told me what you did for her last night after you passed out; how you protected her inside the hospital when they were drawing her blood and then when the Lighter came."

"I was just doing what I knew you'd do for me if the situation were reversed and it was Lillian."

Except that kissing part. Grrr. It ticked me off just thinking about her lips on alien boy.

"I don't understand why I feel this way. I mean it's like my stomach is in knots just watching her lay on you, even though I know nothing is going on. I feel protective, but it's more than that. Like I want to smash something." He snarled - snarled! - and tugged at his hair with his hand. "I feel like a Neanderthal."

I laughed as I said, "You are a Neanderthal! Guys are that way with their girls. Some call it being high-handed or cave man syndrome. I just call it good manners."

"So it's normal for humans to be…possessive?" he said as a gruff confession.

"Yep. I'm possessive as all get out. In fact, let's stop talking about it because it's making me itch to get home."

"Well, let's go home then," he replied and stretched. "I'm so done with this trip and we're still alive which means we weren't followed."

"Sweet." I leaned over to shake Marissa, but he stopped me.

"Please, just let her sleep if you don't mind. She'd been so restless and odd since she helped Margo and I'm really worried that maybe she pushed it too far. Maybe rest was what she needed and she'll wake up feeling better."

"I'm dandy. You drive us to the casa and I'll lullaby your girl." He sent me a wry look that said 'cheap shot'. I grinned. "I know, sorry. And by the way, what you're doing, letting her be comfortable and sleep on me even though you don't like it…proves you're not a Neanderthal." He smiled and chuckled silently. He opened his mouth and I knew what would spew out. "Are we almost done with the male bonding? Because I'm ready to go home, big man."

"Fine," he said and rolled his eyes in his Jeff way. "Fine, fine." He got in the driver's seat. The engine was already on and the heat kicked on higher. "It snowed all night. It might be a rough ride," he told me.

"Whatever. As long as we don't end up in the ditch, I'm good."

We stayed quiet and drove. I had almost fallen back asleep when I felt him jerk the van to a stop. I wanted to sit up to see what was going on, but figured Jeff would bite my head off. But then I heard Jeff's angry breaths. Then he exited the van. I knew something was up. So I slid slowly and gently out of from under Marissa's head. She didn't even notice. She kept right at it.

I crawled over Simon and Billings. As soon as I opened the door and hopped out I pulled it closed, but didn't latch it so the noise wouldn't wake anyone. I straightened and cursed to myself. Jeff was standing in the middle of the snow covered road, in a short sleeve t-shirt like a freak show, as he stared down three enforcers. Two guys and one female. And they looked strangely familiar.

I made my way to them and they looked me over quickly before going back to Jeff.

"We have to do an ear check to let you pass through. We've had lots of rebel break-ins lately and Malachi is cracking down," one of them was saying.

"Here," I told them and thrust my head to the side for them to see. "All human and anti-rebelliony. Let's get going, big guy," I told Jeff, but it was a no-go as I knew it would be. But a guy can hope can't he?

"Not so fast. We have to check for marks on every person that passes through." He looked at me and did a double take. "You look so familiar."

"I was thinking…wait. I met you at the enforcement facility. My mentor was Billings."

"Oh yeah," he drawled and smiled, but then stopped. "Wait. We never saw you or Billings again after the explosion. We've all been reassigned to other facilities. We thought you died with the casualties."

"Nope, still kicking. But no offense, we got blew up the first day, man. I figured that job wasn't for me."

They laughed and nodded. "Yeah, I guess that wasn't really in the job description was it."

"They left that part out of the manual, and I don't blame them," I said. They chuckled again and I prayed it was working.

"Well, we've always got spots if you're open to coming back one day."

"I'll think about it. So, can we get through? Heat's broken in the van and it's freezing, man."

Jeff got the hint and crossed his arms over his chest, he pretended to shiver.

"I guess so. It's not like you would work for the enforcers if you were a rebel right?" he joked and I laughed to placate him.

"Nah, man. I don't think that would work out. Thanks. Maybe we'll see you around."

"Yep."

I waved and we made our way back to the van. But when Jeff started to drive passed, the woman yelled and pointed. The enforcers drew their guns and I started to tell Jeff to gun the gas, but knew they'd follow us. I rolled down my window and heard her yelling, "That's our van. They are the ones who stole our van."

That's where I recognized her from. She was Lily's mom! The ones who ran Sherry and them off the bridge putting their van at the bottom of the river.

Wow, what a witch. I wondered where her husband was.

I leaned out the window, though they fired a couple shots at us, and let my magic hands work. I blasted the two enforcer cars that were parked beside each other on either side of the road. They both landed on their tops as the enforcers scattered and glared at the van like we'd been unprovoked.

"Now, they won't follow."

"Nice work," Jeff said as he looked back to see what I'd done, and then slammed on the brakes once more.

There was big guy standing in the road. Lily's dad, that crazy lady's husband. He had on a Kevlar vest stacked with bullets and a huge gun that made me wonder what he was compensating for. Then he pointed it at the van and started shooting.

Rally The Troops
Chapter 28 - Lillian

I watched as Daniel rallied our troops, so to speak. He was so focused, even though he was getting glares and rolled eyes in undulated waves throughout our group.

He kept glancing at me and I kept pretending like he wasn't.

He had been fighting the Lighter right in this spot before and the Lighter saw me as I looked on helplessly as to what to do. He had thrown Daniel and came at me so fast I didn't know what to do. As he held me and made his way up the stairs backwards, Daniel, Max and Ryan had spoken quickly. Then when I was dragged outside I figured Daniel was coming to save me, but I never saw him. Strange, I thought.

Then they'd all showed up on the roof and ambushed the Lighters. The first place he'd looked when he landed was a quick flick of the eyes to me and then on with his work.

Now, after he dragged me back down in to bunker, he was attempting to explain to everyone how the Lighters operated. They said they had called for back-up and Daniel confirmed that they had.

We had no idea what that meant though. Did they have CB radios in their heads or something? He said they have a way to reach out and communicate with others but it was on an individual basis. They can't broadcast to a wide audience of Lighters, only the Taker can do that. So they had called a few reinforcements, but no one knew how many or how long it would take to get here. But as long as we took them all out, our location should be safe.

He told them in brief detail what the Taker was doing. Malachi was tricking people into turning 'rebels' in and instead of getting the reward money, he was consuming them after torturing them for information. He was also consuming all the 'rebels' who were brought in, too. So far, from Daniels rough calculation, he'd killed over two thousand humans, just this past month alone.

My stomach rolled with that thought.

I tried to pay really close attention to what he was saying. I needed to know what was happening.

"You'll need to keep things quiet and dark so they won't be aware of your ambush. They need to think they are sneaking up on you."

"Why do you keep saying 'you' and 'your' like you're not one of us now?" Max said miffed. "You *are* one of us now, right?"

"I apologize. Thousands of years of talking about Keepers and humans as 'them' and 'you' are hard to break." Max nodded and waved for him to continue. "*We* need to be quiet and ready when they come. I can't hear them anymore, I can't listen to their call or hear their minds, I can't even read yours anymore. So I won't be able to help you much with that respect."

"Why?" Calvin asked.

"Why what?"

"Why can't you hear them anymore?"

Daniel, Max and I exchanged looks. We hadn't talked about what Lily did and no one knew how much to say about what had happened. Would people be afraid of her?

"Uh…" Daniel muttered.

"Daniel can't hear them because he's no longer one of them," Max interjected with certainty. I gawked at him and so did Daniel. "Look at his eyes. He's one of us now."

A few leaned forward and gasped at the silver eyes that stared back, no longer black pockets of evil. Daniel shifted uncomfortably and then said, "Ok. Back to the plan. Like I said, I can't hear them, but I can still detect when they are near. I feel them, so I will try to give you as much warning as possible. We need to gather weapons and station people at entry points and hiding spots. And we need to hide the women and children."

"Hey," I yelled, tired of being put out of the loop for my own good. Ann and Kathy barked something at him too and he looked at us exasperated. Max intervened.

"Keepers stay, humans go. Lillian, come on. Don't fight me on this. We'll spend our focus worrying about you instead of taking out Lighters."

"Fine," I said brightly. I had no intentions of sitting back while the others fought. There had to be something I could do even if it was hand ammo to the guys or throw knifes…ok, that was stupid. There had to be something I could…something Daniel had said to me once was playing back in my head. Yes…that, I could do. Though Cain would never forgive me and it would be a fight to get Daniel to help me.

I kept my thoughts to myself and tried to keep listening. Merrick and Miguel eventually joined us and stood by Daniel. They helped in the planning too and before we knew it, we were set for war.

We got started on getting all the ammo and stakes together. They asked a few of us to make 'bombs' or 'grenades'. Which were chemicals and a professional strength tile cleaner that burned your skin if you touched it that we poured into balloons. So ghetto, yet effective. They wouldn't stop the Lighters, but it would stun them long enough to hopefully get a shot in. All the Keepers and guys planned to wear long sleeves and hats and hope that whoever was aiming, aimed correctly.

After a while, everybody took their positions and I, and the rest of the lowly females, took to the back room with Sherry and Ellie, who looked just awful. I thought Ryan would have a hard time leaving her there like that, but he was amped for revenge. He kissed her pale forehead gently and then his face turned murderous as he stalked out to the commons room.

Daniel, who had practically dragged me to the back room to make sure I went, was antsy, too. He kept shifting and switching feet. I asked him what was wrong.

"I just don't want this to end badly for your people."

"We're ready, like you said. And you're here. Between you and the Keepers, they should be able to handle it, right? Unless there's something you're not telling us."

"I just don't know how many are coming. It is unpleasant and foreign to feel so blind and unknowing."

He looked so unsure and unsteady. I grabbed his hand to offer some comfort and immediately regretted it. He looked at me hopeful and intrigued.

I pulled my hand back as I told him, "Daniel, don't read anything into it. It's just something humans do to comfort each other."

"Comfort," he murmured. "Then why did it feel so good?"

"Yikes," I replied and pulled my hair back with my hands. "Daniel, you've got to stop saying things like that. I told you."

"We can be friends, yes?"

"Yes. Only friends."

"And friends can still hug each other, right?"

That reminded me so clearly of something Cain had said to get me to kiss me once. *Drunken party friends can still kiss, right?* I bit my lip at the ache for him. And then looked at Daniel. If I was honest, I did feel something for him. Especially now, when he was open and honest and waiting for me to reach out. I just did not understand this pull…this connection with him that I'd felt ever since I did whatever it was that made him want to be different.

I pulled my arms around his middle, since he was too tall for a neck hug. I tried to stay neutral. This was just a friend, going off to battle, and I wanted to hug him to comfort him and send him off. But when he pressed his hands to my back and buried his face in my hair, I knew that my neutrality was one sided. He inhaled deeply, bending me back a little to press me further against me.

"How can this be wrong when it feels so right for you to be against me?" he whispered.

"Daniel, you're confused." I tried to lean back, but he held me tight. "I know it...feels good, but everything that feels good doesn't mean that it's ok to do it."

"If I die and hell is awaiting me, is it too much to ask that it smells like Jasmine?"

I almost lost it. He was so honest and carefree with his words. He wasn't censored or altered by years of the world and peers and TV molding his mind. He said exactly what he thought with no mind to consequence or decorum. It was refreshing, but also dangerous. I had to get him to stop saying those things.

I pushed him back a little and looked at his face. "You can't say things like that to me, Daniel. Please."

"But it is the truth. You want me to lie?"

"No, I want you to grow a censor button," I muttered and he looked confused. "Humans don't just blurt out every little thing that they think and feel. You have to think about what you say and whether it's appropriate or not."

"Maybe that's what's wrong with your world," he said factually and not unkindly. "Maybe if everyone were a little bit more honest with each other, you would have been a more organized and peaceful planet."

"I can't argue with you, there. But you can't say things like that to me anymore either, ok?"

"So I'm allowed to feel them, just not say them?"

"Um...yes." What else was I supposed to say?

"As you wish," he said and let me go. "I'll go join the others to prepare."

"Be careful, ok?"

"As you wish," he said and smiled, but then backpedaled. He came forward and grasped my arms. His eyes went black. "You be careful. Stay back here and don't attempt to jump into the fray. It would hurt me very much if you were harmed."

"Wouldn't dream of it," I answered.

"Does that mean yes?"

I laughed. "Yes."

"Alright then." His eyes turned back to silver as he turned and left. I knew right then who was going to help me with my plan when the time came. Good old Daniel.

I walked over to Sherry and Lily. They were sitting on the bed with Ellie. She looked pale and terrible. She was on her belly, a big gauze bandage over her back. Sherry was rubbing Lily's hair with one hand and patting Ellie's hand with the other. She didn't look good either.

"Sherry," I said and she jumped and gasped. "Sorry. Are you ok?"

"I'm just so on edge. I don't know what's wrong with me. One minute I'm fine, then the next I'm crying, then I'm wanting to break someone's fingers. I'm losing it," she squeaked.

"It's a lot to deal with," I soothed and sat next to Ellie's head. "We're all losing it a little, I think." I was gonna lose it if Cain didn't come home soon. "How's she doing?"

"She's bad. Miguel said the Lighter hit her spinal cord."

"Oh no..."

"We'll have to wait for her to wake up to see what the damage is."

"Poor, Ryan," I muttered and then turned red with embarrassment. "I mean, poor Ellie too, I just-"

"I know," she said. "I get it. Ryan was just starting to be normal again." She rubbed her temples. Then she groaned and fell forward a little bit. I jumped to catch her, but she was still upright.

"What's going on with you?"

"I have no idea. My head is killing me." Then she sat up and rolled her shoulders. "All better now. Weird."

"Yeah. Weird."

"So what are they doing out there," she asked as if nothing had happened at all.

"They're getting ready for the Lighters."

Lily played with her doll between us. She was kneeling on the floor and then reached up to touch Ellie's hand, putting Ellie's hand on the doll like she was playing with it. Then I remembered what Lily had done. I mouthed "Heal her?" to Sherry and she sat up straighter.

"Lily," she said softly. "Do you think you might want to heal Ellie like you did Daniel?"

"I can't. I alweady twied."

"What do you mean?"

"She's got something wong with her, mommy."

"I know, bug, that's why I want you to heal her."

"No. She's got something wong with her. She's like a wall. That's what she said."

"Who said? You're not making sense, Lily," she said softly.

"I asked her if I could make her better, but she said she was a wall. I don't know," she spouted and shrugged her shoulders.

Sherry and I just looked at each other. I didn't want to push a four year old to discuss something she clearly didn't understand, but I was more confused than when we started. We both stayed quiet. As did pretty much everybody.

Polly and Piper were still in the corner like earlier, playing cards. And they were bickering, which was nothing new. Pap and Mrs. Margaret were bickering, too. They were sitting over a chess board and whisper-yelling to each other about what moves were legal and what not. Paul was nursing an icepack on his face while Katie fed Sky. When I looked back at Sherry, she winced at Paul.

"I did that," she said. "I better go make sure he's ok."

As she got up, we all heard the noise and stood as still as oak trees. There was a pounding on something. The door? Then a rumble and a boom shook the building and echoed around us.

Lightning.

The Lighters were here and the war had already begun.

A Long Shot
Chapter 29 - Cain

I pulled Jeff's neck so that he was leaning over the middle console with me. I reached my foot over and pressed the gas further down. Jeff yelled, asking me what I was doing.

"I'm running down the bastard."

"He's a human!" he spouted.

"A human who's shooting at us!" He grunted and I peeked up just as fat boy jumped out of the way. "Dang!" I moved my foot over to press on the brakes. Simon's head popped up and I yanked him back down just as another shot went through the side window. That's was when I realized that Marissa and Billings were still asleep. How? I didn't know.

"What are you doing? Let's just go," Jeff commanded.

"No way. That's twice that the guy has tried to kill us. He's going down."

I leapt out the side door, hearing Simon's urging me to stay inside, and peeked around the side of the van. Right before I blasted the guy with my sonic hands, Simon pulled a decoy and blurred around the back. Dang it! I ran to catch up and saw him trip. His face was shocked and just as he was trying to get up, I ran in front of him. The guy pulled the trigger and I knew a bullet was going to shred through my chest, but it was instinct to try to protect myself anyway. My palms lifted and stopped the bullet midair about two feet from my face. It fought against the blast of energy, but I held on. I saw the guy's eyes widen just before he flew backwards. He went way up into the air, just as the Lighters had done before. But when he landed in a heap on the ground, I knew he wouldn't be getting back up. The bullet eventually started to recede and then fell away from me on the highway. I sagged at the strain and pain in my arms. Normally it was one blast from my palms, but I'd held onto this one. I had been a couple feet away from getting my head blown off. That would bring the beast out in a guy. So maybe I should stop being a pansy and start practicing my gift like the others. Who knew what else I could do and as much as I hated to admit it. I must've been given this gift for a reason.

I turned to my Keeper to expel my revelation on him, but he was sitting, head bowed.

"Simon, funs over, man. Come on."

169

"You saved me."

"Yeah...it's cool. You can buy me a gift basket later."

"No. It's my job to save you!" he roared and stood up on his shaky legs. "But my body...this old, useless, decrepit body tripped over itself. Do you understand you could have died! I've never been able to help you. I was a fool to think that this body could do what needed to be done."

"Simon," I said in surprise. "Come on, it's fine. It all worked out."

"No thanks to me," he growled and then looked down the road. The enforcers and the lady were running our way. They were still a good half mile away. "Let's go."

"It's the thought that counts?" I tried again as we climbed into the back of the van.

"Actually, no. It's not," he replied and lay down in the back of the van, facing away from me.

I shrugged. Dude needed to chill.

Jeff got us home fast. And we could see the freaking fight going on all the way down the road. I squinted to see what was going on. Lighters, lots of them. And they were treating the place like a Demolition Derby.

"What time is it?" Marissa sat up, her hair a twist and spike of craziness. "Did I miss anything?"

"Nope," I said wryly. "The fun's just starting." Billings and Simon sat up too and we watched as Jeff sped us to the scene. As soon as the van hit the brakes, I slammed open the door and we took off toward the tussle.

I saw Merrick and a Lighter in a tiff. The Lighter kept trying to be sneaky, blurring around to stab Merrick in the back. So I bolted his way and when I got close enough, I threw one hand up to blast the sketchy bastard.

He went tumbling into Ryan's line of sight from a corner of the building. I saw Ryan move to one side and then Calvin fried him with his fire fingers. Then Ryan went right back to being in front and protecting his charge. Sweet set-up.

I was engulfed in big, burly, Keeper arms while off in La-La land.

"Dude, what will the wife think?" I joked as I patted his back.

"Ah, man, I'm glad y'all are ok. I was worried sick."

"You're early," I yelled as we ran towards another Lighter.

"So are-" he grunted "-you," he replied gruffly as he staked one of them through the belly as I held him.

"We ran into trouble times ten. You?"

"We didn't fare so well either."

I was grabbed from behind. I flipped him over my head for Merrick to stake him as he landed on the ground.

"Everyone ok?" I asked.

"Yep. And we got three more." He nodded his head to three people, two dudes and a redhead, who looked like a siren from the depths of hell as she staked a Lighter through his chin up through his skull. Even I winced, but she smiled as she closed her eyes to the bright light. Then hunted immediately for another one. Sheesh...

"Yippee. Well, we had some casualties, but all still here." I nodded towards Billings who was flanking Marissa with Jeff on her other side. I saw someone throwing water balloons. Miguel. Miguel was launching water balloons at Lighter's like hand grenades and then as they screamed at whatever was in the balloon, Kay staked them.

"Well, I'm just happy you're ok," Merrick was saying. "Lillian would be mighty unhappy if something happened to your sorry hide."

"That hurts, Merrick," I mocked and blasted a Lighter with me palm as he blurred up behind Merrick. "Dude, how did you survive at all without me here?"

"Shut up," he laughed and staked him.

It got awfully quiet. We looked around to see all of the Lighters were gone, burned up and dust. We stood waiting all scattered around the field, our eyes roaming for more. I spotted Daniel by the back door and did a double take. What the... When did he get here? I growled at the thought of him being here with Lillian without me.

Merrick must've seen my gaze burning. He said, "He's really helped us. He told us they were coming so we could ambush them. He set this whole thing up."

Someone must have told the ones downstairs that the battle was over because everyone started pouring out into the snow from the back door. Sherry and Lily bolted towards my man and he wasted no time getting to them. Josh went to Racine, Max went to Jeff and Marissa, Pap and Mrs. Maggie went to Simon, Frank went to Calvin and I could imagine that conversation. Calvin bragging about getting to fight and Frank groaning about not being able to.

Then my heart walked out that door, searching with wide blue eyes that made me smile like an idiot. Daniel made his way to her and she seemed relieved. I arched an angry eyebrow at that scene, but quickly changed it to one of happiness as she saw me and took off around Daniel, not even touching him, as she bolted to me. I made quick strides myself and the oomph in my chest from colliding with her was the best kind of pain.

"Oh, Cain..." She kissed my lips, my chin, my neck. "Oh, Cain. I'm so glad you're here."

"I'm glad you're glad," I joked and kissed her with gusto. Gah, how much had I missed this? Her lips...it was like kissing her for the first time. Like I'd never felt her softness before, or her need for me. I was starving for her.

It jacked me like a punch to my gut. I found myself pulling her tightly to me and kissing her deeper. My arms searched for her flesh. She whimpered and I jerked out of reflex, but she kissed me harder and wrapped an arm around my neck. Her hand grazed my hair…

Oh, boy. We had to stop. Now.

So as much as it pained me, I pulled back to look at her flushed face. She blinked in a daze and I couldn't help but smile smugly as I hugged her to me. When I lifted my eyes, the tame, turned Lighter was watching us with a semi-disgusted and semi-pissy expression. Well good, buddy, I thought, get your own.

He turned away and I sensed that I had issued some kind of challenge with my stare. Hmm. I took a deep breath and just wanted to fall into bed with my girl, but since when did we get a break around here?

I picked her up and carried her inside. We parked it on the stairs and I reveled in the way she clung to me as if she never wanted to let go. When I caught Lighter boy gazing at us once again, I'd had enough of that.

So, call me whatever Neanderthal-ish name you must, but I lifted her chin and melded her mouth to mine. She responded vigorously, making me a smug and happy guy.

She tugged once on my lip ring with her teeth and I groaned gruffly. She pulled back and started to apologize, but an apology wasn't what I wanted. As I maneuvered her into my lap on the dark stairwell, I had plenty of ways in mind to make her see just how much I enjoyed that.

"Cain," she whispered. Maybe it was more of a plea.

"Yes, lovely?" I said while still kissing her.

"This is crazy."

"I'm fine with crazy," I said and kissed the dip under her chin, then her neck.

"People can see…if they're looking," she said, her breathlessness making me ache.

"Then they need to avert their nosy eyes."

But just as I was thoroughly enjoying myself, I heard someone clapping. I reluctantly pulled away to see what was going on and saw Sherry bringing out a plate of cookies. Then she grabbed her head with a wince, dropped the whole plate of cookies from her fingers…and Merrick caught her before she fell to the floor.

A Pocket Full of Posers
Chapter 30 - Sherry

My head ached like I'd been hit. It was the strangest thing. I felt hands all over me and tried to pry my eyes open. I kept hearing someone groaning and wished they'd shut up. It was hard enough to concentrate without all that…that was me. Then it all of sudden just stopped. I opened my eyes and looked at Merrick as he knelt above me. He exhaled in relief as I opened my eyes and pulled me into his embrace.

"What…" I almost asked what happened, but like someone had plugged me in, I knew everything in an instant. I gasped and scrambled up. I ran. I flew with all my might down the hall, hearing them yelling and running after me. I got to one pantry door and threw it open. It was empty. I opened the next, empty. The third…oh no…it was empty, too.

By the time I got done with them all, we were supposed to have nine pantries full of food to help tie us over for when the need warehouses opened to feed all these people. It still wouldn't have been near enough, but it was a start. Now, we only had one. One! That wouldn't last us two months.

"I should have realized…" Merrick said beside me and gripped his hair angrily in his fingers. "I should have noticed you were acting strange."

I turned a rage filled roar to Piper, who stood there smugly.

"How could you? Do you have any idea what you've done?"

"I know exactly what I've done!" she yelled back. "I've ended you. You've killed all these people now. They'll starve because of you."

"What's going on, man?" Cain asked Merrick. I looked around and realized that no one understood what was wrong except Merrick and I. And as I looked up at him as he stood beside me, he shook with his rage and hatred for his sister. I gripped his hand.

"She knew I was the only one checking the food, planning the meals. Piper got Polly to compel me," I explained. "The pantries are empty." I heard their gasps and mutters of outrage. "Polly made me see a vision, a compulsion, so I'd believe they were full every time I checked back here. They've been slowly removing the food over the past few weeks."

"I should have seen the compulsion on you," Merrick said in regret and rubbed my fingers with his thumb in a soft apology. "It's why you've been so strange lately." Then he turned his gaze to Piper. "What did you do with the food, Piper?" When she stayed silent, his voice got harder. "If you wanted to go home so badly, then you should have just done it. You didn't need to hurt all these people!" Merrick roared.

"It was the only way to get you all to come with me though. See," she stepped forward towards him, "with all these humans gone, you won't have a reason to stay here."

"You are the most delusional, selfish, evil creature I've ever met. And I've met the Taker, Piper. You can go to hell!"

She cringed back against the wall.

"Where's your thirty pieces of silver, Judas?" Jeff asked her angrily as Kay said, "Piper how could you do that! You took the oath, as we all did!"

"That was your very last chance," she murmured in a sulk and never looked away from Merrick.

"Oh really?" Merrick scoffed. "For what?"

"To be redeemed. To be with your own kind. To come with me to the After."

"Never. Going. To. Happen."

She nodded and sneered, "Then I'm glad I did what I did."

"Just go home, Piper! Get yourself a new body, something. Just leave."

"Not on your human life," she barked. "I'm not leaving just so you can live happily ever after while I drown in misery."

"Well if you won't leave, I will." All heads jerked to Simon. He was looking at the floor. He looked up and met Cain's eyes. "I've done nothing but cause problems for you since I got here. I can't protect you in this body."

"Simon," Cain tried and sighed. "It's alright. We're all here together and we can help."

"It's not alright!" Simon yelled. "You may not care or want to be my charge, but you are. My conscience buzzes for you constantly because I can't do my job! I can't be your Keeper in this decrepit vessel." He closed his eyes and said in a whisper, "Take me home."

Then in a slow hazy glow, his body began to take on a yellow hue. His eyes closed and all the Keepers sucked in quick, surprised breaths before they all fell to their knees. But it wasn't out of respect or reverence. Something made them do it. They all watched with faces of mixed variety as Simon's body slowly undulated and waved, almost unnaturally. Then with wide eyes, he dropped to the floor.

Kay scrambled over to him and looked at his face. She bowed her head and closed his eyes. "Fare thee well, brother. He's gone."

"Fare thee well, brother," the other Keepers murmured.

"What?" Cain asked harshly. "What do you mean he's gone?"

"He went home."

"Home? Home as in..." He pointed up. "You can do that?"

"If we make the decision to go home, yes we can. If we shed the body and decide."

"But it won't last," Jeff said and looked at Merrick and Kay. "Why would he do that? He can't stay there, he'll go mad."

I remembered the time Merrick had explained to me about it. That's what Simon had done. He'd gone home, but Merrick said their conscience would drive them crazy if they didn't answer the call.

"Simon...left," Cain muttered. "What does that mean for me?"

"We don't know...just..." Jeff had no idea what to say, and we all could see that. He resorted to patting Cain's shoulder.

While Cain and Jeff went back and forth about Simon, I turned to Merrick. I didn't even need to say anything. We were screwed, no other word for it. There would be no way to gather enough food now and we'd never survive on the amounts the need warehouse gave each person that could go and collect food. And our measly garden was a joke in terms of feeding a crew this size. It was only supposed to supplement.

He pulled me to him and let me squeeze him until my arms shook. The compulsion was gone, I felt like myself again. I was no longer twitchy, anxious and strange feeling. Like I was about to burst for no apparent reason. But I was upset, for sure. There were no breaks for us, ever.

I looked over and didn't know if I should mourn Simon or not. If he was happy and ok or not. It was just too much to handle, really. Too much in one day to deal with. And out of the corner of my eye, I saw Piper trying to sneak away. Before I could say something, Miguel grabbed her arms.

"Where shall I put the traitor?" he said loudly.

"Lock her up in the room on the far end," Jeff said and glared at her. "Where's Polly? Get her, too."

"I thought you said we'd be kicked out?" Piper protested.

"So you can run and tell the enemy where we are?"

"I wouldn't do that," she sneered back.

"Oh? Like you wouldn't try to starve us either? Take her, Miguel, before I do something I've never done before."

"Right."

He marched her down the hall and the rest of us moseyed our way back to the commons room.

"She must have gotten Polly to compel someone else to help them," I told Merrick. "I doubt those two carried all that food away by themselves. Where is Polly by the way?"

Miguel heard us as he came back and set right out to find her.

"I'll start looking everyone over for signs of compulsion," Merrick said and bent to kiss me.

Everyone was watching Lily, who sat in the middle of the room with her doll and her little wooden horse, so innocently. I saw as Miguel sat down with her and watched her play with her horse.

"What did you decide to name her," he asked.

"Pixie," she said and giggled, falling over into his shoulder. "Isn't that so cute!"

"It sure is," he said and laughed softly watching her.

Danny and Celeste sat by her too as Cain and Lillian parked it on the big couch by Billings. His arm was in a cast and he looked pretty uncomfortable. I decided to grab him some Ibuprofen.

He was eternally grateful, taking the pills and the glass of water and downing it quickly.

On my way to the kitchen to see what we had in the pantries there, I caught - on the sly - Rylee's look of awe and intrigue at Miguel and Lily on the floor. I looked back and agreed. They were quite a sight, opposites in every way.

I went to the kitchen and looked around. I'd been thinking of making something for Lillian when the compulsion started to unravel.

Ah, what were we going to do now? The food...

I decided to make some coffee, though even that wouldn't help things now. As soon as it was done brewing, I made a cup and sipped the black energy. I held its warmth in my hands and left the kitchen, still gloomy.

When I came back into the commons room, I noticed Cain and Lillian were totally involved with each other and nothing else. His hand traced a path in her hair around her ear, over and over as he looked contemplative. No doubt thinking about Simon and all the crap we'd been through. Her eyes were closed and she just leaned against him.

Cain had fallen hard. It was the sweetest thing ever. Well almost...

I peeked at Merrick, but saw Jeff and Marissa in the corner behind him. He was soothing her, rubbing her arms, and she was looking green again. I wondered what we were going to do with her. She was getting worse, not better.

Lily pranced up to me and grabbed my hand, yawning into her fist. I made my way to Merrick and said, "What are we going to do about Marissa? Something's wrong with her."

"Nuttin's wrong with her!" Lily said and laughed loudly. "I told you I was gonna be an aunt. Aunt Rissa's gonna have a baby, silly!"

The whole place stopped. I swore the earth stopped spinning. Marissa's eyes bulged before they landed on Jeff and pleaded.

"Is that true?" he asked roughly.

"Please don't be angry with me."

"Is it true? Are you?"

"It wasn't on purpose."

"Marissa," he said in exasperation.

"Yes!" she sobbed and sucked it in. "Yes, I'm pregnant."

I'm not sure what she expected from Jeff, but from her expression it wasn't anything good. I felt a small sting in my chest at my own loss, but as I looked down at my Lily that all went away.   I glanced back up and watched along with everyone else. Jeff was still. As still as a man could be.

"I'm the father?" he asked.

"Of course you are, fool," she said and swiped her tears off her chin before biting her lip and stepping towards him a little. She sighed when he wrapped his arms around her gently, his eyes focusing on her flat belly.

"You're going have a baby?" he whispered and smiled. Then he absolutely beamed. "You're going to have a baby? That's why you've been so sick?"

"Yes, *we're* going to have a baby."

He kissed her and then smiled the smile of a man who was more happy than he knew what to do with.

Then he promptly fainted.

Merrick and Max got Jeff on the couch and awake. Marissa knelt at his side, a ball of worry and amusement. He sat up and took her face in his hands.

"Was I dreaming? Please say no."

"No," she answered and laughed softly. She let him kiss and cradle her to him. I couldn't remember ever seeing him as happy and satisfied and...human before.

Danny went and turned on the console record player. I thought about telling him that we weren't in the mood. That even with Jeff's happy news, it had still been a sucky day.

But then I realized it was exactly what we needed.

I looked up at Merrick and he smiled that slow grin that said he knew me and knew what I wanted. Or needed. Per Trudy's tradition, Celeste and Danny, and Paul and Kate twirled and laughed. Merrick pulled me to him and held me close as we stood still, but enjoyed the music next to the stairs. I closed my eyes as I let his calming warmth seep into me. Etta James crooned 'At Last' and I opened my eyes to look around. Jeff and Marissa were happy, Cain and Lillian were sweet, Calvin and Lana were talking. She saw me looking and signed 'Are you alright?' I nodded, but she gave me a look to show she didn't believe me. I smiled and got Calvin's attention. I mouthed, 'You wanna dance?' The look of disgust and quick shake of his head was pretty adorable.

I laughed and looked at Merrick, who was watching me closely. How ridiculous were our lives now? Fighting Lighters in an ambush, realizing we could possibly starve now at the fault of one of the people who came to save us, a Keeper and a Special were going to have a baby…and now we were dancing and swaying…

Ridiculous, but wondrous.

"Are you alright?" Merrick asked softly. "You look very calm. Too calm for someone who's been through what you have today."

"I wasn't the only one." I bit my lip. "What are we going to do?" I whispered. He pulled me tighter and spoke into my hair.

"I don't know," he answered roughly.

"We have to figure out a way to get more food…something… we just have to-"

"We will," he said, his voice a hard command as if speaking to the situation itself. He pulled his lips through my hair and pressed them to my mouth. It was the softest of kisses in comparison to his rough words. With a hand playing in the ends of my hair, he said, "I promise you I'll do everything I can."

"I know."

Then our moment was interrupted by the ringing of a bell. Daniel was by the stairs and he jerked, crouching into a defensive position, not knowing what it was.

"No one's in the store," Jeff announced and we all stilled. That was right.

Then we heard a Lighter, loud and clear as a bell through the door as he said, "Knock, knock. Anybody home?"

Pompous Jackhole
Chapter 30- Cain

When they busted in the door, I thought that was it for us. Then after the hit, they ran, which was intriguing because we knew it was a trap. We knew they wanted us to follow them. So naturally, that's what we did. After stuffing everyone else in the back room, of course.

Lillian wasn't happy. We'd just gotten back together and all, but it had to be done.

So we'd walked out to meet the Lighters. All the Keepers, Miguel, Josh, Danny and I looked across the expanse of snow and wondered what they had up their sleeves.

A car's tires crunched in the driveway, passed the van and it came to a stop in the middle of the back yard. I whistled out of sheer appreciation. The windows to the sleek, black Mercedes CLS were tinted dark. As the back door opened, I started to gnaw on my lip ring.

I didn't even have to know what the guy looked like to know that this pompous jackhole was the Taker. All the Keepers tensed and the air around us seemed to cut even more with a chill. The snow swirled around him like it could feel his power.

"So...this is the infamous rebel base I've been searching for? You know, I've got to give you props. Crandle's notes on you did not do you justice. Bring them," he barked to someone.

I felt a chill down my spine at what he meant by that. I'd been watching the door. I hadn't seen anyone go in... They marched our loved ones out single file. They didn't hold them, they let them run to us. They wanted us to be with the woman, I realized. To see the terror in their eyes and feel helpless as they slaughtered us. I pulled Lillian behind me as she reached me in a sprint, and saw Merrick do the same to Sherry and Lily.

"What a sweet sight," the Taker sang.

"Can it, Taker," Merrick barked. "Get on with it."

"But I like games," Malachi crooned and smiled. "In fact, I'd like to play one now." He pointed around sporadically and said, taunting, "Eenie...meenie...miney...." he pointed last to Racine, "mo."

Two Lighters blurred to her side, jerked her arm, careful not to touch her skin, and threw her through the air to land in front of Malachi. He shook with

179

excitement as he took her fragile body in his hands. She looked so pale and weak still. We had to do something.

"It's been too long since a Keeper has run through my veins," Malachi said to her sweetly. "I'm sorry that it's over for you now."

"This ain't over," Josh yelled and tossed two balloons towards the Taker. "Not by a long shot."

The Lighters, the mindless idiots that they were, didn't react, they just watched with a horrified expression. Racine pulled from Malachi and the balloons hit the Taker's chest.

He gasped and grasped at his chest only to start laughing. He looked up at the sky and shook his head, as if he were thoroughly enjoying himself. I started to move forward. I knew the end game for Racine was coming, but I saw Josh bounding forward. He ran like he had a football tucked under his arm but boy, he was booking it. When the Taker's eyes made their way back down to Racine and he reached for her, Josh was on him. He tackled him to the ground and Racine watched for a split second before she scrambled to them, but she was too late.

I saw Merrick and Jeff start to lurch forward, but...

Malachi thrust his arm into Josh's chest as he sprawled on top of him. I heard Josh's gurgle and it reminded me of the soldiers I'd seen die more times that I wanted to admit. Malachi removed his hand and pushed Josh off, a gaping, red, messy hole in his stomach was all that was left.

Racine had crumpled and was screaming, but the Taker made no move for her. She rocked on her knees as she mourned her charge. Sherry screamed too and Merrick turned to her. I heard Lillian's whimper and sob from behind me and reached back to soothe her. But there really wasn't much comfort to give as Malachi straightened to a stand.

One of the Lighters brought him a washcloth and helped him take off his shirt. Malachi shook himself as if disgusted, but looked at us with a satisfied expression.

"Not by a long shot, indeed," he mocked. "They go down so good, but can be so messy." Then he smiled and opened his arms. "Now, who's next?"

A Girl In Sheep's Clothing
Chapter 31 - Merrick

As Sherry fell apart in my arms, I watched as Racine collapsed. All my brother's and sister's hearts ached for her. To lose a charge was the epitome of agony and disgrace. She'd been sick, her body weak, she couldn't have helped the situation, but there would be no way to console her.

I glanced around and saw Lillian creeping away from Cain. I gave her a funny look and she waved me off as she made her way behind all the people watching the horror unfold. Then she grabbed Daniel's hand and dragged him inside. What in the worlds?

"Do I have to come and take you like prisoners or will you go out like heroes and volunteer?" Malachi asked with a satisfied sneer.

I urged Sherry to take Lily, putting them behind me again and ran through scenarios in my head of how this could go down. The image of me smashing his face kept coming front and center. I shook my head and scolded myself. I needed to get in the game. I went forward for Racine. The Taker didn't stop me. He smiled at my boldness and nodded, allowing me to take her.

I picked her up in my arms, her sobs an uncontrollable array of cries and groans. She lay limp as I took her back to our people. Out of the corner of my eye, I saw Cain reach back for Lillian, but when he found nothing he turned. He cursed and turned in circles, his gaze flicking over our group. As I stood back up, leaving Racine huddled on the cold ground, I saw Cain's face harden into a menacing scowl of anger.

I turned and saw why. Lillian and Daniel made a hasty move to Malachi. Cain started to head for her, but stopped. I heard the conversation in his head and balked at Max's explanation. He'd tried to stop them, but they wouldn't listen to him.

Calvin was fighting Ryan, trying to come forward. He yelled, "I'll burn him up. Let me through!"

"No, Cal. You couldn't get close enough."

Cain went white as the snow we were standing on and then yelled, "No, Lillian. No."

"Don't growl at me," she yelled back. "This is why I'm leaving. I'm tired of you all treating me like I'm some…" she stopped and looked at us. Her voice was

181

hard, but her face was pleading us, with her back to the Taker. "Child," she eventually said and mouthed 'I love you' to Cain and bit her lip before turning and letting Daniel lead her with a hand on her arm.

Malachi looked her over and it was obvious he was pleased with what he saw. "And what is this?"

"I'm sorry I betrayed you by living with these…rebels." She knelt on her knees and bowed her head. "I was scared and had nowhere else to go. I wanted to turn them in, but they don't have a phone and they watched me every second. Forgive me, my lord."

"I usually hate to be called that, but from your lips it sounds fitting. And what shall I do with you, you intriguing human?" he said low and suggestive.

Lillian looked up at him and though I couldn't see her face, I heard her purr, "Whatever you'd like, my lord."

I blurred to Cain as I heard his guttural grunt, to keep him from screwing it all up. Yes, Lillian's plan was a leap, a big leap, and I wanted to kill Max and Daniel for helping her orchestrate it, but if Cain flew off the handle and went after Malachi, he'd be dead before he got the chance to scold her for it.

He was strong as he yanked and pulled against me.

"Let me go, Keeper," he growled.

"Just wait," I whispered harshly, knowing I was such a hypocrite because if Sherry had pulled this crap, there was no one on this earth who could stop me. "If you do this, her sacrifice was for nothing. Let's just see what she has planned."

He grabbed my collar and he whispered back, "Sacrifice? That's exactly what I'm talking about. I'm not letting her go with him, not for a second. I don't care if that tame Lighter is with her or not!"

"Cain. Wait."

I turned slightly to see what was up. Malachi was helping Lillian off the ground.

"I had planned to kill them all myself, but I think I'd rather play with this one," he told one of his minions. "We'll be back at the house. You take care of this…situation." When the Lighter obeyed and started to make his way to us, Malachi grabbed his arm. "Do not fail me again in this matter."

The Lighter nodded and then looked at us. He snapped his fingers and his brothers came forward to the line with him. Some more that we hadn't even known were there leapt from the roof and came around the side of the store. Lillian let Malachi lead her to the car and that was it. I let Cain go, throwing my hands into my hair, because there was no way I wanted to let Lillian get in that car with Malachi anymore than he did. I blurred faster than Cain, but the Taker was strong. He placed Lillian in the backseat and grabbed my neck.

"Get the other one," he barked at Daniel who grabbed Cain's arm and twisted it behind him. Malachi threw me back to land in the snow, then he got in the car, shutting the door, and turned his back on us to focus on Lillian.

"I will kill you if you let her leave in that car. Do you understand me?" Cain yelled at Daniel. Daniel put his face close to Cain's.

"By letting her help to save her family and friends, I am giving her something you never have; pride and glory."

"You are such a frigging idiot if you think that's why she's doing this. She doesn't care about glory or pride! Those are Lighter wants, not women who are just being stubborn to try to save their family. She thinks she'll lure him away and we'll be safe after he's gone, but she's wrong. He knows where we are now. Daniel, I will kill you, I swear it, if anything happens to her because of this stunt."

"If she perishes because of my actions, I'll let you kill me."

"Why?"

"Because she asked me to help her and I feel that I can not say no. She is…everything to me." Cain inhaled angrily. "If I knew what love was, I would imagine it was this."

"Ok, fine. You love her? Don't let her go in that car."

"I promised." Then he pushed Cain back with enough force that he skidded in the snow as Daniel climbed into the other side of the car. Before Cain could reach the car again, they were driving away. He yelled and fell to his knees when he knew there was no hope.

"Oh, no…she's not coming back. Why would she do that?"

"Because she loves you and she knew we'd all die if Malachi fought us like that," I told him, and then tapped his shoulder to get his attention. "Incoming."

The Lighters Malachi had left behind were all too eager to finish the job. They were nine of them left and I guessed they thought it would be easy.

We organized in our minds and told everyone else to go at them all together. We circled them and at the mark of Jeff, we ran with weapons raised and gifts blazing. With about fifteen of us rushing them at once, they were surprised and started to backpedal. To regroup maybe. We weren't having it. Especially Cain. He was ruthless, and using his anger and betrayal to fuel his fists and stakes. The battle was surprisingly short. The last Lighter went down as Cain straddled him and he kept staking the ground even after the lightning blast signaled that the Lighter was dust.

He sagged more on the ground and beat his fist in the snow several times. Calvin yelled to him, "I'm sorry. I tried! I wanted to smoke that Taker, Cain. I wanted to kill him for you."

"It's ok, Calvin. Because I'm going after her." He stood. "And after I kill that Taker, I'm gonna kill a Lighter named Daniel, then I'm gonna bring Lillian home and lock her butt up for the rest of her life."

Calvin gulped at Cain's growled words. Ryan pulled him under his arm and took him back inside. No one else knew what to do either so they started making their way inside. Except the usual stragglers and tag-alongs. Miguel, Sherry, Danny, Celeste, Jeff and Marissa came to stand behind us. I reached back, knowing that Sherry was right behind me, and gripped her fingers in mine. She knew she wouldn't be going with us. And even after the speech I made earlier out of anger and fright, I always relented later and went back to forbidding her to come with us.

Human hypocrisy and a flip-flop attitude was definitely something I'd adhered to, haphazardly or not.

I held my hand out to Cain and he looked up at me, his eyes a mess of emotion and anger.

"I can go alone," he said, knowing it was more than a hand-up that I was offering.

"Not a chance."

"You have a family to think about. You shouldn't go out unless you have to."

"You and Lillian are my family, too. Besides, Sherry would never let me let you leave alone. Let's go."

His look was one of annoyance and as much affection as a human male could muster for another. He took my hand, palm to palm in a grip, and let me haul him up.

"Let's get going. I'm pretty sure he'd take her back to the Mayor's Manor, but I don't want them to get too far ahead."

Sherry turned me to her and pulled me down to hug me around my neck. "Be careful, Keeper," she whispered and pulled back to see my face to make sure I agreed. I smiled gratefully at her.

"Thank you for not fighting me on this."

"You have to go. I love you," she said, her voice strong, but shaky. We had to go. The further Lillian got away, the slimmer the chances were of getting her back.

"Are you going to be ok? I know....Josh..."

"I'm fine. What else can I be? I can't bring Josh back and I can't stop you from doing what you have to do."

"I'm sorry, baby," I soothed and kissed her neck as I hugged her hard. "I'll be back soon and we'll...deal with all this."

She nodded and then walked to Cain. He hugged her just as hard as I had. As she said something to him that I couldn't hear, he closed his eyes and then pulled back to look at her. She nodded and then he nodded. I looked around, but someone must have taken Lily inside already. So after one more peck from Sherry, who walked slowly to Racine and helped her inside, Cain, Jeff and I went after the Taker and Cain's girl as everyone else inched inside to await our return.

Down, Down, Down
Chapter 32- Lillian

"Come with me, now," I had told him. I pulled Daniel into the store back door and prayed that Cain hadn't seen me leave. Daniel's skin was cold, but somehow still warm. That doesn't make any sense, but I felt his warmth for me as he gripped my hand and let me tow him.

"I have a plan," I told him as I pushed him into the corner. And as I laid my plan on him, his mouth opened in surprise. His eyes went black and when he started to protest and give me safety talks I punched the guilt card. I hated to do that, but it wasn't as if we had all the time in the world.

"If you care about me as much as you say, then please do as I ask. I can't let them be hurt and you told me so yourself that Malachi was a sucker for the girls."

"He is, but-"

"No buts. Do this for me."

I knew I had him when he exhaled and his sickly sweet breath brushed across my face. Then he got a look on his face, like he had an idea. "I will do this with you," he said, "but this is dangerous. I will not let anything happen to you, but I may have to sacrifice myself so that you may get away. So I require one thing before I do this task." I nodded my agreement. "Your lips," he whispered and moved too quick for me to do anything before he was pressing his cold lips to mine.

His arms held me like I was made of glass. Glass that you wanted to protect without cracking, but crush into your soul for safekeeping.

His cold was once again odd. His skin was cold, but I felt his warmth all over me, seeping and making me feel…strangely calm. The sweet breath I smelled earlier tasted the same as it smelled, but not in a bad way. When one of his hands came up to my face I knew I had let it go too far already.

I pushed against his chest a little, but he held on. He tentatively opened his mouth and mine with it. He grunted once as he pulled me a bit tighter and then released me slowly and gently. He looked down into my face with a slight wince, as if he was waiting for me to slap him. Then he said in a gruff voice, "You taste exactly like I thought you would. Like what I imagine…warmth would taste like."

186

I held in my gasp at his words. Hadn't I thought similar things just seconds ago about *his* warmth? I sighed and said, "You can't ever do that, again, Daniel. I mean it."

"I know, but I had to do it once. This seemed like the most opportune time without there being consequences."

I wanted to laugh at the sheer ridiculousness of that, but kept my composure. He said the sweetest things, whether he realized they were sweet or not. Cain was gruff and protective and definitely could be sweet sometimes, but Daniel was so honest with his no-filter thing. Completely open. Oh, gosh…he'd just kissed me. Ok, worry about that later.

"Ok, let's get going."

"Wait. The Taker can read your mind. You mustn't think of anything but what a girl in your position would think about when you face him."

"Ok. Do the blur thing and go into the bunker, get what we need."

He was back in seconds with what I'd asked him to bring. He placed them gently into his pockets and let me lead the way out the door. But before we made it Max tried to stop us.

"Are you playing hero, Lillian?"

"I have to do this, Max. Don't get in our way."

"Cain will be very upset by this."

"I understand that," I squeaked, "but I have to do this." When he started to hold his hand out to stop me, I got hard. "Don't make me tell Daniel to lay you out so we can pass."

He sighed harshly and waved his arm in flippancy as he said, "Go ahead. It's not like anyone listens to me anyway."

I glanced back at Daniel to make sure he was still a go. His eyes blazed black and he nodded.

I could barely look at everyone as I made my way to the Taker. I wrapped my arms together over my chest to stop my hands from shaking. To be honest, I was surprised that Sherry wasn't pulling this stunt. Maybe I beat her to it. Maybe she was just too tired from being tortured.

I heard Cain's yell. His tortured expression when I looked his way was almost too much to bear. But it also sealed my resolve. I had to do this for him. He had been through so much and yes, he would be angry if something happened to me and yes, he said he loved me. He loved…me, and I loved him. And though Daniel had just kissed me and I, maybe, had felt a spark of something because of his honesty and utter realness I realized one thing: Cain was real because of his love for me and his want to keep me protected and happy at any cost, even his own. Daniel was real because he didn't know any better and he was sweet only by happenstance. He had no idea what half the things even meant that came out of his mouth. He was trying to figure it all out. He wasn't in love with me, he was infatuated with the first person to make him feel. And for all I cared, he could find a new muse, because Cain, and the look on his face right now, not of betrayal, but of pure terror for me, was all I cared about.

He was real. And I was bound and determined to keep him safe, even if that meant sacrificing myself. If the plan worked like a charm, I'd be back before nightfall. If it didn't, well…I hoped Cain understood that I had to do this for him. For them all.

I remember yelling something hateful and mouthing 'I love you' to Cain. It was risky. I could've broken down right then, plan failed. But my resolve held and as I turned to face Malachi I immediately thought about leaving, hating the store, being hungry, loving his shiny car; things I hoped would make him believe me.

And here I sat here with the Taker now, my pretty, grateful smile in place. I waited for the perfect opportunity to strike the match on my plan. He could read our current thoughts so I had to think of the plan only right before we needed to act. We'd have only seconds to throw the gear into motion.

He ran his hand up my thigh, causing Daniel to jerk in response. But this was my part to play, my scene to portray. I was the silly girl in love with the power the Taker emitted.

"So," Malachi drawled, "what's your name, little one?"

"Lillian," I answered softly.

"Mmm, Lillian. Very….wholesome," he sang. I looked up at him and watched him. I was with the Taker, the leader of all evil, so I looked my fill, wondering what all the fuss was about. He never looked up into my face, not once. He watched other things of mine, and though I was repulsed I kept my smile in place and a constant stream of 'ooh's and 'ahh's and 'gosh, he's so cute's playing through my head.

"Thank you," I murmured and tucked my hair behind my ear, but it made me ache to do so. Cain loved it when I did it and to use it for this purpose made me feel dirty.

"I prefer blonds, truly, though it's been a while. They are always a surprise. They are either meek and pure or wild and precarious. I wonder what you'll turn out to be," he murmured and leaned closer to me in the seat. He pulled me by my leg and I slid across the seat surprisingly easy, reminding me that though he looked like a pompous twerp, he was the leader of all evil.

"I'm not sure which I am, my lord. Surprises are always fun though, right?"

He laughed at my remark, clearly enjoying the banter, and then said, "Oh, yes." When he planted his face into my neck and I felt his disgusting, cold tongue on my skin, I knew this was it.

"Now, Daniel," I said loudly. I tried to push Malachi away, but he held tight. I hoped that Daniel carried out our plan, and that I didn't burn up in the process. Either way, this Taker was going to die.

You're On, Pippy
Chapter 33 - Sherry

I felt anxious as I helped Racine inside and placed her on the couch with Miguel's help. He looked down at her and checked her pupils. She just lay there.

"She's down for the count, and I don't mean boxing."

"I know," I said. "Oh…poor, Josh. Racine will blame herself."

"Yep," he agreed. "Josh was worried about her on the run. I hope she gets that; he was just protecting her. That is goes both ways. The Specials care about the Keepers, too."

I nodded and then swayed for no apparent reason. Miguel steadied me, that was when I realized that I was about to fall.

"Whoa. What's up?" Miguel said and peeked down into my face. "Are you goin' to fall out too?"

I wrapped my arms around him in a sudden bout of vulnerability.

"Are you alright? Talk to me, love," he said into my hair.

"It's just so much, Miguel," I told him, my voice catching and curving. I looked up at him. "I don't think I can't handle this anymore. How much more can we take?"

"Sure you can." He grimaced and smoothed an awkward finger over my cheek to catch a tear. "You're the strongest sheila I know. Plus, what are we supposed to do? Play dead like a bunch of armadillos or come out swinging? I prefer to swing."

"Yeah, me, too. Though it's not like I could do any damage," I said and he chuckled. "I'm just so tired of living like this."

"Just…" He sighed and looked around, as if for help. "You're just upset because Merrick blew off with Cain. We're all a little knackered and worn out right now. And with Josh… Major things are going down right now. Just give that body of yours a minute to process."

"Ok."

"It'll all be apples soon, true?"

"Sure," I answered having no idea what that meant, but figured it was along the lines of 'it'll be ok'.

"Well, I don't believe you, but unfortunately I have to take a decko on Ellie. You want to come with?"

"No," I whispered and shook my head. "I'm alright," I said and tried for a smile.

I heard him sigh. He squeezed my hand and said as he walked off, "I'll be back in a bit, love."

After a while, I heard Lily's voice and snapped out of myself. She was standing at my feet and grabbing at my hand.

"Mommy, I'm hungry."

"Ok, bug," I said and took her to the kitchen. After making her a bowl of noodles and setting her at the table I went to the doorway of the kitchen and looked out at the commons room. Everybody was scrambling around and anxious. Should we be packing to head out of here since the Taker knew where we were and he left? Was our hideout compromised? Should I go and box up some food? Should I check on Racine? Should I be worrying about Lillian? Should I go to the shower and cry until my eyes were red for days?

I couldn't think. So I just stood there and let everyone worry around me.

At some point, the pastor came over and tried to talk to me. After a few pleasantries that I forced out, he could tell I wasn't with the program and left with my directions as to where the bathrooms were. His daughter and that other man didn't say a word to me nor I them.

I thought about the last time I'd been in this doorway, with Josh. Bantering about dating…so mundane…so normal. He was gone.

Marissa eventually came up. Jeff was gone with the rest of them and she was wringing her hands in that way that she did. I could tell her skin was sallow and she looked like she could be sick at any second. The mother hen in me took over.

"Are you ok?"

"No." She shook her head furiously. "No, I'm not. It's going to be worse now, when Jeff leaves. I can't think about anything but Josh…that could've easily been Jeff or any one of us."

I pulled her to me and hugged her tightly. She was getting scrawny, what with her being sick and all, and it would only get worse now. I closed my eyes and refused to think about the food crisis yet. One thing at a time.

Miguel and Ryan were back with Ellie, the boys were gone, Racine was incapacitated, Polly was gone, Piper really was the devil, and Josh…oh… I squeezed my eyes shut tighter to stop the burn.

Everyone else was running around but the redhead. I pulled back from Marissa and smiled to make sure she was ok. She smiled back, barely but when I let go she swayed. I couldn't remember the redhead's name so I waved at her and when I got a curled lip as a response, I knew she wasn't bestie material, but I waved her to me anyway.

"What?" she asked.

191

While I held Marissa's arm and started to cart her to one of the couches I asked, "Can you get her a glass of water, please?"

"I guess. Though it's rude to ask guests for help on the first day," she said and smiled the smile of a girl who'd been through too much crap. We all had, so I didn't fire back. I just helped Marissa sit down and she slumped into the sofa back.

The redhead supplied the glass and looked down at Marissa as she sipped it. "Thank you," I told her. "I'm sorry if I was rude earlier. I'm Sherry. Your dad married my husband and me."

"I heard all about it after we ran into your hubs," she replied and rolled her eyes, her hands going to her hips. "Daddy was going on and on about how it was true love." She scoffed. "No such thing, no offense."

"I'm sorry," I said and straightened, "but how am I not supposed to take offense to that?"

"I'm just saying."

"Well don't, please. That man and his," I motioned in the air with finger parenthesis, "*true love* for me is all I've got left."

"And the little girl too, right? I saw her before." She smiled, but it was distant. "She's a beauty."

"Yes, she is," I said softly. Then I stuck out my hand and tried again. "Sherry."

"Rylee," she answered and shook. "So, you guys have built a little army down here, huh? Who's running this shindig?"

"That'd be me, ginger." We both turned to find Miguel, and he was scowling at Rylee. "From go to whoa."

"Black belt," she drawled and laughed. "This is your operation?"

"Not just mine, but I put some elbow grease on weapons and training."

"Really?" She frowned in an over exaggerated way. "I'm surprised you've made it this long. No offense."

"Hey," I said in Miguel's defense. "Tacking on 'no offense' after everything doesn't make it ok to say it. Miguel has saved my life more times than I can count."

"I can help," she said as if I hadn't spoken at all. "I'd love to *help you* teach these suckers how to not be dead."

"Maybe I'll let you help, but you need to show these people a little respect. They've been through a donkey's years of trouble."

"Haven't. We. All." She shuffled and took a little pocketknife out. She played with it and started twirling it in her fingers. "Not all of us have been so lucky to be stuck in some basement and be coddled by each other."

"Not all of us started off that way," Miguel growled back. I put my hand on his arm, no doubt he was thinking about his wife. "We've all lost."

"Some of us were too innocent to even understand that we were dying, much less know the why of it."

"I beg yours? You're innocent?" Miguel scoffed and then turned hard and yelled. "I lost my wife, right in front of my eyes!"

She lifted her shirt, a long scar along the front. "This is what they took from me."

At first I didn't understand what she meant. Then it clicked into place. Marissa, who was on the couch, suddenly stood and gasped as she covered her mouth.

"Your baby," Miguel murmured and stepped toward her a little, looking more sorrowful than ever. "They killed your baby?"

"I was five months along. They didn't care that I was pregnant. I had just come home to be with my dad and they caught us at the church, asking us about rebels. They gutted me and left me for dead, right there in the sanctuary."

"Oh, no, no," Marissa muttered and made a noise like she'd be sick. I put an arm around her.

"I'm so sorry," Miguel said sincerely. "I'm sorry for what I said and I'm sorry for what happened to you." He took a deep breath and began. "They killed her right in front of me, my wife. I couldn't do a thing to stop them as they held me down. With all my training, with all my skills, it wound up being a hill of beans."

She looked at him and though her face was hard, her eyes were seeking. She looked at us all and crossed her arms over her chest.

He smiled sadly. "Pardon me," he said and swiftly walked back passed the stairs.

"Don't pity me!" she yelled, chocked full of emotion as he walked off.

He turned back to look at her. Everyone did, well, because she yelled. He replied, "Compassion isn't pity. I am sorry, but that doesn't mean that I'm going to take it easy on you." He smiled and I knew what he was doing. She was hard and rough and gruff. She needed to keep a certain level of that so he was giving it back to her. "You caught me off guard the first time around, which was cod wallop. I won't make that mistake again. You can count on that, bluey."

"You're on, Pippy."

"Pippy?" he barked back and lifted a black brow.

"Well, you're from England aren't you?"

"Northern Australia," he answered blandly.

"Oh," she said and frowned. "You need to work on that accent, mate."

He groaned and went to go back to the hall. But right before he turned, he looked back. Their eyes met and he smiled a crooked 'game on' smile before leaving. I looked back at her and she was looking at her feet. And bless her, there was a hesitant smile on her face, too.

I shifted my gaze to Marissa, but she was staring at Rylee's clothed belly with wide eyes.

"Marissa, are you gonna be sick again?"

"Uhuh," she said and ran to the kitchen trash can. I followed and patted her back as she was sick over and over. I'd heard a little bit of what she'd done for Margo. I knew that when she used her power that she dispelled her own energy. She must have used a lot to still be so sick, and with the pregnancy, too.

Then I went to the sink and got Marissa a wet cloth. She pressed it to her face and groaned in relief. She thanked me and I smiled, but didn't really mean it. I kept the brave face in place and looked around for something to do so I wouldn't go nuts waiting for Merrick to return.

Playing Hero
Chapter 34 - Cain

"What if he doesn't wait until they get to the house? What if he just does it in the car?" I groaned.

"Does what exactly?" Jeff asked.

"Does it matter!" I yelled back as I shifted gears angrily. "Whatever he's going to do with her isn't something I want. I'm going to murder him."

"Calm down, Cain," Merrick said from the back of the Jeep. "You need a clear head, man. She'll be alright. She's smart. And... Daniel's with her."

"Don't you frigging say his name to me, Merrick," I barked and glared at him in the rearview mirror. "I'm gonna murder him, too."

He lifted his hands in surrender as he and Jeff started talking. They drummed on about Marissa being sick this whole time and babies about the mishaps we'd had on our run. I heard Merrick say something about stairs and falling and laundry chutes, but I wasn't listening.

Lillian was so gonna get it. She was in so much trouble. She had to know how pissed I'd be. She had to know-

The explosion ahead of us jerked all our heads that direction.

"Oh, no," I heard Merrick say. I punched the gas. I hoped with everything in me as we made our way to the wreckage that we'd find something still alive to save. The closer we got the more you could see what was going on. It wasn't an explosion, it was lightning. Lots of it.

Merrick and Jeff gasped and sat forward. "The Taker," Merrick said. "He's dead. Go, Cain, go!" he yelled as he bumped my seat with his fist.

I realized I'd slowed down a little in my awe. I punched the gas again and within a minute we arrived on the scene. We all stumbled out of the Jeep and I gaped in horror at the destroyed car. The lightning had torn it to shreds. Somehow the backdoor creaked open, then fell off its hinges as it hit the pavement. Daniel fell out of it too, grabbing at his arm. It was practically torn off...or burned off.

The driver stumbled out and Merrick jumped on him in his stunned stupor. He never stood a chance. As the lightning rang out, I ran. But Daniel blurred to the other side, beating me to her. He ripped the door open and lifted Lillian's body from the back seat. I almost fell to my knees. She was so bloody and burned

195

everywhere. Her pants and shirt were charred and almost non-existent. I went straight to him.

"Give her to me you bastard." I meant to growl, but it just came out desperate. "I think you've done enough."

"She's alive," he said and handed her to me gently, but quickly and I was surprised there would be no fight from him.

"You won't be for long," I told him, expecting him to run or say something about my not caring enough about her.

But then he said, "We must get her home to your little Lily."

I looked down at Lillian and heard them talking around me.

"Lily?" Merrick asked and came forward. "What for?"

"She's a healer. She saved my life. Your Sherry didn't tell you?"

"No, my Sherry didn't tell me and don't pretend to know more about my girls than I do."

"We must get her to Lily, now," he begged. Lillian's cheek was black and dirty. Her arm on my chest was so messed up; burned beyond repair. I almost broke down right there, but I thanked God that she was unconscious. At least she wasn't feeling this.

Without a word I went and climbed into the Jeep with her in my lap. She was beyond help, I knew that and I was almost ashamed because I was so calm instead of rip-roaring the place down. I just held her. She brought me out of my funk, she made me feel real love - the kind that you use the actual words for - and now, she killed herself for me.

It was sad, but I couldn't even remember being this devastated when my parents died. This wasn't the first time that she'd saved me either. But she was alive, like Daniel - that bastard - had said. But I didn't see how and it couldn't be for much longer.

We were moving. I glanced up to see everyone else was in the Jeep, too. Merrick drove as Jeff sat in the back with me. He had Lillian's feet in his lap and he patted them when he saw me looking, as if to say, 'We all care and we're here for you.' I nodded my gratitude to him and then looked back to her face.

I smoothed her hair, taking the familiar trail behind her ear. Her eyes opened and at first, I thought I was hallucinating. Then she smiled at me.

"Either I'm in Heaven or the plan worked," she croaked.

"Do I look like a frigging angel?" I joked in a hoarse reply.

"Abso-frigging-lutely."

I laughed and then stopped because the shaking might hurt her.

"What did you do?" I asked in a groan and shook my head.

"We borrowed a bomb and a few matches."

A bomb....ah. Those stupid water balloon acid things that Miguel had come up with. I stared at her, looking deep.

I said everything I couldn't say out loud with my stare. That I was so angry at her, that she was a stubborn woman who needed a good spanking, and not of the kinky variety, that the fact that she used Daniel and not me in her plan - even though it would never have worked that way - cut deep, that her plan did work and she saved a lot of people, that I loved her so much I didn't know how to act and if she died, the big guy might as well take me, too, because I'd be useless here without her.

She nodded and started to cry. "I know," she said. "I'm so sorry. But I had to save you."

"Baby, " I told her as sternly as I could, "you are not cursed. Stop trying to make up for something that you didn't do or cause."

"I know."

"Do you? Because it sure looked like you were playing hero again to me. But you're gonna make it. You're gonna be fine," I told myself more than her.

She just smiled, barely, and hooked her hand around my neck. She brought my head down to rest against her forehead and then...she started to rub my head and scalp. She was comforting me, though she was burned and in pain and I wasn't even sure if she'd make it, she was trying to soothe me. I choked up, and I mean big time. I let her do it, because I knew she needed to. For some reason the girl needed it. So I let her and felt wet drops on my arm. I looked down. Those were mine.

When her hand started to quiver and strain with the motions, I knew I was about to lose her. She could barely hold her hand up and when I lifted my head again, her eyes were fighting her lids.

I grabbed her hand gently and kissed her knuckles, leaving them pressed against my mouth and cried. I couldn't remember the last time I'd cried, really I couldn't. But with Lillian drifting away in my arms, I cried for all the things I should have cried for before. My parents, my youth, my fiancé's betrayal, all the heartache we'd had since the Lighters took over. And I cried the hardest for the love I was losing right there in that Jeep. I rocked her and felt the last squeeze of her fingers before she was limp; completely, utterly still. I rocked her harder and as I let myself go and sobbed silently into her hair, I hummed to her that song that she loved so much. The song that I'd played and afterwards she'd told me it was her favorite. Collective Soul's 'Run'.

I held on and didn't let go. My brain was under the notion that as long as I held her she was still with me. I had almost forgotten that I wasn't alone until I heard a quiet, almost secret, sorry in my mind. I peeked up and saw Jeff. I couldn't think though. I turned my gaze back to L and ran my fingers across her eyebrows, something I'd never done before and wished I had. If I had the chance, I'd explore every part of her, just so I could say that I knew her completely. I'd ask her every question I ever wondered about.

Someone tried to take her. I looked up and saw that we were parked at the back of the store. I held her tight and growled to warn them off. She was mine.

"Ok, ok," Merrick said. "Let me help you out."

I let him and then I carried her inside the bunker and down the stairs. Everyone watched and parted a way, covering their mouths and whimpering, but I ignored them and took her right to the couch. I thought about taking her to our room, but I wanted them all to see her sacrifice. She did this for them.

When I placed her down, I kept my hand on her and refused to let go. I felt a hand on my shoulder and then arms around me from behind. I knew it was Sherry without even turning.

Before we'd left, Sherry had said in my ear, "She's been waiting for you. Waiting for someone who was worthy of sacrificing for. She loves you, and I can imagine what's going on in her head right now. Probably that life would be worthless without you."

"Funny, I feel the same way about her," I'd said.

"Exactly," she'd answered back.

Then she'd gone inside and I'd gone to get my girl. Now I had her, and her hand that was usually warm and smooth, was getting colder by the minute.

"Get Miguel," someone behind me said. It should have pissed me off that everyone was standing around and I was crying like a baby, but it just didn't matter.

"It's too late," Jeff murmured and when I looked up at him, he blanched. "I'm sorry, man." He turned back to whoever it was. "Go on and get him."

"No, you're right," I said, my voice a cruel, gruff copy of my former self. "It's too late."

"Too late for what?" Lily said as she was suddenly beside me.

"Lily, come here," Merrick said and held his hand out, but she didn't go.

"But Aunt L doesn't want to go yet," she answered and we all gawked at her. What in the...

"Lily," Sherry said softly, going to her side. "Can you do what you did earlier, with Daniel? Can you do that to Lillian?"

Mine and Merrick's eyes snapped to Daniel. He was still burned badly and though I hated his guts with a passion that belied my calmness, he nodded once to convey that it was the truth.

Lily didn't answer Sherry, she just went up to Lillian and put a small hand on her cheek. "She's still in there," she whispered and smiled at me. "Uncle Cain, she's dweaming about you." I almost lost it again with the frigging tears, but held fast.

"What are you doing, Lily bug?" I asked softly and then gasped, as did we all, as Lillian bucked, then her skin started to change. Her charred complexion smoothed over and her color came back to the peach that I knew. Her clothes were still tattered, but underneath the shreds and burned cloth her skin was healed and beautiful again. I watched her face, knowing what was going to happen, but unable to believe until I saw it for myself. When her eyes opened, it was with a flutter.

She didn't waste a second of precious time as she glanced over to me. She bolted up and grabbed onto me around my neck and I was too stunned to do anything but squat there. When I felt her first breath of relief against my neck, I let my arms touch her. She was real, alive, warm. She was here. I squeezed her to me and cried some more like the big baby that I was apparently becoming.

She leaned back and touched my cheek. She looked at the wetness like it was alien, and I guess for me it probably was.

"I'm sorry," she said in a groan. "I'm so sorry."

"It's over," I said and kissed her forehead. If I kissed her lips now I wouldn't be able to stop, so that would have to wait until later. I ran my fingers over her eyebrows and smiled. One down, a million more places to go.

"I was dreaming…that we were on a boat and you were singing. I could've sworn... There was an older lady there. She was talking to…" She glanced over at Lily.

We all sat back and looked at Lily. Everyone had mixed expressions and I saw it then, the reason no one had said anything about Lily's gift was because people would be scared of her.

Lily asked Daniel if he wanted to be healed again.

"No, young Lily. I deserve these wounds," Daniel said looking at Lillian, only at Lillian.

"I asked you to," she said quietly and gulped.

"But your Cain was right. You can't just give people everything they want. That's not what love is." I tightened my fist at his use of that word, but he turned to go. "I'd like very much to lie down."

He went to the hall, people parted the way for him to go, and he went to his room I assumed. Good, I thought. His beat-down that was coming as sure as I knew the sun would come out tomorrow needed to be later anyway. More important things right now.

I hugged Lily to me. I didn't say anything, because I didn't think I could. Lillian hugged her, too, and then everyone just stood there. Lily looked around and when no one else said anything else she said cheerfully, "You're welcome!" And then she skipped away to Merrick, who was in the back.

I looked back to Lillian and asked the first thing that came to my head. "Do you need anything?"

"I'm starving," she said quietly, tucking her hair behind her ear. "I know that's so stupid after everything that just happened, but I really am hungry."

"It's not stupid."

"I'll get you something," Sherry said and smiled as she squeezed my shoulder. I'd forgotten she was still at my back. She got up and took Lily with her to the kitchen with Merrick following.

I realized I was still holding Lillian in my death grip and loosened up a bit. She stopped me.

"Don't ever let me go again," she said and nestled into my chest.

"You can bet on that, gorgeous."

"Did all that really just happen?"

"Yeah," I breathed. I thought about something. "Hold on a sec, ok?"

I ran to catch up with Sherry. I tapped her on the shoulder and told her I'd take whatever she made. She smirked and handed me a bowl of noodles.

I took them and hastily made my way, grabbed L's hand and gently guided her to our room. I wasn't spending another second sharing her. She was mine tonight.

Beauty From Ashes
Chapter 35 - Lillian

Cain barely let me eat my noodles before he was pulling me to him. I thought there was a night full of caresses and kisses in my future, but he just removed my shoes and socks. Then pulled me to him and held me tucked under his chin. His hands roamed in a protective and relief filled manner.

He exhaled several times only to squeeze me when he did. I didn't really know what to say to him. I felt guilty yet happy, safe yet scared, horrified yet honored all wrapped into a messy package. If I hadn't done what I did, we'd all be dead, I had no doubt. There was no way we'd have gotten the drop on the Taker like that. And he knew of Calvin's fire hands, because of the old Taker's memories. He never would have let him get close enough.

But I still felt wretched for putting Cain through it.

I reached up to rub his head, but he stopped my hand only to kiss my fingers and hug it to his chest.

"I'm soothing you tonight," he said finally. "I'm taking care of you. You risked everything for us."

"For you," I told him. He bent to see my face. "I still would want to have done it if you weren't here, but I'm not sure I would have had the courage to. But with you...I did it without hesitation." I pulled him to me to lean against my head. "I don't think I'm cursed anymore."

He jolted at that and smiled a little in surprise before saying, "It's about time. Why not?"

"Because, there's no way that you could be associated with a punishment. You're my Keeper," I kept going though he sighed raggedly, "and I know now, after everything that happened with Lily and...this is where I'm supposed to be. Everything I've ever done or been through took me to this moment."

He sighed again and pulled me back to him. I was starting to see if there was going to be any action, I'd have to instigate. He was in a strange mood, with good reason.

I kissed his neck, right on his Adam's apple, before leaning back and kissing him on his lips. I thought he'd fight me or pull a you-need-to-rest move, but he didn't. He let me lead him. He didn't push or pull, he just let me do what I wanted.

His hands never left the sides of my neck and face, though mine wandered quite a bit.

I pulled him over me and that was when he finally spoke.

"L, I want to. Gah, do I ever want to, but I won't do this in response to you almost dying. Especially since you took off with Daniel to do it."

His voice had been steady, not angry. He was more hurt by my actions than mad.

"I used him," I said quietly.

"What?"

"I knew he'd help me because of the crush he has on me." I swallowed as the devious deed sunk into me. "I used him."

"He used you, too. He wanted to show you that he was better than me. He thought that by letting you do it, that you'd think he treated you better and didn't try to control you." He grunted. "Like me."

"He kissed me," I confessed in a whisper and waited for the yelling or slamming door. I knew I probably just ruined our night together, but it felt wrong to keep it from him for another second. I felt my hands start to shake on his collar as he stayed silent. I licked my lips and said, "I'm sorry. I told him that he couldn't ever do that again-"

He kissed me hard and ardently, his lips twisting and demanding as he lifted up on his knees to be closer to me. He wasn't angry? I couldn't take it, even though the assault was delicious, I pulled back. "You're not angry?"

"Oh, I'm furious," he said, his breath splaying across my face. "But I'll deal with Lighter boy tomorrow. Dead men aren't my concern right now."

He tried to come at me again, but I pushed a little and he stopped immediately. One more difference between him and Daniel; Cain stopped and headed my requests. Daniel took what he wanted and headed the requests that suited him, not me.

"You're not mad at *me*?"

"You told me," he said steadily. "You could have never said a word and I'd probably never have known about it."

"Yeah," I agreed, "but that wouldn't have been right."

"And that is why I am in love with you," he growled, a strained and guttural noise that if you'd heard it, you wouldn't have understood based on the words he was saying. But I felt his chest rumble, I felt his fingers sweeping my hair, his lips claiming tiny expanses of my skin...one peck at a time.

That girl who broke his heart - I could think of no good words for her - but she had made him leery of relationships. Because though he said he didn't love her, the fact that she had cheated on him after accepting his promise, showed that words were useless. You had to put action behind them.

So I let him kiss and press me until I was flushed every color of rouge. Then he leaned back on his knees and asked if I needed anything. Was I hungry still? Thirsty? Comfortable? Did I want to sleep?

"I just want you," I said and tugged on his lip ring, now that I knew he loved it so much. His answering groan almost made me laugh. And now, as I lorded my guile over him, I felt beautiful and gorgeous and amazing, like he always said I was. Even with my charred clothes.

He asked if I wanted to get out of my clothes and....oh, boy, what a question. He laughed and shook his head before saying, "I'll close my eyes."

I took off my shirt and what was left of my jeans. One whole leg was almost gone anyway. Without looking, he took his shirt off over his head and helped me pull it on. When the collar went over my face I almost groaned aloud at the smell. It was the best mixture of wicked and angelic I'd ever come across. And though angelic wasn't a word I'd associate with Cain, he was angelic with me. Careful, considerate, calculating.

When he pushed me back to our pallet gently and once again tucked me in the cage of his now bare arms, I felt like a million bucks. A million bucks that had been through a washing machine cycle filled with rocks, but a million bucks nonetheless.

Cain was all the wealth I needed, right here is this concrete room. He was the catalyst in my life, just as Daniel had been a catalyst for our war, just as Lily had been a catalyst for the balance of life and death that was no longer clear cut, just as Piper had been a catalyst in her own right for more than one reason.

The scales tipped and we answered it. We wouldn't go down without a fight, no matter how bleak, no matter how hopeless. Cain had said once that he always went out swinging no matter the situation or circumstances. That was a good motto.

But I didn't swing when Cain inched towards my lips once more, as if asking if I still awake. I grabbed on and didn't let go for the rest of the night as he held me like I mattered, treated me with utter respect and reverence, and his fingers crawled over *almost* every inch of my skin in an exploration that was long overdue.

I was in and out of sleep all night. So was Cain. He woke several times in a fit of dreams. I'd wake him and he'd grab me as if checking to make sure he wasn't still dreaming. He kept me against him all night and once again, I felt bad for putting him through all that.

"I love you," I whispered into his chest, my fingers dancing lightly over his skin, after he'd gone back to sleep. "I'm sorry for everything. I'm not sorry I saved you though and I'd do it again in a heartbeat. But I love you, so much."

I let me eyes drift closed and then heard his rumble, "Ditto that last part." I smiled and snuggled in, hearing him continue to tell me what I already knew. "I love you, too, lovely."

Going Out Swinging
Chapter 36- Sherry

I leaned my neck back and let Merrick's lips move against and graze my skin there. I couldn't think of anything that felt better than his kisses on my neck. The tingles and shocks they induced… But then he found my mouth again and I knew I was wrong.

I loved Merrick like that; rough and possessive and commanding. He was always like that after a fight, or a battle, or when he'd been away from me. We'd had all three of those in the past couple days. So, needless to say, I was thoroughly enjoying the session.

As he kissed me over and over, I told him things with my hands while my mouth was occupied. With my fingers in the flesh of his arms, I told him that I loved him and loved what he was doing. With my hand in his hair, I told him that I'd missed him. With my legs wrapped around him, I told him to never leave me again, though that was a request that neither of us could fill.

Afterwards, I was probably the most exhausted I ever remembered being. I pondered the events of the day as he traced circles into my back with his fingers. Racine had eventually gotten up and even eaten a small bowl of noodles, albeit silently. Then she went to bed. Daniel never came out of his room and that was probably a good thing considering he was on Cain's hit list. We'd talked briefly about the food crisis, but the end of the night, everyone was just tired and had enough so we decided to have a meeting tomorrow. Ryan has stayed with Ellie all night. I'd checked on them and he was content to sit on the end of her bed with her feet in his lap. Billings took some pills from Miguel, even after the pills I had given him, but apparently those had more kick. He started singing and asking everyone to dance, eventually passing out on the sofa. Marissa told us about the hospital, how Billings must be sensitive to medicine and we all have a good, needed laugh at his unconscious expense. And Jeff. Good old Jeff was going to be a daddy, and had passed out in front of everyone like a grandma at a P. Diddy concert.

I smiled at that thought.

"Hmm. Grinning in the dark is always a good sign," he murmured against my hair.

"How do you know what I'm up to, Keeper?"

"Because I know you. And I could feel it. Thank you for...that, wife."

"I love it when you call me that," I said and moved my hand against his chest.

"I know," he rumbled.

"I know that you know," I replied and giggled.

"So, are you going to tell me what Lily did? Or are you going to try to bargain?" he asked and sat up to look at me.

"No bargaining. I don't think I want to know what happened to you out there. Not anymore." I shook my head. "It's too hard to let you go when I know exactly what can happen." I sighed and once again felt torn about the whole thing. Lily had this amazing gift, but it could also be a curse. I told him everything.

He listened and nodded, his fist ramming through his hair a few times when I told him about what she did for Daniel.

"Wow. I've never heard of anything like that before. She's..."

"I know," I agreed, knowing he'd say that. "It's all unprecedented."

"I'm sorry I wasn't here." He pulled my back closer to his chest. "I'm sorry you had to deal with that by yourself."

"It's ok," I answered and turned to kiss his jaw. "It'll all be ok."

"So...are you tired?" he asked me low and nipped my earlobe.

"Merrick!" I scoffed. "We've been up for hours already."

"So. What's another hour? Come on, wife."

I groaned and laughed. "So I go from being cut-off to non-stop?"

"Husband's prerogative."

I laughed and just as I gave in and let him brace himself over me, his kisses replacing all humor with want, we heard a noise outside our room. We stilled.

"It's probably one of the kids walking around or something," Merrick whispered against my lips.

Then we heard it again, and it was grunting like fighting. Then yelling.

Merrick scrambled up and threw on his discarded jeans. He peeked out the door, told me to stay, and then blurred away. I pulled on his shirt quickly and peeked out, too. They were a couple others peeking as well and we all shrugged at each other.

I made my way to the end of the hall and saw Daniel locked in a fight with a Lighter, right there in the middle of the commons room. How the heck had he gotten in here? Merrick searched and I knew what he was looking for. I saw a stake on the TV stand, yelled for him and tossed it to him. It was dark, but he could see it.

As there was a pile of people on both sides of the commons room watching I wondered how the Lighter had gotten in. Daniel and Jeff dragged him outside, so as not to destroy our house with its lightning, and expelled him quickly. They blurred back in and locked the trap door back.

"Who opened this door for him?" Merrick barked.

"I did!" Polly said and appeared from the kitchen. "Had to. Made me."

What was she babbling about? But Merrick's face twisted and he went to her. We'd never found Polly before when we looked for her. We assumed she'd ran away to escape punishment or went on a preemptive banishment. But there she was and something was clearly wrong with her as she stared off at nothing on the wall, not looking at any of us.

"Piper gave me to them. Had to, made me."

Merrick lifted her shirt and there was a patch on her ribs. I covered my mouth. It was the first time I was sorry for Polly. Wait a minute....

"Did you say Piper gave you to them?" I asked, my voice shrill.

"Piper...gave me to them. I had to...made me..."

"She must have done it when they were down here earlier." Merrick shook his head. 'Why would she do this?" he groaned. "To her own charge? She knows she'll die now."

"Cause she's a heartless b-"

"Celeste," Danny cut her off and looked at us. "She's in the commons room and she's seen us all. She was walking around outside and led one of them to us. It's over. We have to leave here."

"You're right," Merrick grunted unhappily. "You are right." He let out a slew of curse words along with Piper's name and I winced because he never talked that like, but I didn't blame him.

"What are we going to do now?" Kay asked and put an arm around Celeste. "Where will we go?"

"Wait," Max said and shook his head, always the skeptic. "Piper couldn't have done this. To her own charge? No. No way. Maybe Polly is mistaken."

"Not a chance, Max," Jeff said. "She did this and you know it as well as I do. She won't be a prisoner anymore either. I'll take care of her myself," he ground out. He glanced around at us all, he reached back for Marissa, but his gaze landed on Merrick. "We've had a good run, brother, but we better get a move on."

"Polly..." Merrick said and sighed, fisting his hair into an unruly spike.

"I'll do it, Merrick. I'll get it over with," Miguel said and Celeste whimpered behind him. Her eyes watered and Danny pulled her into his side. "Sorry, Celeste. I didn't mean to sound so callous about it...with your mom only been gone for...."

"It's ok. It has to be done." She sniffed and then gasped and looked out into the hall passed the stairwell. "Josh?"

"No," Josh's voice said. Then he appeared and I felt an urge to hug the crap out of him like he always did me. Josh. He was no longer mangled and in the

207

training room on the floor, waiting a burial. He was walking, talking, right there in front of us, alive and the cause of our gasps. But then he said, "I'm not Josh."

Merrick and Jeff went to him, but before anything was done or said, another guest made an appearance. Ellie emerged from the hall in a stumbling run, yelling. Ryan chased after her. Just as he made it to her, she collapsed on him. "They're coming. I sense them, but if you kill them all, you'll be safe."

"What are you-"

"It will be Lighters," Marissa said and squinted as if looking at something, "and Markers and something we've never seen before. No one else will know we're here, so Ellie is right. If we destroy them all we'll be safe. But they are coming and there are many of them. Soon." She looked at Ellie and said softly, "What are you?"

"I'm some kind of wall for their senses."

"That's what the Lighter was going on about?" Danny asked. "My gift wouldn't work on him when he was holding you in the yard."

She nodded, breathing hard and fast. She must've still been in pain from the wound. "He knew what I was then. I suspected something was wrong with me for a while. But when the Lighters took me, they never sensed or said anything so I just thought I was imagining it. But I wasn't. I feel it…"

"You're a Shield," Merrick said and cocked his head. "Funny. I can't sense a gift on you either. I guess it works against all of us." He clucked his tongue. "But you're right. If we can get the ones that are coming, then none of the others will find us. They won't sense or be able to be directed here by Lighter senses because you'll shield all that. But you also make it where we can't sense them either, so we need to stay on our toes."

"They'll be here within the hour," Marissa announced, causing everyone to take a breath.

"Ok," Merrick replied, looking at me then at Ellie. "Thank you, Ellie. It's ok. We'll take care of it."

She nodded and exhaled, like she was glad that they believed her. She let Ryan wrap his arms around her to help hold her up and she sagged against him. He kissed her forehead and whispered things to her, but I focused on Merrick.

"So," Merrick started, "we need to get together a plan for when they come. Get some more grenades and things ready."

"Ah," I groaned. "Really, how much more can happen to us in one day?"

Then my whole world shifted. My whole life changed in a heartbeat. A painful and gut wrenching heartbeat.

A Lighter had planted and hid himself at the back of the stairwell and emerged from the darkness…ramming a switchblade right into the back of the love of my life.

I screamed.

My feet moved faster than I thought possible and though Danny and even Cain tried to pull me back as Jeff and Max wrestled the Lighter, nothing could do the job. I knelt and a sob that hurt my stomach and throat let loose.

"No, no, no," I murmured and leaned down into Merrick's face. "Baby, we talked about this."

But my Keeper didn't answer me. My fingers shaking, I reached for his neck, for his pulse. There was none and I collapsed on him. I couldn't think or hear or feel except to scream. The tears were extra hot, like they knew the burn in my chest was worse at this loss.

It couldn't be…it wasn't true…please no…

Then I felt a rub on my shoulder. I glanced up to see Cain. He was grimacing and biting on his lip ring. He nodded his head towards the hall and I saw Lily coming down the hall. I hated what popped into my head: Ask her to save him. Was she going to be forced to save every person who got hurt for now on? But Merrick wasn't hurt. He was dead. And he was her daddy.

I tried to speak, but could find no words. Cain braced me from behind so I wouldn't fall over. I must have swayed.

I wanted to tell Lily to come to me, to let me hold her, but instead, I watched as she walked with purpose.

"Don't hurt him, Uncle Jeff. I need him," she said of the Lighter.

"Lily, I don't-" Jeff tried.

"I need him."

She knelt down next to Merrick and looked at him sweetly and touched his cheek. Then she looked up at Jeff, who was still wrestling the Lighter, and held her hand out.

"What?" Jeff said. "What, Lily?"

"I have to touch him."

He glanced at me and I have no idea what I did; nodded, shook my head, just sat there. I was devoid again, but for good reason this time.

But then Lily…she touched them both at the same time and an arc of white light leapt from the Lighter's body to Merrick's, which jumped at the intrusion. It lasted all of ten seconds.

Was this a dream? Was it too much to hope that Lily had saved him even though he was gone? What was she? She could take life from one creature and give it to another? She looked at me and said, "Evil taketh away, good giveth another day. Mrs. Twudy told me that."

Lillian had said something about an old lady talking to Lily… and I had been having those dreams of Mrs. Trudy. What was going on?

I was shocked, confused and hysterical as I waited to see if Lily was going to bring him back. With my fingers fisted into his shirt to ground myself, I watched his face to see if he'd open those green eyes and tell my heart to beat again. I waited.

And then….and then…

THE END FOR NOW...

The thank yous could go on for miles.
First of all, my God and my family. The readers who have picked up this book and my others as well are the reason I do this. It's been SO much fun getting to know all different kinds of people from all over the world who have read something of mine. It's humbling in every sense of the word and I thank you for allowing me to be a little piece of your world. You guys are the best and I love to hear from you! You rock!

Be sure to check out the other books in the Collide Series

Be sure to follow Shelly on one of these venues for updates, sneak peeks, information, new releases and giveaways.

www.facebook.com/shellycranefanpage
www.twitter.com/authshellycrane
www.shellycrane.blogspot.com

Shelly is a bestselling YA author from a small town in Georgia and loves everything about the south. She is wife to a fantastical husband and stay at home mom to two boisterous and mischievous boys who keep her on her toes. They currently reside in everywhere USA as they happily travel all over with her husband's job. She loves to spend time with her family, binge on candy corn, go out to eat at new restaurants, buy paperbacks at little bookstores, site see in the new areas they travel to, listen to music everywhere and also LOVES to read.

Her own books happen by accident and she revels in the writing and imagination process. She doesn't go anywhere without her notepad for fear of an idea creeping up and not being able to write it down immediately, even in the middle of the night, where her best ideas are born.

Shelly's website:

www.shellycrane.blogspot.com

PLAYLIST

Song   Artist
1. The End Is Where We Begin : Our Lady Peace
2: Song For A Waitress : Jason Reeves (Cain & L's Song)
3. Called Out In The Dark : Snow Patrol
4. Angel : Jack Johnson (Sherry's Song)
5. Soul Meets Body : Death Cab For Cutie (Ryan's Song)
6. The City And The River : The Rescues
7. Room @ The End Of The World : Matt Nathanson
8. Hope You Found It : Jason Walker
9. In My Arms : Plumb (Lily's Song)
10. Edge Of Desire : John Mayer
111. So Close, So Far : Hoobastank
12. Lights : Ellie Goulding
13. Echo : Jason Walker
14. Many Shades Of Black : The Raconteurs
15. Chasing Cars : Snow Patrol (Merrick & Sherry's Song)
16. Hold You In My Arms : Ray Lamontagne
17. The Sound Of Winter : Bush
18. Everything : Tyler Ward
19. Rainy Day : Plain White T's
20. Shelter : Jars Of Clay (The Bunker Family's Song)
21. Something To Die For : The Sounds (Jeff's Song)
22. While We Wait : Jack Johnson
23. Lose Control : House Of Heroes (Miguel's Song)
24. We Won't Give Up : The Afters
25. In No Time : Mutemath
26. All The Same To Me : Anya Marina
27. Everlasting Light : The Black Keys
28. Angel In Disguise : The Red Jumpsuit Apparatus (Merrick's Song)
29. Back Against The Wall : Cage The Elephant
30. Hero - Jars Of Clay (Cain's Song)
31. Destroyer : David Gray

Made in the USA
San Bernardino, CA
07 May 2014